On Suicide

GREAT WRITERS ON
THE ULTIMATE QUESTION

On Suicide

GREAT WRITERS ON
THE ULTIMATE QUESTION

Edited by John Miller

with special assistance by Genevieve Anderson

CHRONICLE BOOKS : SAN FRANCISCO

Printed in the United States of America.

On Suicide: great writers on the ultimate question/
edited by John Miller, with special assistance by Genevieve Anderson.
p.   cm.
ISBN 0-8118-0231-0 (pbk.)
1. Suicide—Literary Collections. 2. Suicide in literature.
I. Miller, John, 1959-   . II. Anderson, Genevieve.
PN6071. S8705   1993
808.8'0353—dc20   92-17510
CIP

Page 271 constitutes a continuation of the copyright page.

Editing: John Miller
Book and cover design: John Miller
Composition: John Miller
Cover Image: Mark Rothko, Untitled, 1955,
oil on canvas, 91 3/4 x 69 inches.
From the collection of Mr. and Mrs. Graham Gund.
Photo by Greg Heins.

Distributed in Canada by Raincoast Books,
112 East Third Avenue, Vancouver, B.C. V5T1C8

10 9 8 7 6 5 4 3 2 1

Chronicle Books
275 Fifth Street
San Francisco, CA 94103

CONTENTS

SPECIAL THANKS TO ANNIE BARROWS

FOR PUSHING THIS THROUGH.

ADDITIONAL THANKS TO

PETER BYCZKOWSKI, BETH GARNETT

AND ANDREA JUNO

ROBERT COLES

—

Introduction

I N T H E   1 9 5 0 s I had the
great privilege of knowing, spending time with William Carlos
Williams. That was, alas, a time of personal decline for him, even
though he managed during that decade to finish his lyrical masterpiece,
Paterson. He had suffered a stroke in the 1950s, and had become quite
depressed. I had written my undergraduate thesis on the first two
books of *Paterson* and had sent my effort at understanding his work to

---

Robert Coles is a psychiatrist, teacher, and prolific writer. He has written over fifty
books, on topics ranging from Catholic Worker Dorothy Day to author James Agee,
from children's books to his own volumes of poetry. Coles won a Pulitzer Prize for his
1980s series, Children of Crisis. *Coles's interest in suicide grew in part out of conver-*
sations with two other doctor-writers, William Carlos Williams and Walker Percy.

him at the suggestion of my college tutor, Perry Miller. The result was
a note scribbled on one of the doctor's prescription forms—an invitation to "drop by." I did so soon enough, and before long my whole life
was changed as I started taking pre-med courses with a career in pedi-
atrics as my goal. When I got to medical school I wrote him letters, and
I visited him. Sometimes he'd be friendly, warmly interested in my
pitiable struggles to do well in science, engagingly direct about his own
struggles with his writing, with his desire to keep doing readings of his
poetry, no matter the difficulties in speaking left him by the stroke, and
not the least, with "the blackness," he once called it, the dark moods
that seized him, and no question, threatened his life.

　　The better I got to know Dr. Williams, the more I heard about
those moods; and the more I heard about his view of both life and of
death. "I've had a lucky time here on this earth," he once told me—
and then a fateful pause, while he turned his eyes away from me,
toward a window across the room. Suddenly, during that silence, I
learned more about him as he felt then, about his mood, his state of
being, than I'd been learning for some time from the occasionally spirited
talks we'd been having. The very way he returned his eyes to me and
the place in the room where we sat (the parlor of his house on Ridge
Road, Rutherford, New Jersey) and fussed with his glasses, which he
kept taking off and cleaning and putting back on, told me a lot. Here
was someone who was doing a lot of solitary thinking; who was trying
to figure out what his life had meant, and so doing, had been experiencing his fair share of doubts, misgivings, apprehensions; and finally,
who was not by any means convinced that any future ahead of him
would turn out to be valuable, even as he was struggling to get a (visual)
fix on what the future was likely to be. As such thoughts (about his
thoughts) crossed my mind (later to be written in a letter to my parents,
both of whom loved Dr. Williams' poetry, and too, his fiction, the stories
and the novels), I suddenly heard another comment from a man who

was then, who still is (I say unashamedly), a great hero of mine: "On some days I'm not sure there's any point [for me] to live, to living—just to stay alive." No more—a return of the eyes to that window, with its view of the street. I noticed how awkwardly he sat, hunched, his feet crossed at his ankles, his head turned at an angle that must have been uncomfortable for him to sustain, and his words, too, in that sentence, just a bit disjointed. I wanted him to say more, even as I felt utterly inadequate with respect to what I ought think or say in response. He said no more, though—at least on that personal score.

   Within moments we were, at his initiative, talking about poets, poems—a subject on lots of people's minds at the time: his friend, Ezra Pound, the nature of his craziness, and what it meant, in view of the government's charge of wartime treason. Years later, 1973 to be exact, I sat with Flossie Williams in that same room and heard her memories of her husband's state of mind during that period, 1955: "He was quite 'low' at times, back during those years! The doctors called him 'depressed', He hated that word! They wondered if he was 'suicidal', 'Oh,' he said, 'such a catch-all word!' Then he added —'a waste-basket.' Then, he explained: 'toss one life after another into it, as if they're all the same, that way!' I remember him smiling. The poet in him and the doctor in him, both, had made a point to me!"

   Now it was her turn to fall silent for a while, even as we both remembered Bill, thought about a thought he had left to us—one earned out of his life, his intelligent, suffering introspection at the end of it. As always, Dr. Williams had spoken fiercely and brilliantly, if tersely, on behalf of the individual, on behalf of human particularity—and by implication, had given the back of his hand to those who want to take words such as "depression" or "suicidal" and give them a sweeping, unqualified, all too categorical authority. For him, the experienced, wise clinician, the man of letters, comfortable with irony and paradox, at ease with life's uncertainties, inconsistencies, even contradictions, its continually contingent nature, its fateful, chancy unpredictability, the static, flat mannerisms of the language of the social sciences or of psychopathology were of little help, indeed. I suspect that if he were now with us he'd also have no great use for the popularized version of psychiatry that makes up so much of our general cultural life these days: newspaper advice columns; self-help groups and books, with their dragnet voyeurism and exhibitionism—as if, to paraphrase Sophocles, the whirl of the odd and the loony is *our* king.

Today, were Dr. Williams alive, I fear the righteous indignation he could summon, the good clean anger he could show, would also be more than aroused by the glib way all too many of his fellow Americans, inhabitants of a 20th-century secular world, think about, talk about suicide. Even as I read the pieces that make up this book, and thought about what I might want to say in response to them, I couldn't help but notice the prominence on the best-seller lists of a self-help book dealing with suicide, no less. Nor could I ignore all the discussions of the subject that have been appearing in magazines, and of course, on those aforementioned talk shows, which a friend of mine, moved to an irritation that explodes into rage every once in a while, calls our "modern American circus, a replacement for Barnum and Bailey." In all of that one hears and sees the prescriptive mode, the labeling mode, and too, the self-righteous mode. Want yet another answer, another solution? Need to *know*, period? Interested in *doing*? (No "God forbid" is spoken as *that* question is asked!) Want to "talk about it?" So it goes—"groups" and more "groups," and plenty of phrases and stages, phrases and formulations, and these days, even some recommendations, some lists of what to do, when, where and how.

Meanwhile, there are the poets and essayists and novelists and philosophers who appear in the pages that follow—with their collective offering of complexities, riddles, mysteries, ironies: a properly thick, textured, provocative soul-searching. As I read these selections,

so intelligently and sensitively assembled, and as I kept thinking of Dr.
Williams, I decided to let my struggle to understand his struggle to
understand his encounter with the shadow of death be my response to
this extraordinary assembly of choices, attitudes, ruminations, evoca-
tions, thoughts and second thoughts. But I have another moment to
share with the reader—one more recent, and one equally dear and precious to me, and one that connects with the life of a writer who is a
member of this book's company. It was a great privilege, also, for me to
know Walker Percy for many years—and hear him often talk about
suicide: his father had taken his life, as had others before him, in the
family. Toward the end of Dr. Percy's own life, as he lay dying of cancer,
I talked with him, said goodbye to him—and heard from him this:
"Well, on suicide: to live a life to its natural end, a life that is a mysterious gift—that is our choice, as so many philosophers have reminded
us; but it is also our responsibility, our obligation to the giver of that
gift." There was much more: a wonderfully, spirited, rambling, at once
funny and serious series of comments, observations, asides, so worthy
of Pascal's *Pensées*, I thought as I heard them. Perhaps every reader
won't accept the religious implication of that remark of Dr. Percy's, but
his emphasis on mystery, on responsibility to others, to another, if not
Another, is I feel edifying, even inspiring—given the self-centeredness,
the self-preoccupation that informs so much of the talk about suicide
these days. Even as life is a gift to us, one to be cherished to the end,
one that is awesome in its uniqueness—so are the reflections, the
stances and epiphanies which follow: a most generous collection,
broad and deep and touching and provocative, and yes, one dares
think, decidedly providential.

PHILLIP LOPATE

Suicide of a Schoolteacher

LL THIS HAPPENED
a while ago, in 1979. At the time I had been working for close to ten
years as a writer-in-residence at P.S. 90, a public school on Manhattan's
Upper West Side. My situation there was unique: unlike most writers-
in-the-schools, who are sent into scattershot residences all over the
map, I was allowed—thanks to the receptive staff of P.S. 90 and my
sponsoring organization, Teachers and Writers Collaborative—to sink

---

*"Suicide of a Schoolteacher," Phillip Lopate's piercing account of a co-worker's
death, was originally written for the small magazine* Boulevard. *Lopate has
written several nonfiction books, including* Being with Children
and Bachelorhood. *"Suicide of a Schoolteacher" is included in his brilliant and
curmudgeonly book of essays,* Against Joie de Vivre, *published in 1989.*

roots in one place and to teach anything I wanted. The children and I made films together, put on plays, produced novels and poetry magazines and comic books, ran a radio station. I became entwined with the life of the school, went to Parents Association meetings and staff parties, and felt for the first time in my life a productive member of a community.

If the elementary school world was far more earthbound, less glamorous, than the downtown literary/art circles (around which my career and erotic fantasies still revolved), it nevertheless felt warmer, more communal, richer in drama, and more willing to make a fuss over me personally. This dream of the grade school as maternally nurturing community may have been in part, I see now, a naïve family romance, or a narcissistic projection of my own need to play the favorite son. That not everyone who taught at P.S. 90 was so well served by, or contented with, the milieu was a fact I certainly took in but tended to downplay. In any case, my dream received a jolt of reality one night when Monte Clausen, the schoolteacher I was closest to at P.S. 90, phoned me at home.

"Did you hear about Jay Becker yet?" asked Monte, cautiously.

"No. What about Jay?"

"He killed himself."

I turned off the television. "How?"

"He jumped from his apartment window. The twenty-seventh floor, something like that, of the Amsterdam Towers."

"Jesus." All my life I had prepared myself for a phone call telling me that someone I knew had committed suicide. Now that one had finally come, I was at a loss. "The Amsterdam Towers, that's right around me."

"You knew he'd moved into your neighborhood . . . ?"

"Sure. We used to get off at the same bus stop together." This seemed so inadequate a claim of connection with the victim that I immediately felt ashamed for having said it. I pressed Clausen for details, and we had one of those *Dragnet* exchanges: What time of day did it happen? How did you find out? Underneath my sober tone I sensed a spark of excitement at the gaudiness of the news—perhaps survivor's superiority or simply the pleasure of sharing a choice bit of gossip, which did not seem real to me yet. It was almost as though, now that Jay had made his point, he could dust himself off and go about his business. Side by side with that reaction was the unwanted understanding, like a punch in the gut, that Jay Becker was gone forever.

—

THE NEW SCHOOL year was barely a month old when Jay Becker stayed home for a week. He was extremely conscientious; he had almost never taken a sick day; so we were all surprised when the week turned into an indefinite leave of absence. One of his colleagues, Cesar Gomez, called him at home to see what was wrong. Becker answered readily that he had "emotional problems." Gomez asked Becker whether or not he wanted people in the school to call him, and Jay, after a pause, said yes, he'd like to hear from them.

A teacher who did phone reported that Jay seemed to be getting his problems under control: he had invited his mother to move in temporarily to take care of him.

Sometime in the evening of Monday, October 22, 1979, Jay jumped out the window of his twenty-seventh-story apartment. One assumes that his mother was out at the time. Did she return to find her son on the pavement? Many of these police-blotter details were never clarified, since no one at the school felt he or she had the right to ask his relatives for the full story. Not that it is of any importance whether he jumped at eight or nine o'clock, climbed out the window onto a ledge or crashed through it. In any event, there must have been many curious strollers from Columbus Avenue gathered around the body on that warm October night.

I see two stories here. The first is about a man who couldn't take it anymore, which is of necessity a mystery story without a satisfying solution, since the motives and last thought processes of a "successful" suicide are for the most part denied us. I might speculate in my own way why he killed himself, but anyone else's guess would be as good as mine. The second is about a public school, and how everyone (including myself) dealt with the disturbing private challenge to institutional life that suicide proffers. Here at least I can record what I personally wit-nessed about the community's response to the crisis.

Around midnight, Eduardo Jimenez, the principal of P.S. 90 received a distraught call from Jay's stepfather telling him what had hap-pened. By the next morning, the news had spread through the staff. A gloomy Tuesday; many teachers were in shock. "It can't be," they kept saying. "I just can't believe Jay is dead." Some students had begun to hear rumors, but when they asked for details they got little response. The adults seemed to be afraid of panic breaking out among the children. One fourth-grade teacher, Kate Drucker, who often held long discus-sions with her class about the most serious topics (including death), and who herself is a very analytical, honest woman, told them evasively that she wasn't sure what had happened. She admitted later that a truthful discussion would probably have been the best approach, but she didn't feel like talking about it just yet, she was too shaken up. (That night, Kate told me later, she called everyone she knew, people she hadn't spo-ken to in years, to see if they were still alive.)

The other staff members were equally reticent, as though they were waiting for a policy statement from the main office about how to phrase it—or, even better, an expert opinion from a developmental psy-chologist on what amount of truth the children could absorb at each grade level.

Becker's own class, of course, would have to be informed. Mr. Jimenez went to Room 234, along with the Parents Association president, and told the students that their teacher had died. When they asked the principal how, all he would answer was that it had been an "untimely death," which was tantamount to telling the kids that he had died of death.

An emergency lunchtime staff meeting was called to discuss the crisis. Ed Jimenez, somber on the best of days, seemed especially grim, as well as uncharacteristically subdued. He admitted that he was at a loss, and solicited the advice of his staff. To those who had watched Jimenez laying down the law at staff meetings over the years—sometimes judiciously, sometimes wrongheadedly, but always forcefully— his uncertainty came as a surprise.

A parent suggested that we bring someone in from the nearby Columbia Teachers College or Bank Street School of Education to do a workshop on handling death and grief in the classroom. Someone else remembered that Dr. Myra Hecht, the director of the New York Center for Learning, had once given a valuable talk on this subject. Perhaps she could be prevailed upon to deliver it again, this time with special attention on suicide. "For the kids or the staff?" it was asked. "For both, maybe," came the tentative reply. "You mean two separate workshops?" Someone volunteered to phone Dr. Hecht and see what she was amenable to doing.

After the meeting, Kate Drucker commented: "How screwed up we are that we have to bring in someone from the outside to tell us what we should be feeling and how we should respond at a time like this."

—

BY TUESDAY AFTERNOON, around the lunchroom and the schoolyard, the kids' rumor mill was already in full operation. Some children thought Mr. Becker may have been hit by a car. Another rumor, unfounded but tenacious, was that Becker had been suffering from skin cancer, and that he decided to kill himself rather than prolong the incurable disease. The cancer rumor had probably been started by a well-meaning adult who had sought to justify Becker's suicide (as if unbearable emotional suffering were not enough justification). Some of the parents who knew the circumstances of Becker's death let their children in on the facts; but the next day, when their children told other kids, many of these kids refused to believe them, thinking it was a wild, made-up story. Gradually, they would approach their teachers and say, "Somebody told me this crazy thing that Mr. Becker jumped out the window. That's not true, is it?"

Meanwhile, the school continued to handle Becker's suicide in the way they would a death from natural causes. On Wednesday morning the usual public address messages were canceled, and instead the announcement was made that the school had suffered a great loss. Mr. Becker, a man who had taught and helped children for fourteen years, was no longer with us, and the classes were asked to observe a minute of silence. It was the first of many such moments of silence, a ritual that became almost droll in its ecumenical utility.

What fascinated me was the *denial* of suicide, the reluctance to speak its name publicly. It put me in mind of another situation I had encountered at school. In 1976, after the debacle of Senator Eagleton withdrawing from the vice-presidential race because of previous psychiatric treatment, I thought of doing an educational unit on mental illness. How did the idea of "crazy" differ from society to society? What was the historical evolution of insane asylums? What about Freud's ideas? I could see the creative writing possibilities, using literary models like Gogol's "Diary of a Madman." It seemed a rich subject, one which afforded a chance to reduce the children's fears of their own deviations from the norm. So I was a little surprised when everyone at school—even Clausen, who usually indulged my zaniest notions—reacted with discomfit and total resistance. Since the idea would never work without my colleagues' cooperation, I abandoned it.

I kept thinking about this earlier constraint in connection with the adult reticence to tell the kids about Jay's suicide. How far did the taboo extend? Were we still so close, I wondered, to the barbaric medieval stigma attached to suicide? Perhaps the theological and legal sanctions that continue to surround the deed, such as refusing to bury the victim in hallowed ground, or requiring hospitals to file a police report, accounted for some of the reticence. But not all: no, there was something unique about suicide, I began to feel, that made a public school singularly ill-equipped to handle it. Schools are dedicated to helping children find their way into life, and an adult self-doubt so deep it denies the worth of life itself cannot help but threaten that environment. Since little children often regard their teachers as semi-parents, and since the offspring of suicides have a greater tendency than others to follow that self-destructive path, the suicide of a schoolteacher could seem a dangerous model. Beyond that, suicide is a defiantly private expression, a dissonance jamming public discourse, like a monotonously insistent burglar alarm that no one can shut off. The radical nature of the suicide act is that it both draws attention to a distressing problem and simultaneously obliterates the possibility of ameliorating it. By rejecting all human assistance, by announcing in advance that any relief will have arrived too late, it negates the whole *raison d'être* of those in the "caring professions": teachers, nurses, social workers, psychotherapists.

Implicating his or her survivors in guilt, the suicide (how strange the word fuses doer and deed) mocks the shallow understanding of those who thought he or she was doing all right, who mistook a calm scornful smile for adjustment. Revenge, spite, anger, stubborn will-fulness all have their part in suicide. The suicide insists on having the final word. No wonder people at the school found themselves unable to talk freely.

The most frightening part of suicide is its reminder that we are none of us so far from it. Suicide has a suggestive, contagious dimen-sion, as Durkheim showed long ago with his charts, or the suburban teenagers in Texas and New Jersey more recently. But why go so far afield? I had only to look within myself to know my own vulnerability.

At seventeen I had tried to kill myself with pills, and, botching the job, had landed in a locked psychiatric ward. Though this was my only bona fide suicide attempt, it began in me a lifelong relationship with that temptation. It seemed to me I had a "virus" inside me like malaria that could flare up at any moment, and I needed always to be on guard against it. On the other hand, I would court it, even in times of seeming tranquillity. I seemed to derive creative energy from the assertion of suicide as an option. This morbidity left me freer to act or write as I wanted, as much as to say: No one understands me, I'll show them. It also became my little secret that, while going about in the world, and functioning equably as expected, several times a week I would be batting away the thought of killing myself. How often have I thought, in moods of exasperation or weariness: "I don't want to go on anymore. Enough of this, I don't want any more life!" I would imagine, say, cutting my belly open to relieve the tensions once and for all. Usually, this thought would be enough to keep at bay the temptation to not exist. So I found myself using the threat of suicide for many purposes: it was a superstitious double hex warding off suicide; it was a petulant, spoiled response to not getting my way; and it was my shorthand for an inner life, to which I alone had access—an inner life of furious negation, which paradoxically seemed a source of my creativity as a writer.

Added to this was an element of loyalty to youthful positions. Just as a student protester might vow never to become conservative in middle age, similarly, after they released me from the psychiatric ward and people said to me, "Now wasn't that a stupid thing to do?" I swallowed my pride and nodded yes; in my head, however, I swore allegiance to the validity of my decision. If nothing else, I vowed that I would always respect the right of an individual to kill himself. Whether suicide was a moral or immoral act I no longer felt sure, but of the dignity of its intransigence I was convinced.

In any event, I came to believe, rightly or wrongly, that I had a sixth sense in these matters, which is why Clausen's phone call with the news did not entirely surprise me. I had started seeing a look of constant pain in Jay's eyes; I knew more or less what the look meant. I think because he could not bear to have another person see him that way—hunted from within—his eyes fled mine. Whenever our gaze did lock for a moment, it was odd and unbearable. A sympathetic vibration exists between "suicide-heads" that is dismaying, to say the least. After Jay killed himself and everyone kept saying how astonished they were, I felt isolated by having had a presentiment along these lines. It's hard to tell whether the uncanny shiver that comes from sensing, after an act of violence, that one may have foreseen it is mere vanity or something more valid. The matter was complicated by a memory fragment that suddenly surfaced after Jay's death; I was not a hundred percent sure whether it had actually happened this way, whether this was a hallucinatory vision, or a combination of both. Here is what I "remembered," from the previous spring.

We had been standing by the time clock, where we often bumped into each other at the end of a school day. Jay was getting ready to punch out. (As a consultant I was not required to, but I hung around the time clock out of solidarity and a need to imagine myself in the regular teachers' shoes.) I asked him: "How goes it?" He said: "Not so good." "Why, what's the matter?" Then I remember that twisted smile of his, as he faced the time cards, and his saying, "Everything," and adding under his breath, "I'm thinking of killing myself." His tone had just enough of that pessimistic New York irony for me to try to dismiss it as hyperbole. "Cheer up," I said, patting his shoulder, trying to make light of it, "hang in there. Death comes soon enough on its own."

I next remember fleeing the schoolhouse, shaken by what one might call the paranoia of empathy. I had had a glimpse at a pain so palpable it could not be denied, and was revulsed by my patronizing pat on the back, as though a colleague's reassurance could somehow assuage it.

This sensing of Jay's suicidal capacity went no further than species recognition. I did not feel impelled to warn those close to him, or to speak to his therapist if he had one, or even to draw him out about the fantasy, as one is supposed to do with suspected suicides. If anything, I'd been scared away from him. In my defense, we did not have the kind of relationship that could have easily permitted my extracting other confidences; he told me exactly as much as he wanted and then clammed up. Beyond that, I did not really consider myself to have the power to change his feelings. It was his decision to make, to live or die. All I could do was be a witness, and file away my impressions for a later date when I might be able to help him more, if the situation arose. Was this a cop-out? Does it show the error of my frequent position of detachment? Or is it megalomaniacal now to horn in on his death and act as though it was up to me to alter the trajectory of his history? I don't know what my responsibilities are to alleviate the suffering of others. Let me add that barely a day goes by without my picking up uncanny hints of someone's urgent misery beneath the social mask. I am never sure how much of this "intuition" is trustworthy and how much is projection, a distortion for the sake of promoting melodrama or feelings of superiority. I have sniffed suicide in the air a dozen times or more and been proven wrong. This time, however, I was right, and it spooked me.

THE FUNERAL WAS on Wednesday, around noon, and some of the teachers who had been closest to Jay switched their lunch hours with other staff so that they could attend. They piled into taxis and rode the twenty blocks down to Riverside Chapel, on 75th Street and Amsterdam Avenue.

As usual, tabs were kept on who showed up. The principal's absence was duly noted. On the other hand, some of Becker's traditional allies, who were very protective of him, made caustic remarks about certain open classroom teachers who did attend. "What's she doing here? She always gave him trouble when he was alive."

The funeral lasted fifteen minutes.

Jay's mother and stepfather wept. The rabbi spoke of the special relationship between the mother and her departed son, which was unusually close and devoted; of the deceased's having helped children; of his years of dedicated service to the community; his love of fresh air. Not a word about suicide. True, it was a religious service, and since Judaism views suicide as a sin, the rabbi perhaps felt unable to mention it. Nevertheless, it seemed ironic that Jay, who had finally spoken of his pain in a manner impossible to ignore, was still not getting through.

After the funeral, most of the teachers returned to school. A few, who had student teachers covering their classes, went out for coffee, along with some ex-P.S. 90 teachers who had been notified of the service. Two of these "alumnae" were now teachers in other schools; several had gone on to downtown jobs like copywriting or bank-telling, which seemed elegant to them compared with working in an elementary school. They defended their decision to leave teaching.

"Let's face it," said one ex-teacher bitterly. "Kids are takers, not givers."

"No, kids can give you a lot," said a woman still at P.S. 90. "But you have to know how to receive it from them."

"And if you know that, you're probably secure enough not to need their support in the first place," replied the first woman.

Lilly Chu, a more formal teacher who was on sabbatical that year, spoke to me with feeling about how good Jay had been to her. "Once there was a mouse running around the classroom and I was scared stiff. He came in and took care of it. His door was always open. He was such an important part of that school! He was like a rock, always there when you needed him. I'm afraid I got more from him than

I ever gave him. . . . If only I had reached out more."

"But he made it hard to reach out," I answered. "He never asked for help. There has to be something in the person that you can grab on to."

"That's true, but still I think we could have done more. Everyone's in their own world, their own problems. So much sadness in him. Nobody pays attention." Lilly's eyes began watering.

There was much talk, after Jay's death, about "reaching out." As one teacher put it, "To work in the same school and not know he was suffering like that . . . and all he needed was a little friendship." Everyone took it as a given that Jay had died of loneliness, that his death could have been prevented by more human contact. I was not so sure. P.S. 90 is not a particularly cruel, unfeeling environment—quite the opposite. Most suicides have people around them who do say a kind word, offer a helping hand, but it seems to come from a great distance away, and they don't know how to read the gesture. Often they don't want to. The suicide has to screen out or misinterpret a great deal of the kindness that comes his way if he is to get on with the business at hand. He must concentrate all his energies on keeping the tenuous flame of suicide alive inside and feeding it day by day. Sometimes it is not loneliness so much as the need to act decisively, for once, in one's uncontrolled, errant life.

The words "reach out," with their telephone-commercial sappiness, began to get on my nerves. In contradistinction to that line from *Under the Volcano*, *"No se puede vivir sin amor,"* I believed it *was* possible to live without love. Many do in this world, and we mock their endurance by pretending otherwise. Of course it could be argued that I am using the word "love" in too narrow a sense. There are many kinds of love besides human companionship: love of place, love of work, love of culture and beauty, love of God. In my view Jay had known some or all of these. I guessed that he had gotten fatigued, exhausted from some unremitting inner struggle, or from a tormenting superego that told him he could do much better, and that somehow he had crossed the line between the tolerable and the unbearable. Yet even as I balked at the kitschy explanation, "All you need is love," what if an important truth did lie under its sentimentality? Perhaps my old need to defend suicide as a valid action was getting in the way of my understanding the obvious: that Jay Becker had not been cared about or loved enough.

—

THAT DAY I saw two girls I knew in the hallway. They were from Becker's class, and I asked them how his students were taking it. They giggled and said most of the kids were glad! Then they did an imitation of the adults: "We should all talk about this. Mr. Becker died yesterday. Now on to math." They mocked the public address announcements, the solemnity of the principal, everything. These were both fairly sweet, sensitive, and intelligent girls, for the record. Their merry refusal to grieve, chilling and unfeeling as it was, bespoke a survivors' will to be themselves in the face of what they perceived as adult intimidation. I asked the girls if they knew how their teacher had died. "We don't! Someone said—he *killed himself*, but that's probably wrong." They giggled at the scandal of it. I listened without answering; I was too intrigued by their response to reprimand them; besides, I needed to think about it more.

On Wednesday night the annual bake sale was supposed to take place at the school. Some had argued that it should be canceled in deference to the recent tragedy, but others answered that the children and parents had gone to a lot of effort, and why should they be punished? So the bake sale was held in the school cafeteria as planned.

A large crowd swarmed around the tables and bought cake slices and cupcakes, the proceeds of which were to go for the school's legal battle to get back its Title I funding. It was a happy crowd, with the children running around the cafeteria and the parents chatting, and everyone waiting for the judges to award the prizes. Before the judging began, the new Parents Association president, Dave Naumann, a friendly shaggy-bearded man with a huge belly, rose to make an announcement.

He said that the school had suffered a deep loss. "And I don't mean the loss of our Title I designation. A teacher who had served in the school for sixteen years—"

"Fourteen years!" corrected several pedantic children.

"—Jay Becker, who had been suffering from an illness . . . died of that illness on Monday night. Now I'd like us to have a moment of silence—a minute is a long time, I know, so I'm only asking for a moment—to honor the memory of Jay Becker."

Everyone stood at attention, facing different directions, perhaps wondering how long a moment was in Dave Naumann's mind. I thought it a shame that, having gotten everyone's attention, he had waffled at the crucial moment. But later I agreed with others that Naumann had done a brave thing under the circumstances. After all, many had opposed his making any announcement, on the grounds that it would mar a festive event.

Several parents spoke to me that evening. They were worried about the kids in Becker's class. No one seemed to be talking to them, working through whatever problems they might be having with the tragedy. Some of the other teachers had held honest discussions with their classes by this time, but Becker's kids had only been treated to a succession of substitute teachers, starting with his leave three weeks before. The mood in that class had grown anarchic. Becker's kids were being avoided, almost like pariahs contaminated with the unpleasantness of suicide. Maybe, in some unconscious way, people blamed them for what had happened, or—and this, the parents stressed, was particularly dangerous—the children felt themselves to blame. Meanwhile, Jimenez had gone away for a few days on business, and, due to the budget cuts, there was no assistant principal around that year to deal with the problem.

I decided that it was up to me to go into Jay's class the next morning and level with the kids. Over the years I had developed the conviction that it was wrong to shield children from the truth; to the extent that we could even know the truth (and in this case we did), we must tell it to them. What worried me was the thought that this high-minded position might have also satisfied some sadistic impulse in me— the side of truth-telling that takes pleasure in pulling the mask off hypocrisy and disenchanting innocence. Also, I hesitated because I was not a trained psychologist or counselor, only a writing teacher. But this qualm finally seemed cowardly to me. What else was being a teacher but trying to respond as humanly as possible to problems that would not wait for an expert? Besides, I would get them to write.

ON THURSDAY MORNING I came into school early. I was shaking, as though I were about to teach my first lesson at P.S. 90. I ran into Monte Clausen in the main office. I told him that I would probably be criticized like hell for this but that I was going to discuss Becker's death with his class. "Why criticized?" he said. "It's about time someone did. People will most likely be grateful to you. What are you afraid of?"

I couldn't explain my fear. I had the sense that I was about to touch something very explosive and dangerous, partly because my own feelings about suicide might not be under control. "Oh, I guess I'm worried that parents will write letters protesting my exposing their kids to such ugly matters. . . ."

"But you have a role in this school of articulating feelings that no one else will come out and say."

"I do?" I felt relieved that what I thought might be interpreted as provocation had come to be considered approved behavior—my "role," in fact. Articulating the unspoken feelings of a community seemed a much more interesting function for a writer-in-the-schools than the narrower one of imparting writing techniques. I thanked Clausen for saying what he had said, and he wished me good luck.

I spoke to the substitute teacher and asked if I could take over her class for about an hour to discuss Becker's death. She said they were in the middle of long division, but if I came back in half an hour, they would be ready for me. I went down to the teachers' lounge and had a cup of coffee, and when I came back I was shaking a little less.

First I introduced myself to the class, said my name, and reminded them that I was the writing teacher. A third of the kids had worked with me in previous classes; the others recognized me from the halls, or in any event acknowledged my right to be there. I said I wanted to "clear the air" about Mr. Becker's death. When something important happens like that, you just can't sweep it under the rug. You need to bring it out into the open, talk about it, not let it stay bottled up inside. (I heard myself resorting to cliché after cliché, but I clung to them for sup-port, these trite, soothing figures of speech seemed to be absolutely nec-essary to get me started.)

"First of all, how did Mr. Becker die?" I asked.

A few hands. "My father told me he committed suicide."

"That's right. He did."

"How did he kill himself?" several kids called out.

"He jumped out of a twenty-seventh-story window."

There were several gasps. "See, I told you!" one boy cried as he smacked another.

"Was there blood on the sidewalk?"

"Get outta here!" cried David, a sensitive blond-haired kid who was embarrassed at his classmates' gory curiosity.

"I didn't see the spot where he fell," I answered.

"When did it happen?"

"Monday evening."

"What time Monday evening?"

"I don't know, about eight or nine, thereabouts. . . . "

"Somebody said he had cancer."

"To the best of my knowledge, he didn't have cancer. He killed himself for emotional reasons."

The students began talking loudly among themselves.

"What kind of teacher was Mr. Becker?" I asked over the noise.

An explosion of hands.

"He was funny," two girls said, laughing together.

"How, funny?"

"He would always tell corny jokes like—if a boy was talking to a girl, he would say, 'Flirting with the girls, Damon?' And one time he said that Julie shouldn't worry about Damon liking her, because Damon liked only dogs!"

"No, he said Damon only liked girls who looked like dogs!"

"And he brought in a picture of a collie and said that was Damon's girlfriend."

"And he used to say, 'When I talk about my two friends, I mean Danielle and Julie.' And they would get embarrassed."

"He liked the girls better than the boys."

"No he didn't."

"Hold it! Quiet. One at a time. What else about Mr. Becker?" I asked.

"He screamed at you."

"Yeah! We had to put our fingers in our ears and dive under the desks. And one time he yelled at Tracy and Tracy yelled right back at him. He hollered *'Aren't you doing your assignment?'* and Tracy hollered back *'No!'*"

Tracy beamed with pride. She was a cute black girl who had a reputation for fearlessness and trouble.

"What did he do when he wanted to reward you for being good?"

"He would let us go to the park. He would give us extra recess."

"And how did he punish you for being bad?"

"By screaming at us!"

"That's all?"

"That was enough! He would scream till you were sick to your stomach."

I paused a moment. So far, the kids seemed to regard their teacher as a one-dimensional figure. As yet they showed no feeling that a real man had died.

"How did he seem in class?"

"He seemed happy!"

"Did he ever seem not happy? Did he ever do anything that seemed strange to you?"

One little black girl near the front said softly: "Sometimes, when everyone was doing their work in silent period, he would stare out at nothing and look real sad."

"Yeah, he would stare out the window. But only during reading period."

"Or he would look down at his shoe and sorta frown."

"Uh huh," I nodded encouragingly, but there was nothing more forthcoming on the topic. "Why do you think someone would want to kill himself?" I asked.

"Somebody said he was married and his wife divorced him."

"That's true, she did, but that was many years ago."

"Somebody said his wife was still bothering him, even after the divorce."

"I wouldn't know," I said. "But lots of people get divorced. Why would someone go so far as to kill himself?"

"Can't take it anymore," one boy shrugged.

"Uh huh. . . . Why not?"

"Maybe he's depressed," said one child.

"Maybe he has emotional problems," said another.

There was something glib, almost disinterested in the tone of their responses. I've taught certain lessons with children that attained a deep spiritual quality, where each of their answers sounded forth like a bell in a thoughtful silence. This was where I had hoped to bring the discussion, but for the most part the kids were extroverted, noisy, too impatient to listen to each other or take the pain of the subject seriously. I understood there must be a terrific need to avoid that pain at all costs. I was torn between pushing further into it and letting them get away.

"I knew a girl, she hung herself because she got an F on her report card," mentioned the same soft-spoken little black girl in front.

"I once wanted to kill myself," said a boy in the middle rows, "because I did something wrong, and I thought my mother was going to kill me!"

"*She* tried to kill herself!" Tracy pointed happily at a plump white girl across the aisle from her.

"Shut up, Tracy," muttered the girl.

"How?" someone else asked.

"She took a whole mess of pills."

"You and your big mouth, Tracy," said the girl, looking daggers at her supposed friend.

I asked the class how many had ever thought of killing themselves. About ten raised their hands (including the substitute teacher!). It was odd how they could admit to suicidal feelings in themselves but still not identify enough with Becker to feel very sorry for him.

One boy said disenchantedly: "Mr. Becker always told *us* to be good and then he went and jumped out a window!"

"I don't think that it's like 'being bad' to kill yourself," I said. "It's a tragedy, it's a sad thing, but I don't think it's a crime or a sin."

"It *is* a sin," said a tall Hispanic boy in back. "It's breaking one of the Ten Commandments."

I quickly went through the list in my mind, not having remembered any against suicide. "Which one?"

"'Thou shalt not kill,'" he answered.

"But doesn't that mean you shouldn't kill someone else?" asked a boy near him. "Not: you shouldn't kill yourself?"

"I honestly don't know," I said.

"What does 'adultery' mean?" asked one of the girls.

"It's . . . when you're married and you sleep with someone who's not your husband or wife." I turned to the substitute teacher apologetically, as if to say: Well, they're getting an education at least. Then I went to the blackboard, out of some pedagogical instinct (or perhaps to shift the subject from theologically hazardous waters) and showed them the etymological breakdown of the word "suicide," along with homicide, fratricide, parricide, and regicide.

Some children wanted to discuss what happens to a person when he dies: the worms versus heaven. There was a lot of cross-conversation at this point, not all of it germane; those with short attention spans were getting impatient with the strain of a long discussion and tried to sabotage the focus.

"When someone is dead—" I began to phrase the question.

"Don't use that word!" cried a girl.

"Why not?"

"It sounds awful! Gives me the creeps. Use something else."

"Which would you prefer?"

"Passed on."

I began to make a list on the blackboard, based on their suggestions, not sure where this was leading: passed on/retired/into the blue/on vacation/gone but not forgotten. To these, at the bottom, I added my own word: dead.

"Do you think Mr. Becker is in heaven, or in the other place?" asked a boy whimsically. This got a big laugh.

"I don't actually believe in heaven or hell," I answered, "but everyone is entitled to have his own ideas on the subject."

I had noticed that there was a group of children who had been silent for most of the discussion. Just out of curiosity, I asked how many children had had Mr. Becker in class all of the previous year as well as this term. Most of the silent ones, sixth graders, raised their hands. I asked how many of the children had had Mr. Becker only since September. This time most of the noisiest students raised their hands. It was clear that the children who had been in his class the longest felt most complexly about him, and as yet were unable to put their feelings into words. The taboo against sentimentality in this age group may also have deterred them.

"Of those who had Mr. Becker last year," I asked, "do you think your attitude toward him changed over time?"

Yes, several volunteered. One Chinese-American boy explained how he had come to like the man because, when Mr. Becker explained things, he made sure you understood them. He was strict but he really cared if you learned it. *He*, personally, had learned a lot from Mr. Becker.

"Some of the teachers in this school let you get away with murder," said another sixth grader. "But Mr. Becker really taught you. He was the best teacher in the school."

Now the tide seemed to be turning.

"I liked him because, even when he made fun of you, he always knew if he hurt your feelings," said a scholarly girl with glasses. "And then later he would try to cheer you up. I *liked* having Mr. Becker as a teacher, only I didn't like being in this class because of the other kids who spoiled it for me, like—" Her recitation of names was drowned out by the classmates' boos.

I asked them whether they thought that, overall, Mr. Becker was a good teacher, a bad teacher, or in between. For some reason, this question made Becker's critics most uncomfortable. They were unwilling to say out loud that they thought he had been a bad teacher, although some obviously felt it.

I told them I didn't think there was a single teacher who worked well with all kids. There were bound to be some kids who would thrive under one teacher while others would do better with someone else.

"What about Mrs. Reilly?" asked a boy. "I had her in the first grade and she was good with all the kids."

A little wide-eyed girl begged to differ: "She *hits* kids."

Rather than get into a discussion of the merits of Mrs. Reilly, I asked them how they had felt when they heard that their teacher had died.

"I was shocked!" said Danielle, one of Jay's favorites.

"I felt sad the way I would if any man had died," said a fifth-grade boy soberly, "like if someone had been shot on the battlefield. But I didn't really know the man."

Many of the newcomers to the class agreed. They had barely known him, how could they feel much about his death?

I explained that it was not a question of right or wrong feelings. Feelings were like the cards you were dealt in a game, you just had to go with those cards. Sometimes everyone might be crying at a funeral and you might be feeling nothing; that was the card you had been dealt that time. Sometimes a person died and you felt angry at him for leaving you. The important thing was to be honest and know what you were feeling. There was no point in faking it.

I told them I wanted them to write, a request that was met with the usual groans of protest. I threw out two suggestions: One idea was to write a portrait of Mr. Becker as they remembered him, a truthful portrait, not making him look either better or worse than he did while he was alive. The second idea was to write about how they felt and were still feeling about his death.

Paper was handed out, the children set to work. Some worked in pairs, most wrote singly.

I approached the substitute teacher, who had helped maintain some order during the discussion, which was not always easy. She had technically supported my efforts, but at the same time I sensed something like disapproval in her—not exactly disapproval, but a scowling, hard-bitten quality, an angry wall. Substituting does that to some people.

"How has this class been?" I asked, under my breath.

"Rough," she said. "It's a tough situation."

"I'll bet it is."

"I wouldn't have been able to get that much out of them. I didn't think it was my place to talk to them about it."

"Were you surprised," I asked, "at the . . . amount of indifference they expressed at first?"

"I'm always surprised by their amount of indifference. I've been teaching for years and I've never seen a group of kids like this. They're cold. They have no hearts."

"They're avoiding a lot," I countered.

"Maybe you could excuse them that way. To me they're just cold. The other day we were at gym and I said at the end of the period, 'Aren't you going to put away the mats?' 'We didn't take them out, so we're not going to put them back!' I tried to explain to them that if you do something nice for people in this world, it will be better for you in the long run. 'Don't you believe in helping others?' I asked them. They all said, 'No. It's every man for himself.'"

What bad luck these kids had, I thought: on top of everything else, they had ended up with a rather narrow-minded substitute teacher who could see no further than their manners. Oh, I knew what she meant; I've felt that way about kids at times. But this class didn't seem so extraordinarily vicious. A little rowdy, perhaps, having escaped the

strict disciplinary hand of Mr. Becker. A class that starts to get a maver-
ick reputation often takes perverse pride in confirming its notoriety;
something of that "bad seed" swagger was detectable here.

About half of the children wrote short pieces, a few general-
ized, perfunctory sentences that were followed by a drawing of their
former teacher. I don't know if our discussion had already exhausted
what they had to say, or if the challenge of judging an authority figure
objectively on paper was too threatening, or if they were just being lazy.
The other half wrote papers that were more interesting—at the very
least, shot through with revealing flashes. I offer these examples not so
much as gems of children's creative writing, but as documentation that
may shed some light on the various ways children come to terms with
an unusual situation:

*On the first day of school, all my friends and I were waiting to see
what classes we were in. After about fifteen minutes, everybody in my class
went to their new classes, all except me. I was not on the list. I told the principal, and he went to all the classes to see if I was listed. Finally one of my
friends came to tell me that Mr. Becker had called my name when he was calling roll. I was a little disappointed that I had Mr. Becker because he had a bad
reputation of yelling so much. When I got into the room and of course he was
yelling, I said to myself, "it's going to be a long year." After about a week of
school I liked Mr. Becker, and I thought that everybody was wrong about him.
Then he started coming on strong with his yelling. I once heard that he was a
little deaf, that's why he had to yell so loud. When Mr. Becker died I felt sad
but not too sad because I didn't know him that well.*
—David

*At times he acted very strange. When he walk he puts his hands in
his pockets and looks down at the floor like if he was very very sad.*
He was a very good teacher. He knew when he was going to be

absent. He was absent every day and Mr. Jimenez said he'll be back next year and then 3 weeks later Mr. Jimenez came in with 2 parents and said that he died but he didn't want to tell that he committed suicide.

—Lorraine

Mr. Becker was much more different than the other teachers I had and know about. He was very positive. He had a special touch to make kids like himself. Mr. Becker had no right to kill himself, he should have been proud of his work. Many amount of kids since the last 14 years have gone to fantastic schools. His pupils had a lot of liking for him.

Mr. Becker might of yelled a lot but the kids he yelled at deserved it. Every kid in school except for kids in his class think he's a loudmouth but he really isn't what kids think he is. He let us do things that no other kids got. We went outside and every time we went out we went to the park! Personally I liked him.

—Jonah

When I heard Mr. Becker died I was really surprised almost shocked. I couldn't believe it. Mr. Becker will be gone forever. You won't hear him yell or scream again.

Most people didn't like him. I admit I didn't like him that much but not enough to hate him or be happy he died.

I'm very unhappy he died. I wish he hadn't.

—Kim

Mr. Becker was a very strange man he always wanted things done his way. When we had a spelling test if you made a certain mistake like if you added a s he would count it wrong. And he always squinted his eyes like he couldn't see and he always put his hands in his pockets. And yelled like he couldn't hear his self.

—Wendy

When I heard that Mr. Becker died, I was very surprised because he had been with this school for 14 years, and now when I come into this class he jumps out the window. Last year when I was just going into fifth grade, Mrs. Goldstein got hit with a block. The girl that threw the block, meant to throw the block at a boy named Donald, but he ducked and it hit Mrs. Goldstein and she fell off her chair and was knocked out. Mrs. Goldstein went to the hospital and never came back to our school. And the girl that threw the block was in lots of trouble and got transferred to another school.

So the same thing happened this time but Mr. Becker jumped out a window.

—Damon

Mr. Becker is a very good or you could say was a very good teacher. It's a shame that I could not have written is, but I hate to say I had to write was.

I wish he did not kill himself because he was the best teacher in the school.

—Ian

SLOWLY THE ACHE began to recede.

A month after his suicide, people had stopped talking about Jay. Everything had been said. And resaid. What was the point of dwelling morbidly on it? seemed to be the sentiment. I could see their point. When all was said and done, the school staff had done everything that could be expected and more.

Still, Jay's suicide continued to preoccupy me. By now I had begun to wrestle with Becker—to identify with and argue with him. If he had waited longer, things might have gotten better for him. What arrogance, to assume it would all stay the same. I kept trying to enter his consciousness to understand why he did what he did. How does one arrive at a final conviction that there is no hope? What part of the decision was rational, mental, and what part physiological? I imagined a psychic pain growing inside him (myself) that demanded some physical outlet. Suicide must have been his attempt to give Pain a body, a representation, to put it outside himself. A need to convert inner torment into some outward tangible wound that all could see. It was almost as though suicide were a last-ditch effort at exorcism, in which the person sacrificed his life in order that the devil inside might die.

At the simplest level, I imagined Jay a victim of a screaming inside his head. When the screaming grew too intense, he jumped.

I had no such inner scream, but a continuous subvocal nattering, and at times I pretended to turn the volume up on it so that I might experience what Jay's distress would have been like. With the cold weather and shrinking of daylight, I felt a contraction of hope. That fall I decided to go to Yom Kippur services; the main sin I confessed to on Kol Nidre night was despair. (Didn't Catholicism also consider it the sin against the Holy Ghost?) I was experimenting with suicidal consciousness, walking for a while in Jay's footsteps. From the outside everyone saw me as tranquil, productive, satisfied, I had so tricked them into believing my confident act that they could not perceive the suffering underneath. Was suicide the only way I could ever get them to take my pain seriously? I wondered melodramatically. Of course, part of the reason people could not "credit" my misery was that it didn't go that deep, compared to others'. Yet I supposedly had all this friendship and good fortune coming toward me, and then I would turn the corner and not feel it.

Why did I, who, if I wanted to be honest about it, had a much wider support network of love and admiration than Jay, keep trying to minimize the difference between us? Perhaps if he and I were equally bereft, then I no longer had to feel guilty about being more advantaged, my debt would be cleared toward him. In part, my flirtation with suicide was also a way to absorb the shock of his passing. Sometimes we mime on a minor level the death of someone we know—take to our beds with a lingering cold when a friend has died of AIDS. I also needed to manufacture grief (or sorrow, which kept turning into self-pity) because I felt bad about not being more upset by his not being around. Maybe I was also competing with Jay Becker on some unconscious level, jealous of the attention he had gotten by killing himself.

Though I preferred to think of Jay as in some sense my opposite (shrill, inflexible), he kept turning up in my head as an undesired aspect of myself, an alter ego I was trying to push down. His self-contempt held up a frightening mirror to my own tendencies toward self-dislike. I suspect, too, that, because he was older and stronger-voiced than I, I was projecting onto him some of my feelings toward my older brother. Though in daily life I get along well with my older brother, we have had at times a very troubled, treacherous, competitive relationship, and in dreams he still often threatens to harm or kill me; the obverse is that subconsciously I have wished him dead on occasion. Who knows whether there was not some disguised relief experienced at Jay's (my brother's) death, for which I felt doubly culpable?

Preoccupied by all this, I tried my usual method of coping with distress, which is to write about it. I had in mind an objective reportorial essay, with myself kept firmly in the background, for some magazine like *The Atlantic* or *The New Yorker*. But as soon as I put pen to paper I felt my insides shaken up. I couldn't find the right entryway into the story, I couldn't get enough distance from it; everything was so interconnected mentally that hundreds of possibly irrelevant details begged to be written down. I was also disgusted at the idea of capitalizing on Jay's suicide, making something opportunistically, journalistically "topical" out of still open wounds. So I put away my notes for a little while, until I could feel calmer, more objective. That little while stretched into eight years; and it is only now, at forty-four—Jay's age when he jumped—that I am at last ready to take it up again.

I think there was another reason for my having been unable to write the essay then. I had come to a decision, around the middle of the school year, to leave P.S. 90. Running the P.S. 90 project for Teachers and Writers had been the best job I'd ever had, maybe ever would have, but after ten years of doing it, I felt "burned out," if you will. I had exhausted my pedagogic fantasies; I couldn't think of any new projects. On the one hand, I needed to break away from a place in which I felt almost cloyingly, undeservedly loved, and try new risks; on the other hand, I was tired of being so poorly paid, getting less after twelve years as a consultant than a starting teacher's salary. It was time to "graduate" to a university post.

Jay's death had seemed a warning sign to get out—of P.S. 90, of New York City, of my solitariness, if possible—before it was too late. I heard from a poet friend, Cynthia Macdonald, about a job that had opened up in the new creative writing department at the University of Houston; I applied for it, was interviewed in March, and was accepted. Knowing I would be leaving, I did not feel I could in good conscience write about P.S. 90 as though still an inside member of that community. I had already said good-bye to it. Like Jay, I, too, was walking out on the kids, the school. Any attempt to write about my connection to that ongoing institution would be dogged by elegy and guilt.

—

IN TOLSTOY'S DEATH of Ivan Illych, one of the noblest works of fiction, the protagonist is "redeemed" by his mortality. Before dying he learns what he was put on earth for, and by extension, so do we, the story's readers, at least for a wrenching, consoling moment. But I keep forgetting the Tolstoyan point. What *is* it that we are put on earth for? After all these pages, I can redeem neither Jay Becker's life nor his death.

THAT JUNE THE school was featured on the cover of *New York* magazine under the headline "Twelve Public Schools That Really Work." The photograph, which showed every kid in class with his or her multi-ethnic hand straining to the bursting point to answer, had obviously been staged. To me there was something ludicrous about a city magazine's consumerist mania to find the twelve best of everything, be it late-night rib joints or neighborhood schools. But while we took the compliment with a grain of salt, knowing how inaccurate such media hype can be, we also acknowledged that P.S. 90 was a pretty good public school, all things considered. Typical was the defensive pride of one speaker at graduation exercises: "We didn't need *New York* magazine to tell us we were special. We knew that already."

At graduation, Ed Jimenez said in his principal's address: "This school prides itself on being a caring community. That's one thing that never changes. We care about the children, we care about each other. We continue to hold a belief in humanistic education, the importance of the individual in the learning process." True, but on the other hand, I mused (in the way one has of framing objections to any speaker's rhetoric), what about the vitriolic tensions among the staff, or an individual like Jay, who slipped between the cracks of our caring?

Nine months after the warm October night of Monte Clausen's phone call, a staff party was thrown to celebrate the end of the school year. Jimenez, with his ill-at-ease attempts at facetious banter, was trying to circulate, play the gracious boss, though his very presence made certain staff members deeply uneasy. They had not even wanted to invite him. He had, however, been so kind to me at graduation exercises, reading aloud one of my poems and wishing me the best in my new, post P.S. 90 life, that I made it a point to chat with him for a long while, conspicuously distancing myself from those who were getting their revenge by cold-shouldering him at the staff party. By the same token, making small talk with Jimenez could be an arduous affair, and some of my friends on Malcontents' sofa were giggling at me, and I longed to join their bitchy confab.

By the time I finally did make it over there, the mood had grown quiet.

Kate Drucker was saying what a hard year it had been. The staff hadn't organized anything like the previous year's fun activities: no Vest Day (when everyone had dressed elegantly and worn a vest), no lunch-hour volleyball game for teachers. Somehow the spirit just hadn't been there this year.

"Why is that, do you think?" I asked.

PLATO

—

Phaedo

ECHECRATES. Were you with Socrates yourself, Phaedo, on the day when he drank the poison in prison, or did you hear about it from someone else?

PHAEDO. I was there myself, Echecrates.

ECHECRATES. Then what did he say before his death? And how did he die? I should like to hear, for nowadays none of the Phliasians go to Athens at all, and no stranger has come from there for a long time, who

---

Plato's Phaedo, *written around 390 B.C., tells the story of Socrates' imprisonment by the Athenians on charges of impiety and corruption of local youth. Condemned to death by poison, Socrates spent his last hours discussing the immortality of the soul with his disciples, including Phaedo, who sat beside Socrates as he drank the hemlock.*

could tell us anything definite about this matter, except that he drank poison and died, so we could learn no further details.

PHAEDO. Did you hear about the trial and how it was conducted?

ECHECRATES. Yes, some one told us about that, and we wondered that although it took place a long time ago, he was put to death much later. Now why was that, Phaedo?

PHAEDO. It was a matter of chance, Echecrates. It happened that the stern of the ship which the Athenians send to Delos was crowned on the day before the trial.

ECHECRATES. What ship is this?

PHAEDO. This is the ship, as the Athenians say, in which Theseus once went to Crete with the fourteen youths and maidens, and saved them and himself. Now the Athenians made a vow to Apollo, as the story goes, that if they were saved they would send a mission every year to Delos. And from that time even to the present day they send it annually in honor of the god. Now it is their law and after the mission begins the city must be pure and no one may be publicly executed until the ship has gone to Delos and back; and sometimes, when contrary winds detain it, this takes a long time. The beginning of the mission is when the priest of Apollo crowns the stern of the ship; and this took place, as I say, on the day before the trial. For that reason Socrates passed a long time in prison between his trial and his death.

ECHECRATES. What took place at his death, Phaedo? What was said and done? And which of his friends were with him? Or did the authorities forbid them to be present, so that he died without his friends?

PHAEDO. Not at all. Some were there, in fact, a good many.

ECHECRATES. Be so good as to tell us as exactly as you can about all these things, if you are not too busy.

PHAEDO. I am not busy and I will try to tell you. It is always my greatest pleasure to be reminded of Socrates whether by speaking of him myself or by listening to someone else.

ECHECRATES. Well, Phaedo, you will have hearers who feel as you do; so try to tell us everything as accurately as you can.

PHAEDO. For my part, I had strange emotions when I was there. For I was not filled with pity as I might naturally be when present at the death of a friend; since he seemed to me to be happy, both in his bearing and his words, he was meeting death so fearlessly and nobly. And so I thought that even in going to the abode of the dead he was not going without the protection of the gods, and that when he arrived there it would be well with him, if it ever was well with anyone. And for this reason I was not at all filled with pity, as might seem natural when I was present at a scene of mourning; nor on the other hand did I feel pleasure because we were occupied with philosophy, as was our custom—and our talk was of philosophy;—but a very strange feeling came over me, an unaccustomed mixture of pleasure and pain together, when I thought that Socrates was presently to die. And all of us who were there were in much the same condition, sometimes laughing and sometimes weeping; especially one of us, Apollodorus; you know him and his character.

ECHECRATES. To be sure I do.

PHAEDO. He was quite unrestrained, and I was much agitated myself, as were the others.

ECHECRATES. Who were these, Phaedo?

PHAEDO. Of native Athenians there was this Apollodorus, and Critobulus and his father, and Hermogenes and Epiganes and Aeschines and Antisthenes; and Ctesippus the Paeanian was there too, and Menéxenus and some other Athenians. But Plato, I think, was ill.

ECHECRATES. Were any foreigners there?

PHAEDO. Yes, Simmias of Thebes and Cebes and Phaedonides, and from Megara Euclides and Terpsion.

ECHECRATES. What? Were Aristippus and Cleombrotus there?

PHAEDO. No. They were said to be in Aegina.

ECHECRATES. Was anyone else there?

PHAEDO. I think these were about all.

ECHECRATES. Well then, what was the conversation?

PHAEDO. I will try to tell you everything from the beginning. On the previous days I and the others had always been in the habit of visiting Socrates. We used to meet at daybreak in the court where the trial took place, for it was near the prison; and every day we used to wait about, talking with each other, until the prison was opened, for it was not opened early; and when it was opened, we went in to Socrates and passed most of the day with him. On that day we came together earlier; for the day before, when we left the prison in the evening we heard that the ship had arrived from Delos. So we agreed to come to the usual place as early in the morning as possible. And we came, and the jailer who usually answered the door came out and told us to wait and not go in until he told us. "For," he said, "the eleven are releasing Socrates from his fetters and giving directions how he is to die to-day." So after a little delay he came and told us to go in. We went in and found Socrates just released from his fetters and Xanthippe—you know her—with his little son in her arms, sitting beside him. Now when Xanthippe saw us, she cried out and said the kind of thing that women always do say: "Oh Socrates, this is the last time now that your friends will speak to you or you to them." And Socrates glanced at Crito and said, "Crito, let somebody take her home." And some of Crito's people took her away wailing and beating her breast. But Socrates sat up on his couch and bent his leg and rubbed it with his hand, and while he was rubbing it, he said, "What a strange thing, my friends, that seems to be which men call pleasure! How wonderfully it is related to that which seems to be its opposite, pain, in that they will not both come to a man at the same time, and yet if he pursues the one and captures it, he is generally obliged to take the other also, as if the two were joined together in one head. And I think," he said, "if Aesop had thought of them, he would have made a fable telling how they were at war and god wished to reconcile them, and when he could not do that, he fastened their heads together, and for that reason, when one of them comes to anyone, the other follows after. Just so it seems that in my case, after pain was in my leg on account of the fetter, pleasure appears to have come following after."

Here Cebes interrupted and said, "By Zeus, Socrates, I am glad you reminded me. Several others have asked about the poems you have composed, the metrical versions of Aesop's fables and the hymn to Apollo, and Evenus asked me the day before yesterday why you who never wrote any poetry before, composed these verses after you came to prison. Now, if you care that I should be able to answer Evenus when he asks me again—and I know he will ask me—tell me what to say."

"Then tell him, Cebes," said he, "the truth, that I composed these verses not because I wished to rival him or his poems, for I knew that would not be easy, but because I wished to test the meaning of certain dreams, and to make sure that I was neglecting no duty in case their repeated commands meant that I must cultivate the Muses in this way. They were something like this. The same dream came to me often in my past life, sometimes in one form and sometimes in another, but always saying the same thing: 'Socrates,' it said, 'make music and work at it.' And I formerly thought it was urging and encouraging me to do what I was doing already and that just as people encourage runners by cheering, so the dream was encouraging me to do what I was doing, that is, to make music, because philosophy was the greatest kind of music, and I was working at that. But now, after the trial and while the festival of the god delayed my execution, I thought, in case the repeated dream really meant to tell me to make this which is ordinarily called music, I ought to do so and not to disobey. For I thought it was safer not to go hence before making sure that I had done what I ought, by obeying the dream and composing verses. So first I composed a hymn to the god whose festival it was; and after the god, considering that a poet, if he is really to be a poet, must compose myths and not speeches, since I was not a maker of myths, I took the myths of Aesop, which I had at hand and knew, and turned into verse the first I came upon. So tell Evenus that, Cebes, and bid him farewell, and tell him, if he is wise, to come after me as quickly as he can. I, it seems, am going to-day; for that is the order of the Athenians."

And Simmias said, "What a message that is, Socrates, for Evenus! I have met him often, and from what I have seen of him, I should say that he will not take your advice in the least if he can help it."

"Why so?" said he. "Is not Evenus a philosopher?"

"I think so," said Simmias.

"Then Evenus will take my advice, and so will every man who has any worthy interest in philosophy. Perhaps, however, he will not take his own life, for they say that is not permitted." And as he spoke he put his feet down on the ground and remained sitting in this way through the rest of the conversation.

Then Cebes asked him: "What do you mean by this, Socrates, that it is not permitted to take one's life, but that the philosopher would desire to follow after the dying?"

"How is this, Cebes? Have you and Simmias, who are pupils of Philolaus, not heard about such things?"

"Nothing definite, Socrates."

"I myself speak of them only from hearsay; but I have no objection to telling what I have heard. And indeed it is perhaps especially fitting, as I am going to the other world, to tell stories about the life there and consider what we think about it; for what else could one do in the time between now and sunset?"

"Why in the world do they say that it is not permitted to kill oneself, Socrates? I heard Philolaus, when he was living in our city, say the same thing you just said, and I have heard it from others, too, that one must not do this; but I never heard anyone say anything definite about it."

"You must have courage," said he, "and perhaps you might

hear something. But perhaps it will seem strange to you that this alone of all laws is without exception, and it never happens to mankind, as in other matters, that only at some times and for some persons it is better to die than to live; and it will perhaps seems strange to you that these human beings for whom it is better to die cannot without impiety do good to themselves, but must wait for some other benefactor."

And Cebes, smiling gently, said, "Gawd knows it doos," speaking in his dialect.

"It would seem unreasonable, if put in this way," said Socrates, "but perhaps there is some reason in it. Now the doctrine that is taught in secret about this matter, that we men are in a kind of prison and must not set ourselves free or run away, seems to me to be weighty and not easy to understand. But this at least, Cebes, I do believe is sound, that the gods are our guardians and that we men are one of the chattels of the gods. Do you not believe this?"

"Yes," said Cebes, "I do."

"Well then," said he, "if one of your chattels should kill itself when you had not indicated that you wished it to die, would you be angry with it and punish it if you could?"

"Certainly," he replied.

"Then perhaps from this point of view it is not unreasonable to say that a man must not kill himself until god sends some necessity upon him, such as has now come upon me."

"That," said Cebes, "seems sensible. But what you said just now, Socrates, that philosophers ought to be ready and willing to die, that seems strange if we were right just now in saying that god is our guardian and we are his possessions. For it is not reasonable that the wisest men should not be troubled when they leave that service in which the gods, who are the best overseers in the world, are watching over them. A wise man certainly does not think that when he is free he can take better care of himself than they do. A foolish man might perhaps think so, that he ought to run away from his master, and he would not consider that he must not run away from a good master, but ought to stay with him as long as possible; and so he might thoughtlessly run away; but a man of sense would wish to be always with one who is better than himself. And yet, Socrates, if we look at it in this way, the contrary of what we just said seems natural; for the wise ought to be troubled at dying and the foolish to rejoice."

When Socrates heard this I thought he was pleased by Cebes' earnestness, and glancing at us, he said, "Cebes is always on the track of arguments and will not be easily convinced by whatever anyone says."

And Simmias said, "Well, Socrates, this time I think myself that Cebes is right. For why should really wise men run away from masters who are better than they and lightly separate themselves from them? And it strikes me that Cebes is aiming his argument at you, because you are so ready to leave us and the gods, who are, as you yourself agree, good rulers."

"You have a right to say that," he replied; "for I think you mean that I must defend myself against this accusation, as if we were in a law court."

"Precisely," said Simmias.

"Well, then," said he, "I will try to make a more convincing defence than I did before the judges. For if I did not believe," said he, "that I was going to other wise and good gods, and, moreover, to men who have died, better men than those here, I should be wrong in not grieving at death. But as it is, you may rest assured that I expect to go to good men, though I should not care to assert this positively; but I would assert as positively as anything about such matters that I am going to gods who are good masters. And therefore, so far as that is concerned, I not only do not grieve, but I have great hopes that there is something in store for the dead, and, as has been said of old, something better for the good than for the wicked."

"Well," said Simmias, "do you intend to go away, Socrates, and keep your opinion to yourself, or would you let us share it? It seems to me that this is a good which belongs in common to us also, and at the same time, if you convince us by what you say, that will serve as your defence."

"I will try," he replied. "But first let us ask Crito there what he wants. He has apparently been trying to say something for a long time."

"Only, Socrates," said Crito, "that the man who is to administer the poison to you has been telling me for some time to warn you to talk as little as possible. He says people get warm when they talk and heat has a bad effect on the action of the poison; so sometimes he has to make those who talk too much drink twice or even three times."

And Socrates said: "Never mind him. Just let him do his part and prepare to give it twice or even, if necessary, three times."

"I was pretty sure that was what you would say," said Crito, "but he has been bothering me for a long time."

"Never mind him," said Socrates. "I wish now to explain to you, my judges, the reason why I think a man who has really spent his life in philosophy is naturally of good courage when he is to die, and has strong hopes that when he is dead he will attain the greatest blessings in that other land. So I will try to tell you, Simmias, and Cebes, how this would be.

"Other people are likely not to be aware that those who pursue philosophy aright study nothing but dying and being dead. Now if this is true, it would be absurd to be eager for nothing but this all their lives, and then to be troubled when that came for which they had all along been eagerly practising."

And Simmias laughed and said, "By Zeus, Socrates, I don't feel much like laughing just now, but you made me laugh. For I think the multitude, they heard what you just said about the philosophers, would say you were quite right, and our people at home would agree entirely with you that philosophers desire death, and they would add that they know very well that the philosophers deserve it."

"And they would be speaking the truth, Simmias, except in the matter of knowing very well. For they do not know in what way the real philosophers desire death, nor in what way they deserve death, nor what kind of death it is. Let us then," said he, "speak with one another, paying no further attention to them. Do we think there is such a thing as death?"

"Certainly," replied Simmias.

"We believe, do we not, that death is the separation of the soul from the body, and that the state of being dead is the state in which the body is separated from the soul and exists alone by itself and the soul is separated from the body and exists alone by itself? Is death anything other than this?" "No, it is this," said he.

"Now, my friend, see if you agree with me; for, if you do, I think we shall get more light on our subject. Do you think a philosopher would be likely to care much about the so-called pleasures, such as eating and drinking?"

"By no means, Socrates," said Simmias.

"How about the pleasures of love?"

"Certainly not."

"Well, do you think such a man would think much of the other cares of the body—I mean such as the possession of fine clothes and shoes and the other personal adornments? Do you think he would care about them or despise them, except so far as it is necessary to have them?"

"I think the true philosopher would despise them," he replied.

"Altogether, then, you think that such a man would not devote himself to the body, but would, so far as he was able, turn away from the body and concern himself with the soul?"

"Yes."

"To begin with, then, it is clear that in such matters the philosopher, more than other men, separates the soul from communion with the body?"

"It is."

"Now certainly most people think that a man who takes no pleasure and has no part in such things doesn't deserve to live, and that one who cares nothing for the pleasures of the body is about as good as dead."

"That is very true."

—

WHEN HE HAD finished speaking, Crito said: "Well, Socrates, do you wish to leave any directions with us about your children or anything else—anything we can do to serve you?"

"What I always say, Crito," he replied, "nothing new. If you take care of yourselves you will serve me and mine and yourselves, whatever you do, even if you make no promises now; but if you neglect yourselves and are not willing to live following step by step, as it were, in the path marked out by our present and past discussions, you will accomplish nothing, no matter how much or how eagerly you promise at present."

"We will certainly try hard to do as you say," he replied. "But how shall we bury you?"

"However you please," he replied, "if you can catch me and I do not get away from you." And he laughed gently, and looking towards us, said: "I cannot persuade Crito, my friends, that the Socrates who is now conversing and arranging the details of his argument is really I; he thinks I am the one whom he will presently see as a corpse, and he asks how to bury me. And though I have been saying at great length that after I drink the poison I shall no longer be with you, but shall go away to the joys of the blessed you know of, he seems to think that was idle talk uttered to encourage you and myself. So," he said, "give security for me to Crito, the opposite of that which he gave the judges at my trial; for he gave security that I would remain, but you must give security that I shall not remain when I die, but shall go away, so that Crito may bear it more easily, and may not be troubled when he sees my body being burnt or buried, or think I am undergoing terrible treatment, and may not say at the funeral that he is laying out Socrates, or following him to the grave, or burying him. For, dear Crito, you may be sure that such wrong words are not only undesirable in themselves, but they infect the soul with evil. No, you must be of good courage, and say that you bury my body,—and bury it as you think best and as seems to you most fitting."

When he had said this, he got up and went into another room to bathe; Crito followed him, but he told us to wait. So we waited, talking over with each other and discussing the discourse we had heard, and then speaking of the great misfortune that had befallen us, for we felt that he was like a father to us and that when bereft of him we should pass the rest of our lives as orphans. And when he had bathed and his children had been brought to him—for he had two little sons and one big one—and the women of the family had come, he talked with them in Crito's presence and gave them such directions as he wished; then he told the women to go away, and he came to us. And it was now nearly sunset; for he had spent a long time within. And he came and sat down fresh from the bath. After that not much was said, and the servant of the eleven came and stood beside him and said: "Socrates, I shall not find fault with you, as I do with others, for being angry and cursing me, when at the behest of the authorities, I tell them to drink the poison. No, I have found you in all this time in every way the noblest and gentlest and best man who has ever come here, and now I know your anger is directed against others, not against me, for you know who are to blame. Now, for you know the message I came to bring you, farewell and try to bear what you must as easily as you can." And then he said to us: "How charming the man is! Ever since I have been here he has been coming to see me and talking with me from time to time, and has been the best of men, and now how nobly he weeps for me! But come, Crito, let us obey him, and let someone bring the poison, if it is ready; and if not, let the man prepare it." And Crito said: "But I think, Socrates, the sun is still upon the mountains and has not yet set; and I know that others have taken the poison very late, after the order has come to them, and in the meantime have eaten and drunk and some of them enjoyed the society of those whom they loved. Do not hurry; for there is still time."

And Socrates said: "Crito, those whom you mention are right in doing as they do, for they think they gain by it; and I shall be right in not doing as they do; for I think I should gain nothing by taking the poison a little later. I should only make myself ridiculous in my own eyes if I clung to life and spared it, when there is no more profit in it. Come," he said, "do as I ask and do not refuse."

Thereupon Crito nodded to the boy who was standing near. The boy went out and stayed a long time, then came back with the man who was to administer the poison, which he brought with him in a cup ready for use. And when Socrates saw him, he said: "Well, my good man, you know about these things; what must I do?" "Nothing," he replied, "except drink the poison and walk about till your legs feel heavy; then lie down, and the poison will take effect of itself."

At the same time he held out the cup to Socrates. He took it, and very gently, Echecrates, without trembling or changing color or expression, but looking up at the man with wide open eyes, as was his custom, said: "What do you say about pouring a libation to some deity from this cup? May I, or not?" "Socrates," said he, "we prepare only as much as we think is enough." "I understand," said Socrates; "but I may and must pray to the gods that my departure hence be a fortunate one; so I offer this prayer, and may it be granted." With these words he raised the cup to his lips and very cheerfully and quietly drained it. Up to that time most of us had been able to restrain our tears fairly well, but when we watched him drinking and saw that he had drunk the poison, we could do so no longer, but in spite of myself my tears rolled down in floods, so that I wrapped my face in my cloak and wept for myself; for it was not for him that I wept, but for my own misfortune in being deprived of such a friend. Crito had got up and gone away even before I did, because he could not restrain his tears. But Apollodorus, who had been weeping all the time before, then wailed aloud in his grief and made us all break down, except Socrates himself. But he said, "What conduct is this, you strange men! I sent the women away chiefly for this very reason, that they might not behave in this absurd way; for I have heard that it is best to die in silence. Keep quiet and be brave." Then we were ashamed and controlled our tears. He walked about and, when he said his legs were heavy, lay down on his back, for such was the advice of the attendant. The man who had administered the poison laid his hands on him and after a while examined his hands and legs, then pinched his foot hard and asked if he felt it. He said "No"; then after that, his thighs; and passing upwards in this way he showed us that he was growing cold and rigid. And again he touched him and said that when it reached his heart, he would be gone. The chill had now reached the region about the groin, and uncovering his face, which had been covered, he said—and these were his last words—"Crito, we owe a cock to Aesceulapius. Pay it and do not neglect it." "That," said Crito, "shall be done; but see if you have anything else to say." To this question he made no reply, but after a little while he moved; the attendant uncovered him; his eyes were fixed. And Crito when he saw it, closed his mouth and eyes.

Such was the end, Echecrates, of our friend, who was, as we may say, of all those of his time whom we have known, the best and wisest and most righteous man.

ALFRED ALVAREZ

—

The Savage God

SUICIDE IS A closed
world with its own irresistible logic. This is not to say that people commit suicide, as the Stoics did, coolly, deliberately, as a rational choice
between rational alternatives. The Romans may have disciplined themselves into accepting this frigid logic, but those who have done so in
modern history are, in the last analysis, monsters. And like all monsters,
they are hard to find. In 1735 John Robeck, a Swedish philosopher living

---

*After the poet Sylvia Plath committed suicide, her friend, the novelist and
critic Alfred Alvarez began his classic study,* The Savage God. *The 1970 book
tells the story of Plath's later life and examines the relationship of suicide to
literature. In this excerpt, Alvarez, who attempted suicide himself, grippingly
relives the experience and explains why he chose life.*

in Germany, completed a long Stoic defense of suicide as a just, right and desirable act; he then carefully put his principles into practice by giving away his property and drowning himself in the Weser. His death was the sensation of the day. It provoked Voltaire to comment, through one of the characters in *Candide*: "... I have seen a prodigious number of people who hold their existence in execration; but I have only seen a dozen who voluntarily put an end to their misery: three Negroes, four Englishmen, four Genevois, and a German professor called Robeck." Even for Voltaire, the supreme rationalist, a purely rational suicide was something prodigious and slightly grotesque, like a comet or a two-headed sheep.

The logic of suicide is, then, not rational in the old Stoic sense. It scarcely could be, since there is almost no one now, even among the philosophers, who believes that reason is clean and straightforward, or that motives can ever be less than equivocal. "The desires of the heart," said Auden, "are as crooked as corkscrews." To the extent that suicide *is* logical, it is also unreal: too simple, too convincing, too total, like one of those paranoid systems, such as Ezra Pound's Social Credit, by which madmen explain the universe. The logic of suicide is different. It is like the unanswerable logic of a nightmare, or like the science-fiction fantasy of being projected suddenly into another dimension: everything makes sense and follows its own strict rules; yet, at the same time, everything is also different, perverted, upside down. Once a man decides to take his own life he enters a shut-off, impregnable but wholly convincing world where every detail fits and each incident reinforces his decision. An argument with a stranger in a bar, an expected letter which doesn't arrive, the wrong voice on the telephone, the wrong knock at the door, even a change in the weather—all seem charged with special meaning; they all contribute. The world of the suicide is superstitious, full of omens. Freud saw suicide as a great passion, like being in love: "In the two opposed situations of being most intensely in love and of suicide, the ego is overwhelmed by the object, though in totally different ways." As in love, things which seem trivial to the outsider, tiresome or amusing, assume enormous importance to those in the grip of the monster, while the sanest arguments against it seem to them simply absurd.

This imperviousness to everything outside the closed world of self-destruction can produce an obsession so weird and total, so psychotic, that death itself becomes a side issue. In nineteenth-century Vienna a man of seventy drove seven three-inch nails into the top of his head with a heavy blacksmith's hammer. For some reason he did not die immediately, so he changed his mind and walked to the hospital, streaming blood. In March 1971 a Belfast businessman killed himself by boring nine holes in his head with a power drill. There is also the case of a Polish girl, unhappily in love, who in five months swallowed four spoons, three knives, nineteen coins, twenty nails, seven window bolts, a brass cross, one hundred and one pins, a stone, three pieces of glass and two beads from her rosary. In each instance the suicidal gesture seems to have mattered more than its outcome. People try to die in such operatic ways only when they are obsessed more by the means than by the end, just as a sexual fetishist gets more satisfaction from his rituals than from the orgasm to which they lead. The old man driving nails into his skull, the company director with his power drill and the lovelorn girl swallowing all the hardware seem to have acted wildly out of despair. Yet in order to behave in precisely that way they must have brooded endlessly over the details, selecting, modifying, perfecting them like artists, until they produced that single, unrepeatable happening which expressed their madness in all its uniqueness. In the circumstances, death may come but it is superfluous.

Without this wild drama of psychosis, there is a form of suicide, more commonplace but also more deadly, which is simply an extreme form of self-injury. The psychoanalysts have suggested that a man may destroy himself not because he wants to die, but because there is a single aspect of himself which he cannot tolerate. A suicide of this order is a perfectionist. The flaws in his nature exacerbate him like some secret itch he cannot get at. So he acts suddenly, rashly, out of exasperation. Thus Kirillov, in Dostoevsky's *The Possessed*, kills himself, he says, to show that he is God. But secretly he kills himself because he knows he is not God. Had his ambitions been less, perhaps he would have only attempted the deed or mutilated himself. He conceived of his mortality as a kind of lapse, an error which offended him beyond bearing. So in the end he pulled the trigger in order to shed this mortality like a tatty suit of clothes, but without taking into account that the clothes were, in fact, his own warm body.

Compared with the other revolutionaries in the novel, Kirillov seems sane, tender-hearted and upright. Yet maybe his concern with Godhead and metaphysical liberty consigns him, too, to the suburbs of psychosis. And this sets him apart from the majority of the inhabitants of the closed world of suicide. For them, the act is neither rash nor operatic nor, in any obvious way, unbalanced. Instead it is, insidiously, a vocation. Once inside the closed world, there seems never to have been a time when one was not suicidal. Just as a writer feels himself never to have been anything except a writer, even if he can remember with embarrassment his first doggerel, even if he has spent years, like Conrad, disguised as a sea dog, so the suicide feels he has always been preparing in secret for this last act. There is no end to his sense of *déjà vu* or to his justifications. His memory is stored with long, black afternoons of childhood, with the taste of pleasures that gave no pleasure, with sour losses and failures, all repeated endlessly like a scratched phonograph record.

An English novelist who had made two serious suicide attempts said this to me: "I don't know how much potentially suicides *think* about it. I must say, I've never really thought about it much. Yet it's always there. For me, suicide's a constant temptation. It never slackens. Things are all right at the moment. But I feel like a cured alcoholic: I daren't take a drink because I know that if I do I'll go on it again.

Because whatever it is that's there doesn't alter. It's a pattern of my entire life. I would like to think that it was only brought on by certain stresses and strains. But in fact, if I'm honest and look back, I realize it's been a pattern ever since I can remember.

"My parents were very fond of death. It was their favorite thing. As a child, it seemed to me that my father was constantly rushing off to do himself in. Everything he said, all his analogies, were to do with death. I remember him once telling me that marriage was the last nail in the coffin of life. I was about eight at the time. Both my parents, for different reasons, regarded death as a perfect release from their troubles. They were very unhappy together, and I think this sunk in very much. Like my father, I have always demanded too much of life and people and relationships—far more than exists, really. And when I find that it doesn't exist, it seems like a rejection. It probably isn't a rejection at all; it simply isn't there. I mean, the empty air doesn't reject you; it just says, 'I'm empty.' Yet rejection and disappointment are two things I've always found impossible to take.

"In the afternoons my mother and father both retired to sleep. That is, they retired to death. They really died for the afternoons. My father was a parson. He had nothing to do, he had no work. I begin now to understand how it was for him. When I'm not working, I'm capable of sleeping through most of the morning. Then I start taking sleeping pills during the day to keep myself in a state of dopiness, so that I can sleep at any time. To take sleeping pills during the day to sleep isn't so far from taking sleeping pills in order to die. It's just a bit more practical and a bit more craven. You only take two instead of two hundred. But during those afternoons I used to be alive and lively. It was a great big house but I never dared make a sound. I didn't dare pull a plug in case I woke one of them up. I felt terribly rejected. Their door was shut, they were absolutely unapproachable. Whatever terrible crisis had happened to me, I felt I couldn't go and say 'Hey, wake up, listen to me.' And those afternoons went on a long time. Because of the war I went back to live with them, and it was still exactly the same. If I ever bumped myself off, it would be in the afternoon. Indeed, the first time I tried was in the afternoon. The second time was after an awful afternoon. Moreover, it was after an afternoon in the country, which I hate for the same reasons as I hate afternoons. The reason is simple: when I'm alone, I stop believing I exist."

Although the speaker is well into a successful middle age, the injured and rejected child she had once been still lives powerfully on. Perhaps it is this element which makes the closed world of suicide so inescapable: the wounds of the past, like those of the Fisher King in the legend of the Holy Grail, will not heal over—the ego, the analysts would say, is too fragile—instead, they continually push themselves to the surface to obliterate the modified pleasures and acceptances of the present. The life of the suicide is, to an extraordinary degree, unforgiving. Nothing he achieves by his own efforts, or luck bestows, reconciles him to his injurious past.

Thus, on August 16, 1950, ten days before he finally took sleeping pills, Pavese wrote in his notebook: "Today I see clearly that from 1928 until now I have always lived under this shadow." But in 1928 Pavese was already twenty. From what we know of his desolate childhood—his father dead when he was six, his mother of spun steel, harsh and austere—the shadow was probably on him much earlier; at twenty he simply recognized it for what it was. At thirty he had written flatly and without self-pity, as though it were some practical detail he had just noticed: "Every luxury must be paid for, and everything is a luxury, starting with being in the world."

A suicide of this kind is born, not made. As I said earlier, he receives his reasons—from whatever nexus of guilt, loss and despair—when he is too young to cope with them or understand. All he can do is accept them innocently and try to defend himself as best he can. By the time he recognizes them more objectively, they have become part of his sensibility, his way of seeing and his way of life. Unlike the psychotic self-injurer, whose suicide is a sudden fatal twist in the road, his whole life is a gradual downward curve, steepening at the end, on which he moves knowingly, unable and unwilling to stop himself. No amount of success will change him. Before his death Pavese was writing better than ever before—more richly, more powerfully, more easily. In the year before he died he turned out two of his best novels, each in less than two months of writing. One month before the end he received the Strega Prize, the supreme accolade for an Italian writer. "I have never been so much alive as now," he wrote, "never so young." A few days later he was dead. Perhaps the sweetness itself of his creative powers made his innate depression all the harder to bear. It is as though those strengths and rewards belonged to some inner part of him from which he felt himself irredeemably alienated.

It is also characteristic of this type of suicide that his beliefs do not help him. Although Pavese called himself a Communist, his politics permeate neither his imaginative work nor his private notebooks. I suspect they were merely a gesture of solidarity with the people he liked, against those he disliked. He was a Communist not because of any particular conviction, but because he hated the Fascists who had imprisoned him. In practice, he was like nearly everybody else in this present time: skeptical, pragmatic, adrift, sustained neither by the religion of the Church nor by that of the Party. In these circumstances, "this business of living"—the title of his notebooks—becomes particularly chancy. What Durkheim called "anomie" may lead to a social conception of man infinitely more impoverished than any religious formulation of his role as a servant of God. Yet since the decline of religious authority, the only alternative to the ersatz and unsatisfactory religions of science and politics has been an uneasy, perilous freedom. This is summed up in an eerie note found in an empty house in Hampstead: "Why Suicide? Why not?"

Why not? The pleasures of living—the hedonistic pleasures of the five senses, the more complex and demanding pleasures of concentration and doing, even the unanswerable commitments of love—seem often no greater and mostly less frequent than the frustrations—the continual sense of unfinished and unfinishable business, jangled, anxious, ragged, overborne. If secularized man were kept going only by the pleasure principle, the human race would already be extinct. Yet maybe his secular quality is his strength. He chooses life because he has no alternative, because he knows that after death there is nothing at all. When Camus wrote *The Myth of Sisyphus*—in 1940, after the fall of France, a serious personal illness and depressive crisis— he began with suicide and ended with an affirmation of individual life, in itself and for itself, desirable because it is "absurd," without final meaning or metaphysical justification. "Life is a gift that nobody should renounce," the great Russian poet Osip Mandelstam said to his wife when, in exile after his imprisonment, she proposed that they commit suicide together if Stalin's secret police took them again. Hamlet said that the only obstacle to self-slaughter was fear of the afterlife, which was an unconvinced but Christian answer to all those noble suicides which the heroes of Shakespeare's Roman plays performed so unhesitatingly. Without the buttress of Christianity, without the cold dignity of a Stoicism that had evolved in response to a world in which human life was a trivial commodity, cheap enough to be expended at every circus to amuse the crowd, the rational obstacles begin to seem strangely flimsy. When neither high purpose nor the categorical imperatives of religion will do, the only argument against suicide is life itself. You pause and attend: the heart beats in your chest; outside, the trees are thick with new leaves, a swallow dips over them, the light moves, people are going about their business. Perhaps this is what Freud meant by "the narcissistic satisfactions [which the ego] derives from being alive." Most of the time, they seem enough. They are, anyway, all we ever have or can ever expect.

Yet such "satisfactions" can also be very fragile. A shift of focus in one's life, a sudden loss or separation, a single irreversible act can suffice to make the whole process intolerable. Perhaps this is what is implied by the phrase "suicide when the balance of mind was disturbed." It is, of course, a legal formula evolved to protect the dead man from the law and to spare the feelings and insurance benefits of his family. But it also has a certain existential truth: without the checks of belief, the balance between life and death can be perilously delicate.

Consider a climber poised on minute holds on a steep cliff. The smallness of the holds, the steepness of the angle, all add to his pleasure, provided he is in complete control. He is a man playing chess with his body; he can read the sequence of moves far enough in advance so that his physical economy—the ratio between the effort he uses and his reserves of strength—is never totally disrupted. The more improbable the situation and the greater the demands made on him, the more sweetly the blood flows later in release from all tension. The possibility of danger serves merely to sharpen his awareness and control. And perhaps this is the rationale of all risky sports: you deliberately raise the ante of effort and concentration in order, as it were, to clear your mind of trivialities. It is a small-scale model for living, but with a difference: unlike your routine life, where mistakes can usually be recouped and some kind of compromise patched up, your actions, for however brief a period, are deadly serious.

I think there may be some people who kill themselves like this: in order to achieve a calm and control they never find in life. Antonin Artaud, who spent most of his life in lunatic asylums, once wrote:

If I commit suicide, it will not be to destroy myself but to put myself back together again. Suicide will be for me only one means of violently reconquering myself, of brutally invading my being, of anticipating the unpredictable approaches of God. By suicide, I reintroduce my design in nature, I shall for the first time give things the shape of my will. I free myself from the conditioned reflexes of my organs, which are so badly adjusted to my inner self, and life is for me no longer an absurd accident whereby I think what I am told to think. But now I choose my thought and the direction of my faculties, my tendencies, my reality. I place myself between the beautiful and the hideous, the good and evil. I put myself in suspension, without innate propensities, neutral, in the state of equilibrium between good and evil solicitations.

THERE IS, I believe, a whole class of suicides, though infinitely less gifted than Artaud and less extreme in their perceptions, who take their own lives not in order to die but to escape confusion, to clear their heads. They deliberately use suicide to create an unencumbered reality for themselves or to break through the patterns of obsession and necessity which they have unwittingly imposed upon their lives. There are also others, similar but less despairing, for whom the mere idea of suicide is enough; they can continue to function efficiently, and even happily, provided they know they have their own, specially chosen means of escape always ready: a hidden cache of sleeping pills, a gun at the back of a drawer, like the wife in Lowell's poem who sleeps every night with her car key and ten dollars strapped to her thigh.

But there is also another, perhaps more numerous class of suicide to whom the *idea* of taking their own lives is utterly repugnant. These are the people who will do everything to destroy themselves except admit that that is what they are after; they will, that is, do everything except take the final responsibility for their actions. Hence all those cases of what Karl Menninger calls "chronic suicide"—the alcoholics and drug addicts who kill themselves slowly and piecemeal, all the while protesting that they are merely taking the necessary steps to make an intolerable life tolerable. Hence, too, those thousands of inexplicable fatal accidents—the good drivers who die in car crashes, the careful pedestrians who get themselves run over—which never make the suicide statistics. The image recurs of the same climber in the same unforgiving situation. In the grip of some depression he may not even recognize, he could die almost without knowing it. Impatiently, he fails to take the necessary safety measures; he climbs a little too fast and without working out his moves far enough in advance. And suddenly, the risks have become disproportionate. For a fatal accident, there is no longer need of any conscious thought or impulse of despair, still less a deliberate action. He has only to surrender for a moment to the darkness beneath the threshold. The smallest mistake—an impetuous move not quite in balance, an error of judgment which leaves him extended beyond his strength, with no way back and no prospect of relief—and the man will be dead without realizing that he wanted to die. "The victim lets himself act," said Valéry, "and his death escapes from him like a rash remark. . . . He kills himself because it is too easy to kill himself." Whence, I suppose, all those so-called "impetuous suicides" who, if they survive, claim never to have considered the act until moments before their attempt. Once recovered, they seem above all embarrassed, ashamed of what they have done, and unwilling to admit that they were ever genuinely suicidal. They can return to life, that is, only by denying the strength of their despair, transforming their unconscious but deliberate choice into an impulsive, meaningless mistake. They wanted to die without accepting the responsibility for their decision.

Every so often the opposite of all this occurs: there is a cult of suicide which has very little to do with real death. Thus early-nineteenth-century Romanticism—as a pop phenomenon rather than as a serious creative movement—was dominated by the twin stars of Thomas Chatterton and Goethe's Young Werther. The ideal was "to cease upon the midnight with no pain" while still young and beautiful and full of promise. Suicide added a dimension of drama and doom, a fine black orchid to the already tropical jungle of the period's emotional life. One hundred years later a similar cult grew up around the *Inconnue de la Seine*. During the 1920s and early 1930s all over the Continent, nearly every student of sensibility had a plaster cast of her death mask: a young, full, sweetly smiling face which seems less dead than peacefully sleeping.

The girl was in fact genuinely *inconnue*. All that is known of her is that she was fished out of the Seine and exposed on a block of ice in the Paris Morgue, along with a couple of hundred other corpses awaiting identification. (On the evidence of her hair style, Sacheverell Sitwell believes this happened not later than the early 1880s.) She was never claimed, but someone was sufficiently impressed by her peaceful smile to take a death mask.

It is also possible that it never happened at all. In another version of the story a researcher, unable to obtain information at the Paris Morgue, followed her trail to the German source of the plaster casts. At the factory he met the *Inconnue* herself, alive and well and living in Hamburg, the daughter of the now-prosperous manufacturer of her image.

There is, however, no doubt at all about the cult around her. I am told that a whole generation of German girls modeled their looks on her. She appears in appropriately aroused stories by Richard Le Gallienne, Jules Supervielle and Claire Goll, and oddly enough, since the author is a Communist, was the moving spirit behind the heroine of *Aurélian*, a long novel which Louis Aragon considers his master-piece. But her fame was spread most effectively by a sickly though much-translated best seller, *One Unknown*, by Reinhold Conrad Muschler. He makes her an innocent young country girl who comes to Paris, falls in love with a handsome British diplomat—titled, of course—has a brief but idyllic romance and then, when milord regretfully leaves to marry his suitably aristocratic English fiancée, drowns herself in the Seine. As Muschler's sales show, this was the style of explanation the public wanted for that enigmatic, dead face.

The cult of the *Inconnue* seemed to attract young people between the two world wars in much the same way as drugs call them now: to opt out before they start, to give up a struggle that frightens them in a world they find distasteful, and to slide away into a deep inner dream. Death by drowning and blowing your mind with drugs amount, in fantasy, to the same thing: the sweetness, shadow and easy release of a successful regression. So the cult flourished in the absence of all facts, perhaps it even flourished because there were no facts. Like a Rorschach blot, the dead face was the receptacle for any feelings the onlooker wished to project into it. And like the Sphinx and the Mona Lisa, the power of the *Inconnue* was in her smile—subtle, oblivious, promising peace. Not only was she out of it all, beyond troubles, beyond responsibilities, she had also remained beautiful; she had retained the quality the young most fear to lose—their youth. Although Sitwell credits to her influence an epidemic of suicide among the young people of Evreux, I suspect she may have saved more lives than she destroyed. To know that it can be done, that the option really exists and is even becoming, is usually enough to relieve a mildly suicidal anxiety. In the end, the function of the Romantic suicide cult is to be a focus for wandering melancholy; almost nobody actually dies.

The expression on the face of the *Inconnue* implies that her death was both easy and painless. These, I think, are the dual qualities, almost ideals, which distinguish modern suicide from that of the past. Robert Lowell once remarked that if there were some little switch in the arm which one could press in order to die immediately and without pain, then everyone would sooner or later commit suicide. It seems that we are rapidly moving toward that questionable ideal. The reason is not hard to find. Statistics, for what they are worth, show that in Great Britain, France, Germany and Japan there has been an enormous increase in death by drugs. In a brilliant essay entitled "Self-Poisoning," Dr. Neil Kessel has written:

In every century before our own, poisons and drugs were dissimilar. Poisons were substances which should not be taken at all, the province not of physicians but of wizards. Their properties verged upon the magical. They were, indeed, "unctions bought of montebanks." By the second half of the nineteenth century, science had displaced sorcery and poisons were purchased from the chemist, not the alchemist. But they still differed from

drugs. *Drugs, with few exceptions, though recognized to produce undesir-*
able actions if taken in excess, were not considered lethal agents and were
not used to kill. The growth of self-poisoning has come about in the train of
a rapid rise in the number of highly dangerous preparations employed ther-
apeutically, together with a great contemporaneous increase in prescribing.

The effect of this medical revolution has been to make poisons both
readily available and relatively safe. The way has thus been opened for self-
poisoning to flourish. . . . Facilities for self-poisoning have been placed with-
in the reach of everyone.

ALONG WITH THE increase in suicide by drugs has gone a propor-
tionate decrease in older, more violent methods: hanging, drowning,
shooting, cutting, jumping. What is involved, I think, is a massive and,
in effect, a qualitative change in suicide. Ever since hemlock, for whatever obscure reason, went out of general use, the act has always
entailed great physical violence. The Romans fell on their swords or, at
best, cut their wrists in hot baths; even the fastidious Cleopatra
allowed herself to be bitten by a snake. In the eighteenth century the
kind of violence you used depended on the class you belonged to: gentlemen usually took their lives with pistols, the lower classes hanged
themselves. Later it became fashionable to drown yourself, or endure
the convulsions and agonies of cheap poisons like arsenic and strychnine.
Perhaps the ancient, superstitious horror of suicide persisted so long
because the violence made it impossible to disguise the nature of the
act. Peace and oblivion were not in question; suicide was as unequivo-
cally a violation of life as murder.

Modern drugs and domestic gas have changed all that. Not
only have they made suicide more or less painless, they have also made
it seem magical. A man who takes a knife and slices deliberately across
his throat is murdering himself. But when someone lies down in front of
an unlit gas oven or swallows sleeping pills, he seems not so much to be
dying as merely seeking oblivion for a while. Dostoevsky's Kirillov said

that there are only two reasons why we do not all kill ourselves: pain and fear of the next world. We seem more or less, to have got rid of both. In suicide, as in most other areas of activity, there has been a tech-nological breakthrough which has made a cheap and relatively painless death democratically available to everyone. Perhaps this is why the sub-ject now seems so central and so demanding, why even governments spend a little money on finding its causes and possible means of preven-tion. We already have a suicidology; all we mercifully lack, for the moment, is a thorough-going philosophical rationale for the act itself. No doubt it will come. But perhaps that is only as it should be in a peri-od in which global suicide by nuclear warfare is a permanent possibility.

—

AFTER ALL THIS, I have to admit that I am a failed suicide. It is a dismal confession to make, since nothing, really, would seem to be easier than to take your own life. Seneca, the final authority on the subject, pointed out disdainfully that the exits are everywhere: each precipice and river, each branch of each tree, every vein in your body will set you free. But in the event, this isn't so. No one is promiscuous in his way of dying. A man who has decided to hang himself will never jump in front of a train. And the more sophisticated and painless the method, the greater the chance of failure: I can vouch, at least, for that. I built up to the act carefully and for a long time, with a kind of blank pertinacity. It was the one constant focus of my life, making everything else irrelevant, a diversion. Each sporadic burst of work, each minor success and disappointment, each moment of calm and relaxation, seemed merely a temporary halt on my steady descent through layer after layer of depression, like an elevator stopping for a moment on the way down to the basement. At no point was there any question of getting off or of changing the direction of the journey. Yet, despite all that, I never quite made it.

I see now that I had been incubating this death far longer than

I recognized at the time. When I was a child, both my parents had half-heartedly put their heads in the gas oven. Or so they claimed. It seemed to me then a rather splendid gesture, though shrouded in mystery, a little area of veiled intensity, revealed only by hints and unexplained, swiftly suppressed outbursts. It was something hidden, attractive and not for the children, like sex. But it was also something that undoubtedly did happen to grownups. However hysterical or comic the behavior involved—and to a child it seemed more ludicrous than tragic to place your head in the greasy gas oven, like the Sunday roast joint—suicide was a fact, a subject that couldn't be denied; it was something, however awful, that people did. When my own time came, I did not have to discover it for myself.

Maybe that is why, when I grew up and things went particularly badly, I used to say to myself, over and over, like some latter-day Mariana in the moated grange, "I wish I were dead." It was an echo from the past, joining me to my tempestuous childhood. I muttered it unthinkingly, as automatically as a Catholic priest tells his rosary. It was my special magic ritual for warding off devils, a verbal nervous tic. Dwight Macdonald once said that when you don't know what to do with your hands you light a cigarette, and when you don't know what to do with your mind you read *Time* magazine. My equivalent was this one sentence repeated until it seemingly lost all meaning: "Iwishiweredead . . . Iwishiweredead . . . Iwishiweredead. . . . " Then one day I understood what I was saying. I was walking along the edge of Hampstead Heath, after some standard domestic squabble, and suddenly I heard the phrase as though for the first time. I stood still to attend to the words. I repeated them slowly, listening. And realized that I meant it. It seemed so obvious, an answer I had known for years and never allowed myself to acknowledge. I couldn't understand how I could have been so obtuse for so long.

After that, there was only one way out, although it took a long time—many months, in fact—to get there. We moved to

America—wife, child, *au pair* girl, myself, and trunk-upon-trunk-load of luggage. I had a term's appointment at a New England university and had rented a great professorial mansion in a respectably dead suburb, ten miles from the campus, two from the nearest shop. The house was Germanic, gloomy and far too expensive. For my wife, who didn't drive, it was also as lonely as Siberia. The neighbors were mostly twice her age, the university mostly ignored us, the action was nil. There wasn't even a television set in the house. So I rented one and she sat disconsolately in front of it for two months. Then she gave up, packed her bags, and took the child back to England. I didn't even blame her. But I stayed on in a daze of misery. The last slide down the ice slope had begun and there was no way of stopping it.

My wife was not to blame. The hostility and despair that poor girl provoked in me—and I in her—came from some pure, infantile source, as any disinterested outsider could have told me. I even recognized this for myself in my clear moments. I was using her as an excuse for troubles that had their roots deep in the past. But mere intellectual recognition did no good, and anyway, my clear moments were few. My life felt so cluttered and obstructed that I could hardly breathe. I inhabited a closed, concentrated world, airless and without exits. I doubt if any of this was noticeable socially: I was simply more tense, more nervous than usual, and I drank more. But underneath I was going a bit mad. I had entered the closed world of suicide, and my life was being lived for me by forces I couldn't control.

When the Christmas break came at the university, I decided to spend the fortnight in London. Maybe, I told myself, things would be easier, at least I would see the child. So I loaded myself up with presents and climbed on a jet, dead drunk. I passed out as soon as I reached my seat and woke to a brilliant sunrise. There were dark islands below—the Hebrides, I suppose—and the eastern sea was on fire. From that altitude, the world looked calm and vivid and possible. But by the time we landed at Prestwick the clouds were down like the black cap on a hanging judge.

We waited and waited hopelessly on the runway, the rain drumming on the fuselage, until the soaking fog lifted at London Airport.

When I finally got home, hours late, no one was there. The fires were blazing, the clocks were ticking, the telephone was still. I wandered around the empty house touching things, frightened, expectant. Fifteen minutes later, there was a noise at the front door and my child plunged shouting up the stairs into my arms. Over his shoulder I could see my wife standing tentatively in the hall. She, too, looked scared.

"We thought you were lost," she said. "We went down to the terminal and you didn't come."

"I got a lift straight from the airport. I phoned but you must have left. I'm sorry."

Chilly and uncertain, she presented her cheek to be kissed. I obliged, holding my son in my arms. There was still a week until Christmas.

We didn't stand a chance. Within hours we were at each other again, and that night I started drinking. Mostly, I'm a social drinker. Like everyone else, I've been drunk in my time but it's not really my style; I value my control too highly. This time, however, I went at the bottle with a pure need, as though parched. I drank before I got out of bed, almost before my eyes were open. I continued steadily throughout the morning until, by lunchtime, I had half a bottle of whiskey inside me and was beginning to feel human. Not drunk: that first half-bottle simply brought me to that point of calm where I usually began. Which is not particularly calm. Around lunchtime a friend—also depressed, also drinking—joined me at the pub and we boozed until closing time. Back home, with our wives, we kept at it steadily through the afternoon and evening, late into the night. The important thing was not to stop. In this way, I got through a bottle of whiskey a day, a good deal of wine and beer. Yet it had little effect. Toward evening, when the child was in bed, I suppose I was a little tipsy, but the drinking was merely part of a more jagged frenzy which possessed us all. We kept the hi-fi booming pop, we danced, we had trials of strength: one-arm push-ups, handstands, somersaults; we balanced pint pots of beer on our fore-heads, and tried to lie down and stand up again without spilling them. Anything not to stop, think, feel. The tension was so great that without booze, we would have splintered into sharp fragments.

On Christmas Eve, the other couple went off on a skiing holiday. My wife and I were left staring at each other. Silently and meticulously, we decorated the Christmas tree and piled the presents, waiting. There was nothing left to say.

Late that afternoon I had sneaked off and phoned the psy-chotherapist whom I had been seeing, on and off, before I left for the States.

"I'm feeling pretty bad," I said. "Could I possibly see you?"

There was a pause. "It's rather difficult," he said at last. "Are you really desperate, or could you wait till Boxing Day?"

Poor bastard, I thought, he's got his Christmas, too. Let it go. "I can wait."

"Are you sure?" He sounded relieved. "You could come round at six-thirty, if it's urgent."

That was the child's bedtime; I wanted to be there. "It's all right," I said, "I'll phone later. Happy Christmas." What did it matter? I went back downstairs.

All my life I have hated Christmas: the unnecessary presents and obligatory cheerfulness, the grinding expense, the anticlimax. It is a day to be negotiated with infinite care, like a minefield. So I fortified myself with a stiff shot of whiskey before I got up. It combined with my child's excitement to put a glow of hope on the day. The boy sat among the gaudy wrapping paper, ribbons and bows, positively crowing with delight. At three years old, Christmas can still be a pleasure. Maybe, I began to feel, this thing could be survived. After all, hadn't I flown all the way from the States to pull my marriage from the fire? Or had I? Perhaps I knew it was unsavable and didn't want it to be otherwise. Perhaps I was merely seeking a plausible excuse for doing myself in. Perhaps that was why, even before all the presents were unwrapped, I had started it all up again: silent rages (not in front of the child), muted recriminations, withdrawals. The marriage was just one aspect of a whole life I had decided, months before, to have done with.

I remember little of what happened later. There was the usual family turkey for the child and my parents-in-law. In the evening we went out to a smart, subdued dinner party, and on from there, I think, to something wilder. But I'm not sure. I recall only two trivial but vivid scenes. The first is very late at night. We are back home with another couple whom I know only slightly. He is small, dapper, cheerful, an unsuccessful poet turned successful journalist. His wife is faceless now, but him I still see sometimes on television, reporting expertly from the more elegant foreign capitals. I remember him sitting at our old piano, playing 1930s dance tunes; his wife stands behind him, singing the words; I lean on the piano, humming tunelessly; my wife is stretched, glowering, on the sofa. We are all very drunk.

Later still, I remember standing at the front door, joking with them as they negotiate the icy steps. As they go through the gate, they turn and wave. "Happy Christmas," we call to each other. I close the door and turn back to my wife.

After that, I remember nothing at all until I woke up in the hospital and saw my wife's face swimming vaguely toward me through a yellowish fog. She was crying. But that was three days later, three days of oblivion, a hole in my head.

It happened ten years ago now, and only gradually have I been able to piece together the facts from hints and snippets, recalled reluctantly and with apologies. Nobody wants to remind an attempted suicide of his folly, or to be reminded of it. Tact and taste forbid. Or is it the failure itself which is embarrassing? Certainly, a successful suicide inspires no delicacy at all; everybody is in on the act at once with his own exclusive inside story. In my own case, my knowledge of what happened is partial and second-hand; the only accurate details are in the gloomy shorthand of the medical reports. Not that it matters, since none of it now means much to me personally. It is as though it happened to another person in another world.

It seems that when the poet-journalist left with his wife, we had one final, terrible quarrel, more bitter than anything we had managed before, and savage enough to be heard through his sleep by whoever it was who was staying the night in the guest room above. At the end of it, my wife marched out. When she had returned prematurely from the States, our own house was still leased to temporary tenants. So she had rented a dingy flat in a florid but battered Victorian mansion nearby. Since she still had the key to the place, she went to spend the night there. In my sodden despair, I suppose her departure seemed like the final nail. More likely, it was the unequivocal excuse I had been waiting for. I went upstairs to the bathroom and swallowed forty-five sleeping pills.

I had been collecting the things for months obsessionally, like Green Stamps, from doctors on both sides of the Atlantic. This was an almost legitimate activity, since in all that time I rarely got more than two consecutive hours of sleep a night. But I had always made sure of having more than I needed. Weeks before I left America, I had stopped taking the things and begun hoarding them in preparation for the time I knew was coming. When it finally arrived, a box was waiting stuffed with pills of all colors, like jellybeans. I gobbled the lot.

The following morning the guest brought me a cup of tea. The bedroom curtains were drawn, so he could not see me properly in the gloom. He heard me breathing in an odd way but thought it was probably a hangover. So he left me alone. My wife got back at noon, took one look and called the ambulance. When they got me to the hospital I was, the report says, "deeply unconscious, slightly cyanosed, vomit in mouth, pulse rapid, poor volume." I looked up "cyanosis" in the dictionary: "A morbid condition caused by insufficient aeration of the blood." Apparently I had vomited in my coma and swallowed the stuff; it was now blocking my right lung, turning my face blue. As they say, a morbid condition. When they pumped the barbituates out of my stomach, I vomited again, much more heavily, and again the muck went down to my lungs, blocking them badly. At that point I became—that word again—"deeply cyanosed"; I turned Tory-blue. They tried to suck the stuff out, and gave me oxygen and an injection, but neither had much effect. I suppose it was about this time they told my wife there wasn't much hope. This was all she ever told me of the whole incident; it was a source of great bitterness to her. Since my lungs were still blocked, they performed a bronchoscopy. This time they sucked out a "large amount of mucus." They stuck an air pipe down my throat and I began to breathe more normally. The crisis, for the moment, was over.

This was on Boxing Day, December 26. I was still unconscious the next day and most of the day after that, though all the time less and less deeply. Since my lungs remained obstructed, they continued to give me air though a pipe; they fed me intravenously through a drip tube. The shallower my coma, the more restless I became. On the evening of the second day the airway was removed. During the afternoon of the third day, December 28, I came to. I felt them pull a tube from my arm. In a fog I saw my wife smiling hesitantly, and in tears. It was all very vague. I slept.

I spent most of the next day weeping quietly and seeing everything double. Two women doctors gently cross-questioned me. Two chunky physiotherapists, with beautiful, blooming, double complexions, put me through exercises—it seems my lungs were still in a bad state. I got two trays of uneatable food at a time and tried, on and off and unsuccessfully, to do two crossword puzzles. The ward was thronged with elderly twins.

At some point the police came, since in those days suicide was still a criminal offense. They sat heavily but rather sympathetically by my bed and asked me questions they clearly didn't want me to answer. When I tried to explain, they shushed me politely. "It was an accident, wasn't it, sir?" Dimly, I agreed. They went away.

I woke during the night and heard someone cry out weakly. A nurse bustled down the aisle in the obscure light. From the other side of the ward came more weak moaning. It was taken up faintly from somewhere else in the dimness. None of it was desperate with the pain and sharpness you hear after operations or accidents. Instead, the note was enervated, wan, beyond feeling. And then I understood why, even to my double vision, the patients had all seemed so old: I was in a terminal ward. All around me, old men were trying feebly not to die; I was thirty-one years old, and despite everything, still alive. When I stirred in bed I felt, for the first time, the rubber sheet beneath me. I must have peed myself, like a small child, while I was unconscious. My whole world was shamed.

The following morning my double vision had gone. The ward was filthy yellow and seemed foggy in the corners. I tottered to the lavatory; it, too, was filthy and evil-smelling. I tottered back to bed, rested a little and then phoned my wife. Since the pills and the booze hadn't killed me, nothing would. I told her I was coming home. I wasn't dead, so I wasn't going to die. There was no point in staying.

The doctors didn't see it that way. I was scarcely off the danger list; my lungs were in a bad state; I had a temperature; I could relapse at any time; it was dangerous; it was stupid; they would not be responsible. I lay there dumbly, as weak as a newborn infant, and let the arguments flow over me. Finally I signed a sheaf of forms acknowledging that I left against advice and absolving them from responsibility. A friend drove me home.

It took all my strength and concentration to climb the one flight of stairs to the bedroom. I felt fragile and almost transparent, as though I were made of tissue paper. But when I got into pajamas and settled into bed, I found I smelled bad to myself: of illness, urine and a thin, sour death-sweat. So I rested for a while and then took a bath. Meanwhile my wife, on orders from the hospital, phoned our National Health doctor. He listened to her explanation without a word and then refused, point-blank, to come. Clearly he thought I was going to die and didn't want me added to his no doubt already prodigious score. She banged down the receiver on him in a rage, but my green face and utter debility frightened her. Someone had to be sent for. Finally the friend who had driven me home from the hospital called in his private family doctor. Authoritative, distinguished, unflappable, he came immediately and soothed everyone down.

This was on the evening of Thursday, the twenty-ninth. All Friday and Saturday I lay vaguely in bed. Occasionally I raised myself to perform the exercises which were supposed to help my lungs. I talked a little to my child, tried to read, dozed. But mostly I did nothing. My mind was blank. At times I listened to my breath coming and going; at times I was dimly aware of my heart beating. It filled me with distaste. I did not want to be alive.

On Friday night I had a terrible dream. I was dancing a savage, stamping dance with my wife, full of anger and mutual threat. Gradually the movements became more and more frenzied, until every nerve and muscle in my body was stretched taut and vibrating, as though on some fierce, ungoverned electrical machine which, fraction by fraction, was pulling me apart. When I woke I was wet with sweat, but my teeth were chattering as if I were freezing. I dozed off almost at once and again went through a similar dream: this time I was being hunted down; when the creature, whatever it was, caught me, it shook me as a dog shakes a rat, and once again every joint and nerve and muscle seemed to be rattling apart. At last I came awake completely and lay staring at the curtains. I was wide-eyed and shuddering with fear. I felt I had tasted in my dreams the death which had been denied me in my coma. My wife was sleeping in the same bed with me, yet she was utterly beyond my reach. I lay there for a long time, sweating and trembling. I have never felt so lonely.

Saturday night was New Year's Eve. Before I even arrived back from the States, we had arranged a party; there seemed no point now, despite everything, in calling it off. I had promised the doctor to spend it in bed, so for a while I held court regally in pajamas and dressing gown. But this was an irritating, self-important posture. Friends came upstairs to see me out of a sense of duty—they had been told I had had pneumonia. Obviously they were bored. The music and voices below were enticing, and anyway, I had nothing now to lose. At ten-thirty I got up, just to see in the New Year, I said. I got back to bed at six the following morning. At ten o'clock I was up again and went down to help clean the house while my wife slept on. The debris of that New Year's binge seemed to me like the debris of the monstrous life I had been leading. I set to work cheerfully and with a will, mopping up, polishing, throwing things away. At lunchtime, when my wife staggered down hung over, the house was sparkling.

A week later I returned to the States to finish the university term. While I was packing I found, in the ticket pocket of my favorite jacket, a large, bright-yellow, torpedo-shaped pill, which I had conned off a heavily insomniac American the day I left. I stared at the thing, turning it over and over in my palm, wondering how I'd missed it on the night. It looked lethal. I had survived forty-five pills. Would forty-six have done it? I flushed the thing down the lavatory.

And that was that. Of course, my marriage was finished. We hung on a few months more for decency's sake, but neither of us could continue in the shadow of such blackmail. By the time we parted, there was nothing left. Inevitably, I went through the expected motions of distress. But in my heart, I no longer cared.

The truth is, in some way I *had* died. The overintensity, the tiresome excess of sensitivity and self-consciousness, of arrogance and idealism, which came in adolescence and stayed on and on beyond their due time, like some visiting bore, had not survived the coma. It

was as though I had finally, and sadly late in the day, lost my innocence. Like all young people, I had been high-minded and apologetic,
full of enthusiasms I didn't quite mean and guilts I didn't understand.
Because of them, I had forced my poor wife, who was far too young to
know what was happening, into a spoiling, destructive role she had
never sought. We had spent five years thrashing around in confusion,
as drowning men pull each other under. Then I had lain for three days
in abeyance, and awakened to feel nothing but a faint revulsion at
everything and everyone. My weakened body, my thin breath, the
slightest flicker of emotion filled me with distaste. I wanted only to be
left to myself. Then, as the months passed, I began gradually to stir into
another style of life, less theoretical, less optimistic, less vulnerable. I
was ready for an insentient middle age.

Above all, I was disappointed. Somehow, I felt, death had let
me down; I had expected more of it. I had looked for something overwhelming, an experience which would clarify all my confusions. But it
turned out to be simply a denial of experience. All I knew of death
were the terrifying dreams which came later. Blame it, perhaps, on my
delayed adolescence: adolescents always expect too much; they want
solutions to be immediate and neat, instead of gradual and incomplete.
Or blame it on the cinema: secretly, I had thought death would be like
the last reel of one of those old Hitchcock thrillers, when the hero
relives as an adult that traumatic moment in childhood when the horror
and splitting off took place; and thereby becomes free and at peace with
himself. It is a well-established, much-imitated and persuasive formula.
Hitchcock does it best, but he himself did not invent it; he was simply
popularizing a new tradition of half-digested psychoanalytic talk about
"abreaction," that crucial moment of cathartic truth when the complex is
removed. Behind that is the old belief in last-moment revelations,
deathbed conversions, and all those old wives' tales of the drowning
man reliving his life as he goes down for the last time. Behind that again
is an older tradition still: that of the Last Judgment and the afterlife. We

all expect something of death, even if it's only damnation.

But all I had got was oblivion. To all intents and purposes, I had died: my face was blue, my pulse erratic, my breathing ineffectual; the doctors gave me up. I had gone to the edge and most of the way over; then gradually, unwillingly and despite everything, I inched my way back. And now I knew nothing at all about it. I felt cheated.

Why had I been so sure of finding some kind of answer? There are always special reasons why a man should choose to die in one way rather than in another, and my own reasons for taking barbiturates were cogent enough, although I did not understand them at the time. As a small baby, I had been given a general anaesthetic when a major operation was performed on my ankle. The surgery had not been a great success and regularly throughout my childhood the thing gave me trouble. Always the attacks were heralded by the same dream: I had to work out a complicated mathematical problem which involved my whole family; their well-being depended on my finding the right answer. The sum changed as I grew, becoming more sophisticated as I learned more mathematics, always keeping one step ahead of me, like the carrot and the donkey. Yet I knew that however complex the problem, the answer would be simple. It merely eluded me. Then, when I was fourteen, my appendix was removed and I was once again put under a general anaesthetic. The dream, by then, had not recurred for a year or two. But as I began to breathe in the ether, the whole thing happened again. When the first sharp draft of gas entered my lungs, I saw the problem, this time in calculus, glowing like a neon sign, with all my family crowding around, dangling, as it were, from the terms. I breathed out and then, as I drew in the next lungful of ether, the figures whirred like the circuits of a computer, the stages of the equation raced in front of me, and I had the answer: a simple two-figure number. I had known it all along. For three days after I came around, I still knew that simple solution, and why and how it was so. I didn't have a care in the world. Then gradually it faded. But the dream never returned.

I thought death would be like that: a synoptic vision of life, crisis by crisis, all suddenly explained, justified, redeemed, a Last Judgment in the coils and circuits of the brain. Instead, all I got was a hole in the head, a round zero, nothing. I'd been swindled.

Months later I began to understand that I had had my answer, after all. The despair that had led me to try to kill myself had been pure and unadulterated, like the final, unanswerable despair a child feels, with no before or after. And childishly, I had expected death not merely to end it but also to explain it. Then, when death let me down, I gradually saw that I had been using the wrong language; I had translated the thing into Americanese. Too many movies, too many novels, too many trips to the States had switched my understanding into a hopeful, alien tongue. I no longer thought of myself as unhappy; instead, I had "problems." Which is an optimistic way of putting it, since problems imply solutions, whereas unhappiness is merely a condition of life which you must live with, like the weather. Once I had accepted that there weren't ever going to be any answers, even in death, I found to my surprise that I didn't much care whether I was happy or unhappy; "problems" and "the problem of problems" no longer existed. And that in itself is already the beginning of happiness.

It seems ludicrous now to have learned something so obvious in such a hard way, to have had to go almost the whole way into death in order to grow up. Somewhere, I still feel cheated and aggrieved, and also ashamed of my stupidity. Yet, in the end, even oblivion was an experience of a kind. Certainly, nothing has been quite the same since I discovered for myself, in my own body and on my own nerves, that death is simply an end, a dead end, no more, no less. And I wonder if that piece of knowledge isn't in itself a form of death. After all, the youth who swallowed the sleeping pills and the man who survived are so utterly different that someone or something must have died. Before the pills was another life, another person altogether, whom I scarcely recognize and don't much like—although I suspect he was, in his priggish ways, far more likable than I could ever be. Meanwhile, his fury and despair seem improbable now, sad and oddly diminished.

The hole in my head lasted for a long time. For five years after the event I had periods of sheer blankness, as though some vital center had been knocked out of action. For days on end, I went around like a zombie, a walking corpse. And I used to wonder, in a vague, numb way, if maybe I had died, after all. But if so, how could I ever tell?

In time, even that passed. Years later, when the house where it had happened was finally sold, I felt a sharp pang of regret for all the exorbitant pain and waste. After that, the episode lost its power. It became just so much dead history, a gossipy, mildly interesting anec-dote about someone half forgotten. As Coriolanus said, "There is a world elsewhere."

As for suicide: the sociologists and psychologists who talk of it as a disease puzzle me now as much as the Catholics and Muslims who call it the most deadly of mortal sins. It seems to me to be somehow as much beyond social or psychic prophylaxis as it is beyond morality, a terrible but utterly natural reaction to the strained, narrow, unnatural necessities we sometimes create for ourselves. And it is not for me. Perhaps I am no longer optimistic enough. I assume now that death, when it finally comes, will probably be nastier than suicide, and certainly a great deal less convenient.

SYLVIA PLATH

Tulips

HE TULIPS ARE too
excitable, it is winter here.
Look how white everything is, how quiet, how snowed-in.
I am learning peacefulness, lying by myself quietly
As the light lies on these white walls, this bed, these hands.
I am nobody; I have nothing to do with explosions.
I have given my name and my day-clothes up to the nurses
And my history to the anaesthetist and my body to surgeons.

The powerful and terrifying poems written by Sylvia Plath shortly before her death were collected in Ariel. *Plath was haunted by suicide from a young age, as is recounted in her autobiographical novel,* The Bell Jar. *She took her own life in 1963 at the age of thirty-one. In 1981, her posthumous* Collected Poems *won the Pulitzer prize. This poem is among her last.*

They have propped my head between the pillow and the sheet-cuff
Like an eye between two white lids that will not shut.
Stupid pupil, it has to take everything in.
The nurses pass and pass, they are no trouble,
They pass the way gulls pass inland in their white caps,
Doing things with their hands, one just the same as another,
So it is impossible to tell how many there are.

My body is a pebble to them, they tend it as water
Tends to the pebbles it must run over, smoothing them gently.
They bring me numbness in their bright needles, they bring me sleep.
Now I have lost myself I am sick of baggage—
My patent leather overnight case like a black pillbox,
My husband and child smiling out of the family photo;
Their smiles catch onto my skin, little smiling hooks.

I have let things slip, a thirty-year-old cargo boat
Stubbornly hanging on to my name and address.
They have swabbed me clear of my loving associations.
Scared and bare on the green plastic-pillowed trolley
I watched my tea-set, my bureaus of linen, my books
Sink out of sight, and the water went over my head.
I am a nun now, I have never been so pure.

I didn't want any flowers, I only wanted
To lie with my hands turned up and utterly empty.
How free it is, you have no idea how free—
The peacefulness is so big it dazes you,
And it asks nothing, a name tag, a few trinkets.
It is what the dead close on, finally; I imagine them
Shutting their mouths on it, like a Communion tablet.

The tulips are too red in the first place, they hurt me.
Even through the gift paper I could hear them breathe
Lightly, through their white swaddlings, like an awful baby.
Their redness talks to my wound, it corresponds.
They are subtle: they seem to float, though they weigh me down,
Upsetting me with their sudden tongues and their colour,
A dozen red lead sinkers round my neck.

Nobody watched me before, now I am watched.
The tulips turn to me, and the window behind me
Where once a day the light slowly widens and slowly thins,
And I see myself, flat, ridiculous, a cut-paper shadow
Between the eye of the sun and the eyes of the tulips,
And I have no face, I have wanted to efface myself.
The vivid tulips eat my oxygen.

Before they came the air was calm enough,
Coming and going, breath by breath, without any fuss.
Then the tulips filled it up like a loud noise.
Now the air snags and eddies round them the way a river
Snags and eddies round a sunken rust-red engine.
They concentrate my attention, that was happy
Playing and resting without committing itself.

WALKER PERCY

The Second Coming

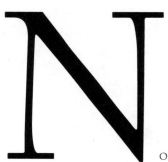

OW HE STOOD alone in the glade after slicing out-of-bounds on eighteen. He was holding the three-iron, not like a golf club or a shotgun now, but like a walking stick. Its blade resting on a patch of wet moss sank slightly of its own weight and the weight of his hand. Tiny bubbles of air or marsh gas came up through the moss next to the metal of the iron.

Once he was in the pine forest the air changed. Silence pressed

The novelist Walker Percy comes from a long line of lawyers—and of suicides. It is little wonder, then, that he writes so passionately on the latter subject in his novels The Moviegoer, The Last Gentleman, *and* The Second Coming. *This excerpt, from* The Second Coming *(1980), has our hero, Will Barrett, finishing up a round of golf when he is physically overcome by a crippling memory.*

in like soft hands clapped over his ears. Not merely faint but gone, blotted out, were the shouts of the golfers, the clink of irons, the sociable hum of the electric carts. He listened. There was nothing but the sound of silence, the seashell roar which could be the *ee*ing and *oh*ing of his own blood or the sound of cicadas at the end of summer which seems to come both from the pines and from inside one's head.

Then he heard a chain saw so faraway that he could not make out its direction yet close enough to register the drop in pitch as the saw bit into the wood and the motor labored.

The golf carts were going away. They had crossed a rise in the fairway. Through the trees he could see their white canopies move, one behind the other, as silently as sails.

He turned his head. Beyond the glade the pine forest was as dark as twilight except for a single poplar which caught the sun. Its leaves had turned a pale gold. Though the air was still in the forest, one leaf shook violently. Beyond the aspen he made out a deadfall of chestnuts. A flash of light came from the chestnut fall. By moving his head he could make the light come and go. It was the reflection of sunlight from glass.

Above him the branches of the pines came off the trunks at intervals and as regularly as the spokes of a wheel.

Lifting the three-iron slowly and watching it all the while, once again he held it like a shotgun at rest, club head high between his chest and arm, shaft resting across his forearm. Now, carefully, as if he were reenacting an event not quite remembered, as if he had forgotten something which his muscles and arms and hands might remember, he swung the shaft of the iron slowly to and fro like the barrel of a shotgun. He stopped and again stood as still as a hunter. Now turning his head and stooping, he looked back at the fence.

But he had not forgotten anything. Today for some reason he remembered everything. Everything he saw became a sign of something else. This fence was a sign of another fence he had climbed through. The hawk was a sign of another hawk and a time when he believed there were fabulous birds. The tiger? Whatever he was, he was gone. Even the wheeling blackbirds signified not themselves but a certain mocking sameness. They flew up, flustered and wheeling and blown about by the same fitful wind just as they had thirty, forty years ago. There is no mystery. The only mystery is that nothing changes. Nothing really happens. Marriages, births, deaths, terrible wars had occurred but had changed nothing. War is not a change but a poor attempt to make a change. War and peace are not events.

Only one event had ever happened to him in his life. Everything else that had happened afterwards was a non-event.

The guitar sound of fence wire stretched above him and the singing and popping of the vines against his body were signs of another event. Stooping now, he was trying to make his body remember what had happened. Suddenly it crossed his mind that nothing else had ever happened to him.

THE BOY HAD gone through the fence first, holding the new Sterlingworth Fox double-barreled twenty-gauge ahead of him, while the man pulled up the top strand of barbed wire. He had gone through the fence, but before he could stand up, the man had grabbed his shoulder from the other side of the fence in a grip that surprised him not so much for the pain as for the suddenness and violence and with the other hand grabbed the gun up and away from him, swung him around and cursed him. *Goddamn you, haven't I told you how to go through a fence with a loaded shotgun? Don't you know what would happen if*—suddenly the man stopped.

Now on the golf links years later he recognized the smell. It was the funky tannin rot of the pin-oak swamp as sharp in his nostrils as wood smoke.

The boy, who had already gotten over the pain but not the surprise, stood looking at the man across the fence holding the two shotguns, still too surprised to feel naked and disarmed without his gun. Nothing would ever surprise him again. Once the surprise was gone and his heart slowed he began to feel the first hint of the coolness and curiosity and watchfulness of the rest of his life. It is possible that his eyes narrowed slightly (he wasn't sure of this) as he put his empty hands in his pockets (he was sure of this) and said:

If what?

They had gone into the woods after singles. The dog had run over the covey instead of pointing it, and the covey had flushed too soon and too far away for a shot, the fat birds getting up with their sudden heart-stop thunder, then angling off tilt-winged and planing into the trees. The man, white-faced with anger, cursed the guide, shot the dog instead of the birds, to teach the dog never to do that again he said, not to hurt the dog bad what with the distance and the number-eight birdshot. The dog and the guide disappeared.

When the man handed the shotgun back to him, his eyes glittered but not in the merry way they did when a hunt went well. He had given the boy the new shotgun for Christmas and he had just finished trying an important lawsuit in Thomasville close by and this was the very place, the very woods where he, the man, once had a great hunt, perhaps even a fabled hunt, with his own father. But this hunt had gone badly. The Negro guide was no good. The dog had been trained badly. The lawsuit was not going well. They, the man and the boy, had spent a bad sleepless night in an old hotel (the same hotel where the man had spent the night before the great Thomasville hunt). The hotel was not at all as the man had remembered it.

Here, said the man, handing him the shotgun and stretching up the top strand of barbed wire. The wire creaked. *I trust you now.*

Thank you. The boy was watchful as he took the gun.

Do you trust me? asked the man.

Yes. No.

You have to trust me now.

Why?

I'm going to see to it that you're not going to have to go through what I am going through.

What's that?

You'll just have to trust me, okay?

Okay, said the boy, eyes wary and watchful. The man sounded almost absentminded and his glittering eye seemed to cast beyond him to the future, perhaps to the lawsuit Monday.

Come over here a minute.

What?

Here. Over here by me.

Oh.

Now, as the boy stood beside him, the man gave him a hug with the arm not holding the gun. He felt the man's hand giving him hard regular pats on the arm. He was saying something. The boy, no longer surprised, did not quite hear because he was reflecting on the strangeness of it, getting an awkward hug from his father, as they stood side by side in their bulky hunting clothes in the wet cold funk-smelling pin-oak swamp. He couldn't remember being hugged before except at funerals and weddings, and then the hugs were perfunctory and the kisses quick cheek kisses and that was all right with him, he didn't want to be hugged or kissed then or now.

And now, standing in the glade with the three-iron, he was wondering idly. *Why? Why is it that I would not wish then or now or ever to kiss my father? Why is it that it was then and now a kind of violation, not the violation of the man grabbing him across the fence but a violation nevertheless, a cheapening besides. Italians and Frenchmen and women hugged and kissed each other and what did it signify?*

What? asked the boy.

The man pulled him close and turned his face down and toward him and the boy smelled the heavy catarrh of his breath with the faint overlay of whiskey from the night before. His father was understood to suffer from "catarrh" and all night long, while the boy lay still, watchful and alert, the man had tossed and breathed out his heavy catarrh-and-whiskey breath.

Two singles went in here. I'll take one and you the other. But the man didn't let him go, held him still and gave him regular hard pats.

The man liked to go after singles after the covey was flushed, veering from the fields and open woodlands which the dogs had quartered and plunge backward into thickets and briars where not even the dogs would go, turning and using his body as entering wedge, the vines singing and popping against the heavy duck of his pants and jacket. When a single got up and he shot it and found it (no thanks to the dogs), and held the bird in his hand for a moment before stuffing it into the game pocket, his eyes would grow merry as if he had set himself an impossible quest and won, had plunged into the heart of the darkness and disorder of the wet cold winter woods and extracted from it of all things a warm bright-eyed perfect bird.

But now the man was standing still, eyes glittering, holding the gun oddly and gazing down at it, the stock resting on the ground, the barrel tilted just back from the vertical and resting lightly in the crotch of thumb and forefinger.

You and I are the same, said the man as if he were speaking to the gun.

How?

You are like me. We are two of a kind. I saw it last night.

Here come the pats again, hard, regular, slow, like a bell tolling.

Saw what?

I saw the way you lay in bed last night and slept or didn't sleep.

You're one of us, I'm afraid. You already know too much. It's too bad in a way.

Us? Who's us?

You'd be better off if you were one of them.

Who's them?

The ignorant armies that clash by night.

The boy was silent.

We have to trust each other now, don't we?

Yes, said the boy, rearing slightly so he could see the man better.

We're buddies, aren't we?

Yes. No. You're wrong. We're not buddies. I don't want to be anybody's buddy.

Okay. Let's go. There are two of them. You take the one on the right.

Okay.

Oh shit, said the man. Last hard pat, sock, wham on the shoulder. *I'm sorry.*

The boy looked up not surprised but curious. He had never heard the man say *shit* before.

Now standing with the three-iron in the glade, he was thinking: he said that one and only *shit* in exactly the same flat taped voice airline pilots use before the crash: *We're going in. Shit.*

Now the man was looking more like himself again, cheeks ruddy, cap pushed back on his head as if it were a summer day and he needed the air, though it was very cold. It was his regular chipper look but when the boy, going forward, looked at him sideways he noticed that his eyes were too bright.

They kicked up two singles but the birds angled apart and the man and the boy, following them, diverged. A lopsided scrub oak, dead leaves brown and heavy as leather, came between them. A ground fog filled the hollows like milk. As the boy moved ahead silently on the wet speckled leaves, his heart did not beat in his throat as it used to before quail are flushed. Then it came, on the man's side of the tree, the sudden tiny thunder of the quail and the shot hard upon it and then the silence. There was not even the sound of a footstep but only a click from the Greener. Now the boy was moving ahead again. He heard the man walking. They were clearing the tree and converging. Through the leathery leaves and against the milkiness he caught sight of a swatch of khaki. Didn't he hear it again, the so sudden uproar of stiff wings beating the little drum of bird body and the man swinging toward him in the terrific concentration of keeping gunsight locked on the fat tilt-winged quail and hard upon the little drumbeat the shocking blast rolling away like thunder through the silent woods? The boy saw the muzzle burst and flame spurting from the gun like a picture of a Civil War soldier shooting and even had time to wonder why he had never seen it before, before he heard the whistling and banging in his ear and found himself down in the leaves without knowing how he got there and even then could still hear the sound of the number-eight shot rattling away through the milky swamp and was already scrambling to get up from the embarrassment of it (for that was no place to be), but when he tried to stand, the keening in his ear spun him down again—all that before he even felt the hot wetness on the side of his face which was not pressed into leaves and touched it and saw the blood. It was as if someone had taken hold of him and flung him down. He heard the *geclick* and *gecluck* of the Greener's breech opening and closing. Then he heard the shot. He waited until the banging and keening in his head stopped. He did not feel cold. His face did not hurt. Using the gun as a prop, he was able to get to his knees. He called out. It had been important to get up before calling. Nobody, not him, not anybody, is going to catch me down here on the ground. When there was no answer, he waited again, aware only of his own breathing and that he was blinking and gazing at nothing in particular. Then, without knowing how he knew, he knew that he was free to act in his own good time. (How did he know such a thing?) Taking a deep breath, he stood up and exhaled it through his mouth *sheeew* as a laborer might do, and wiping blood from his lip with two fingers he slung it off as a laborer might sling snot. Twelve years old, he grew up in ten minutes. It was possible for him to stretch out a hand to the tree and touch it, not hold it. He walked around the tree before it occurred to him that he had forgotten his shotgun. At first he didn't see the man, because both the jacket and the cap had a camouflage pattern which hid him in the leaves like a quail and because the bill of the cap hid his face. The man was part lying, part sitting against a tree, legs stretched out and cap pulled over his face like a countryman taking a nap and there was a feeling in the boy not that it was funny but that he was nevertheless called upon to smile and he might even have tried except that his face suddenly hurt. He did not see the man's gun, the big double-barreled twelve-gauge English Greener. For some reason which he could still not explain, he went back to look for his own gun. It was not hard to walk but when he bent to pick up the gun his face hurt again. When he came back he saw the dark brown stock of the Greener sticking out from the skirt of the man's jacket.

Now the boy was squatting (not sitting) beside the man. He pushed his own cap back as if it were a hot day. He pulled the man's cap off. He was not smiling and his eyes were closed but his face looked all right. His cheeks were still ruddy.

He put his hand under the man's jacket but the Greener got in the way. He pulled the shotgun out by the butt and put his hand under the jacket again and against the man's chest. The heart beat strongly. But his hand was wet and something was wrong. The fabric of shirt and underwear was matted into flesh like burlap trodden into mud.

Now squatting back on his heels beside the man he took his handkerchief from his pocket with his dry hand and carefully wiped the blood from the other hand. Then he pushed his cap back still farther because his forehead was sweating. He blew into both hands because they were cold and began to think.

What he was thinking about was what he was going to do next but at the same time he noticed that he did not feel bad. Why is it, he wondered, that I feel that I have all the time in the world to figure out what to do and the freedom to do it and that what is more I will do it? It was as if he had contracted into the small core of curiosity and competence he had felt within himself after the man had grabbed him across the fence, spun him around, cursed him, and took his gun away. Now he was blowing into his hands and thinking: This is a problem and problems are for solving. All you need to do anything is time to do it, being let alone long enough to do it and a center to do it from. He had found his center.

The guide doesn't live far from here. We passed the cabin. The Negro boy ran home when the man cursed him and shot the dog.

Now he was standing up and looking carefully around. He even made out a speckled quail lying in the speckled leaves. As he waited for the dizziness to clear, he watched the man.

Don't worry, I'm going to get us both out of here. He knew with certainty that he could.

Later, after it was over, his stepmother had hugged them both. *Thank God thank God thank God* she said in her fond shouting style. *You could have both been killed!*

So it had come to pass that there were two accounts of what had happened, and if one was false the other must be true; one which his stepmother had put forward in the way that a woman will instantly and irresistibly construe the world as she will have it and in fact does have it so: that the man had had one of his dizzy spells—he knows with his blood pressure he shouldn't drink and hunt!—and fell; that in falling he discharged the double-barrel, which wounded the boy and nearly killed the man. The boy almost came to believe her, especially when she praised him. *We can thank our lucky stars that this child had the* sense and bravery to know what to do. And you a twelve-year-old—mussing up his hair in front in a way she thought of as being both manly and English—We're so proud of you. My fine brave boy!

But it was not bravery, he thought, eyes narrowing, almost smiling. It was the coldness, the hard secret core of himself that he had found.

The boy and his father knew better. With a final hug after he was up and around and the boy had recovered, except for a perforated and permanently deafened left middle ear and a pocked cheek like a one-sided acne, the man was able to speak to him by standing in the kitchen and enlisting D'Lo the cook in conversation and affecting a broad hunter's lingo not at all like him: I'm going to tell yall one damn thing—Yall? He never said yall. Talking to D'Lo, who stood at the stove with her back to them? I'm getting rid of that savage. He nodded to the Greener on the pantry table. I had no idea that savage had a pattern that wide! So wide it knicked you—did you know that, D'Lo? Hugging the boy, he asked D'Lo. D'Lo must either have known all about it or, most likely, had not been listening closely, for she only voiced her routine but adequate hnnnonnhHM! Now ain't that something else!—which was what the man wanted her to say because this was the man's way of telling the boy, through D'Lo, what had happened and soliciting and getting her inattentive assent to the routineness and even inevitability of it. Such things happen! And I'll tell you something else, the man told D'Lo. When a man comes to the point that all he can think about is tracking a bird and shuts everything out of his mind to the point of shooting somebody, it's time to quit! D'Lo socked down grits spoon on boiler rim. You right, Mister Barrett! Was she even listening? And now the man finally looking down his cheek at him hugged alongside: Right?

Yes Sir. He waited only to be released from the hug.

There was silence. They spoke no more of it. We know, don't we, the silence said, that the man was somehow wounded by the same shot and there is nothing to be said about it.

But how did he miss the bird? How did he wound himself?

While the sheriff was taking care of the man in the swamp, the guide brought the two shotguns, a dead quail, and three empty shells into the dark clean room smelling of coal oil and newspaper and flour paste where the Negro woman was washing his face. She dried it and patted something light and feathery—spiderwebs?—on his cheek. He didn't feel bad but his ear still roared. *"Here dey,"* said the black youth. *They yours and hisn.* He looked down at the kitchen table at the two shotguns, the three empty Super-X shells, and the dead quail. This black boy was no guide. What guide would pick up empty shotgun shells? *You didn't see the other bird?* he asked the guide. *Ain't no other bird,* said the black boy. The white boy said: *There were two singles and he shot twice and he never misses.* The black boy said: *Well he done missed this time.* The white boy heard himself saying: *You just didn't find the bird,* and getting angry and wondering: Why am I worrying about the second bird? *Nawsuh,* said the woman, whose black arms were sifted with flour. *John sho find your bird if he was there. Look, he even found your bullets. Must have been the dogs got him.*

He looked at the Greener on the kitchen table in the shotgun cabin, sat down, broke the breech, and took out the one empty shell and set it next to the shells the guide had found. As he gazed he put one hand to his cheek, which had begun to bleed again, and covered his roaring ear.

NOW IN A green forest glade near a pretty pink-and-green golf links, he touched his deafened ear. Did it still roar a little or was it the seashell roar of the silence of the forest? Holding the three-iron in both hands he tested the spring of its steel shaft.

It was as if the thirty years had passed and he had not ever left the Negro cabin but, strange to say, had only now got around to saying what he had not said for thirty years. Again he smelled the close clean smell of kerosene and warm newspaper.

Now in Carolina in a glade in the white pines he said aloud: *There was only one shell in the Greener,* for some reason smiling a little and examining the three-iron closely as if it had a breech which could be broken, revealing the missing shell. But he only saw the green Winchester Super-X with its slightly wrinkled cylinder smelling of cordite. *What happened to the other shell?* Nothing. There was no other shell. I broke the breech of the Greener and there was only one shell. Why? Because he reloaded after the first shot. He shot the first single. Then there was a pause. It was then that I heard the *geclick* of the Greener breech opening and the *gecluck* of its closing. But why reload with one good shell left? That was all he needed for the second single if I missed it. Because he always liked to be ready. He liked to shoot quick and on the rise. And why, after the second shot, did he reload with only one shell?

Because—He smiled at the three-iron which he held sprung like a bow in front of him.

Because when he reloaded the last time, he knew he only needed one shot.

But why reload at all? He had reloaded before the second shot. After the second shot, he still had a good shell in the second chamber.

Wait a minute. Again he saw the sun reflected from something beyond the chestnut deadfall.

What happened? Here's what happened.

He fired once at the first single. Geclick. Eject one shell and replace it. Gecluck.

He fired the second time at the second single and also hit me. Geclick. Reload. Gecluck.

Why reload if he knew he only needed one more shot? He still had a good shell in the second chamber.

In the Carolina pine forest he closed his eyes and saw green Super-X shells lined up on the clean quilt in the Negro cabin.

There were *four* shells.

FARAWAY THE GOLFERS were shouting, their voices blowing away like the killdeer on the high skyey fairways. It was close and still in the glade. He was watching the three-iron as, held in front of him like a divining rod, it sank toward the earth. *Ah, I've found it after all. The buried treasure*, he thought smiling.

—

SOUTH GEORGIA, ALABAMA, Mississippi... And my father and his near death in the Georgia swamp and my near death and later his death in Mississippi and my being at his death and wanting me to be there, his wanting me to see his brain exploded, expanding like the universe and plastering the attic with neurones like stars in the night sky. Why did he want me to be there? To show me what? Now I know. To show me the one sure sweet exodus. Yes, that's it, that's what he was first giving me in Georgia, then telling me and finally showing me, and now at last I know.

Even D'Lo knew. You po little old boy, what you going to do now? What chance you got in this world? Your daddy done kilt hisself and your mama dead and gone and here you come, po little Willie, what chance you got? She shaking her head and socking down the grits spoon, as he watched her narrow-eyed and even smiling a little, knowing she was wrong. Because he was he and they were they and here he was, free and sure and alert and sly. Nothing, no one, would ever surprise him again. Not they. They least of all. He was free of them.

His father had shot twice in the Georgia swamp, reloaded the Greener, and shot again. But the second shot was a double shot aimed at him. I thought he missed me and he did, almost, and I thought I survived and I did, almost. But now I have learned something and been surprised by it after all. Learned what? That he didn't miss me after all, that I thought I survived and I did but I've been dead of something ever since and didn't know it until now. What a surprise. They were right after all. He was right. D'Lo was right. What a surprise. But is it not also a surprise that discovering you've been dead all these years, you should now feel somewhat alive?

He killed me then and I did not know it. I even thought he had missed me. I have been living, yes, but it is a living death because I knew he wanted me dead. Am I entitled to live? I am alive by a fluke like the sole survivor of Treblinka, who lived by a fluke, but did not really feel entitled to live.

ALBERT CAMUS

—

The Myth of Sisyphus

T HERE IS BUT one truly serious philosophical problem and that is suicide. Judging whether life is or is not worth living amounts to answering the fundamental question of philosophy. All the rest—whether or not the world has three dimensions, whether the mind has nine or twelve categories—comes afterwards. These are games; one must first answer. And if it is true, as

---

French philosopher and novelist Albert Camus is routinely placed in the company of existentialists. Not to his liking, though; Camus believed deeply in the sublime, dogged human spirit. This is perhaps most clear in his essay, "The Myth of Sisyphus." Camus also wrote the novels The Stranger, The Plague, *and* The Fall *and was awarded the Nobel Prize for Literature in 1957. He was killed in 1960, at age 46, in an auto accident.*

Nietzsche claims, that a philosopher, to deserve our respect, must preach by example, you can appreciate the importance of that reply, for it will precede the definitive act. These are facts the heart can feel; yet they call for careful study before they become clear to the intellect.

If I ask myself how to judge that this question is more urgent than that, I reply that one judges by the actions it entails. I have never seen anyone die for the ontological argument. Galileo, who held a scientific truth of great importance, abjured it with the greatest ease as soon as it endangered his life. In a certain sense, he did right. That truth was not worth the stake. Whether the earth or the sun revolves around the other is a matter of profound indifference. To tell the truth, it is a futile question. On the other hand, I see many people die because they judge that life is not worth living. I see others paradoxically getting killed for the ideas or illusions that give them a reason for living (what is called a reason for living is also an excellent reason for dying). I therefore conclude that the meaning of life is the most urgent of questions. How to answer it? On all essential problems (I mean thereby those that run the risk of leading to death or those that intensify the passion of living) there are probably but two methods of thought: the method of La Palisse and the method of Don Quixote. Solely the balance between evidence and lyricism can allow us to achieve simultaneously emotion and lucidity. In a subject at once so humble and so heavy with emotion, the learned and classical dialectic must yield, one can see, to a more modest attitude of mind deriving at one and the same time from common sense and understanding.

Suicide has never been dealt with except as a social phenomenon. On the contrary, we are concerned here, at the outset, with the relationship between individual thought and suicide. An act like this is prepared within the silence of the heart, as is a great work of art. The man himself is ignorant of it. One evening he pulls the trigger or jumps. Of an apartment-building manager who killed himself I was told that he had lost his daughter five years before, that he had changed greatly since, and that that experience had "undermined" him. A more exact word cannot be imagined. Beginning to think is beginning to be undermined. Society has but little connection with such beginnings. The worm is in the man's heart. That is where it must be sought. One must follow and understand this fatal game that leads from lucidity in the face of existence to flight from light.

There are many causes for a suicide, and generally the most obvious ones were not the most powerful. Rarely is suicide committed (yet the hypothesis is not excluded) through reflection. What sets off the crisis is almost always unverifiable. Newspapers often speak of "personal sorrows" or of "incurable illness." These explanations are plausible. But one would have to know whether a friend of the desperate man had not that very day addressed him indifferently. He is the guilty one. For that is enough to precipitate all the rancors and all the boredom still in suspension.

But if it is hard to fix the precise instant, the subtle step when the mind opted for death, it is easier to deduce from the act itself the consequences it implies. In a sense, and as in melodrama, killing yourself amounts to confessing. It is confessing that life is too much for you or that you do not understand it. Let's not go too far in such analogies, however, but rather return to everyday words. It is merely confessing that that "is not worth the trouble." Living, naturally, is never easy. You continue making the gestures commanded by existence for many reasons, the first of which is habit. Dying voluntarily implies that you have recognized, even instinctively, the ridiculous character of that habit, the absence of any profound reason for living, the insane character of that daily agitation, and the uselessness of suffering.

What, then, is that incalculable feeling that deprives the mind of the sleep necessary to life? A world that can be explained even with bad reasons is a familiar world. But, on the other hand, in a universe suddenly divested of illusions and lights, man feels an alien, a stranger. His exile is without remedy since he is deprived of the memory of a lost home or the hope of a promised land. This divorce between man and his life, the actor and his setting, is properly the feeling of absurdity. All healthy men having thought of their own suicide, it can be seen, without further explanation, that there is a direct connection between this feeling and the longing for death.

The subject of this essay is precisely this relationship between the absurd and suicide, the exact degree to which suicide is a solution to the absurd. The principle can be established that for a man who does not cheat, what he believes to be true must determine his action. Belief in the absurdity of existence must then dictate his conduct. It is legitimate to wonder, clearly and without false pathos, whether a conclusion of this importance requires forsaking as rapidly as possible an incomprehensible condition. I am speaking, of course, of men inclined to be in harmony with themselves.

Stated clearly, this problem may seem both simple and insoluble. But it is wrongly assumed that simple questions involve answers that are no less simple and that evidence implies evidence. A *priori* and reversing the terms of the problem, just as one does or does not kill oneself, it seems that there are but two philosophical solutions, either yes or no. This would be too easy. But allowance must be made for those who, without concluding, continue questioning. Here I am only slightly indulging in irony: this is the majority. I notice also that those who answer "no" act as if they thought "yes." As a matter of fact, if I accept the Nietzschean criterion, they think "yes" in one way or another. On the other hand, it often happens that those who commit suicide were assured of the meaning of life. These contradictions are constant. It may even be said that they have never been so keen as on this point where, on the contrary, logic seems so desirable. It is a commonplace to compare philosophical theories and the behavior of those who profess them. But it must be said that of the thinkers who refused a meaning to life none except Kirilov who belongs to literature, Peregrinos who is born of legend, and Jules Lequier who belongs to hypothesis, admitted his logic to the point of refusing that life. Schopenhauer is often cited, as a fit subject for laughter, because he praised suicide while seated at a well-set table. This is no subject for joking. That way of not taking the tragic seriously is not so grievous, but it helps to judge a man.

In the face of such contradictions and obscurities must we conclude that there is no relationship between the opinion one has about life and the act one commits to leave it? Let us not exaggerate in this direction. In a man's attachment to life there is something stronger than all the ills in the world. The body's judgment is as good as the mind's, and the body shrinks from annihilation. We get into the habit of living before acquiring the habit of thinking. In that race which daily hastens us toward death, the body maintains its irreparable lead. In short, the essence of that contradiction lies in what I shall call the act of eluding because it is both less and more than diversion in the Pascalian sense. Eluding is the invariable game. The typical act of eluding, the fatal evasion that constitutes the third theme of this essay, is hope. Hope of another life one must "deserve" or trickery of those who live not for life itself but for some great idea that will transcend it, refine it, give it a meaning, and betray it.

Thus everything contributes to spreading confusion. Hitherto, and it has not been wasted effort, people have played on words and pretended to believe that refusing to grant a meaning to life necessarily leads to declaring that it is not worth living. In truth, there is no necessary common measure between these two judgments. One merely has to refuse to be misled by the confusions, divorces, and inconsistencies previously pointed out. One must brush everything aside and go straight to the real problem. One kills oneself because life is not worth living, that is certainly a truth—yet an unfruitful one because it is a truism. But does that insult to existence, that flat denial in which it is plunged come from the fact that it has no meaning? Does its absurdity require one to escape it through hope or suicide—this is what must be clarified, hunted down, and elucidated while brushing aside all the rest. Does the Absurd dictate death? This problem must be given priority over others, outside all methods of thought and all exercises of the disinterested mind. Shades of meaning, contradictions, the psychology that an "objective" mind can always introduce into all problems have no place in this pursuit and this passion. It calls simply for an unjust—in other words, logical—thought. That is not easy. It is always easy to be logical. It is almost impossible to be logical to the bitter end. Men who die by their own hand consequently follow to its conclusion their emotional inclination. Reflection on suicide gives me an opportunity to raise the only problem to interest me: is there a logic to the point of death? I cannot know unless I pursue, without reckless passion, in the sole light of evidence, the reasoning of which I am here suggesting the source. This is what I call an absurd reasoning. Many have begun it. I do not yet know whether or not they kept to it.

When Karl Jaspers, revealing the impossibility of constituting the world as a unity, exclaims: "This limitation leads me to myself, where I can no longer withdraw behind an objective point of view that I am merely representing, where neither I myself nor the existence of others can any longer become an object for me," he is evoking after many others those waterless deserts where thought reaches its confines. After many others, yes indeed, but how eager they were to get out of them! At that last crossroad where thought hesitates, many men have arrived and even some of the humblest. They then abdicated what was most precious to them, their life. Others, princes of the mind, abdicated likewise, but they initiated the suicide of their thought in its purest revolt. The real effort is to stay there, rather, in so far as that is possible, and to examine closely the odd vegetation of those distant regions. Tenacity and acumen are privileged spectators of this inhuman show in which absurdity, hope, and death carry on their dialogue. The mind can then analyze the figures of that elementary yet subtle dance before illustrating them and reliving them itself.

—

THE GODS HAD condemned Sisyphus to ceaselessly rolling a rock to the top of a mountain, whence the stone would fall back of its own weight. They had thought with some reason that there is no more dreadful punishment than futile and hopeless labor.

If one believes Homer, Sisyphus was the wisest and most prudent of mortals. According to another tradition, however, he was disposed to practice the profession of highwayman. I see no contradiction in this. Opinions differ as to the reasons why he became the futile laborer of the underworld. To begin with, he is accused of a certain levity in regard to the gods. He stole their secrets. Ægina, the daughter of Æsopus, was carried off by Jupiter. The father was shocked by that disappearance and complained to Sisyphus. He, who knew of the abduction, offered to tell about it on condition that Æsopus would give water to the citadel of Corinth. To the celestial thunderbolts he preferred the benediction of water. He was punished for this in the underworld. Homer tells us also that Sisyphus had put Death in chains. Pluto could not endure the sight of his deserted, silent empire. He dispatched the god of war, who liberated Death from the hands of her conqueror.

It is said also that Sisyphus, being near to death, rashly wanted to test his wife's love. He ordered her to cast his unburied body into the middle of the public square. Sisyphus woke up in the underworld. And there, annoyed by an obedience so contrary to human love, he obtained from Pluto permission to return to earth in order to chastise his wife. But when he had seen again the face of this world, enjoyed water and sun, warm stones and the sea, he no longer wanted to go back to the infernal darkness. Recalls, signs of anger, warnings were of no avail. Many years more he lived facing the curve of the gulf, the sparkling sea, and the smiles of the earth. A decree of the gods was necessary. Mercury came and seized the impudent man by the collar and, snatching him from his joys, led him forcibly back to the underworld, where his rock was ready for him.

You have already grasped that Sisyphus is the absurd hero. He *is*, as much through his passions as through his torture. His scorn of the gods, his hatred of death, and his passion for life won him that unspeakable penalty in which the whole being is exerted toward accomplishing nothing. This is the price that must be paid for the passions of this earth. Nothing is told us about Sisyphus in the underworld. Myths are made for the imagination to breathe life into them. As for this myth, one sees merely the whole effort of a body straining to raise the huge stone, to roll it and push it up a slope a hundred times over; one sees the face screwed up, the cheek tight against the stone, the shoulder bracing the clay-covered mass, the foot wedging it, the fresh start with arms outstretched, the wholly human security of two earth-clotted hands. At the very end of his long effort measured by skyless space and time without depth, the purpose is achieved. Then Sisyphus watches the stone rush down in a few moments toward that lower world whence he will have to push it up again toward the summit. He goes back down to the plain.

It is during that return, that pause, that Sisyphus interests me. A face that toils so close to stones is already stone itself! I see that man going back down with a heavy yet measured step toward the torment of which he will never know the end. That hour like a breathing space which returns as surely as his suffering, that is the hour of consciousness. At each of those moments when he leaves the heights and gradually sinks toward the lairs of the gods, he is superior to his fate. He is stronger than his rock.

If this myth is tragic, that is because the hero is conscious. Where would his torture be, indeed, if at every step the hope of succeeding upheld him? The workman of today works every day in his life at the same tasks, and this fate is no less absurd. But it is tragic only at the rare moments when it becomes conscious. Sisyphus, proletarian of the gods, powerless and rebellious, knows the whole extent of his wretched condition: it is what he thinks of during his descent. The lucidity that was to constitute his torture at the same time crowns his victory. There is no fate that cannot be surmounted by scorn.

—

IF THE DESCENT is thus sometimes performed in sorrow, it can also take place in joy. This word is not too much. Again I fancy Sisyphus returning toward his rock, and the sorrow was in the beginning. When the images of earth cling too tightly to memory, when the call of happiness becomes too insistent, it happens that melancholy rises in a man's heart: this is the rock's victory, this is the rock itself. The boundless grief is too heavy to bear. These are our nights of Gethsemane. But crushing truths perish from being acknowledged. Thus Œdipus at the outset obeys fate without knowing it. But from the moment he knows, his tragedy begins. Yet at the same moment, blind and desperate, he realizes that the only bond linking him to the world is the cool hand of a girl. Then a tremendous remark rings out: "Despite so many ordeals, my advanced age and the nobility of my soul make me conclude that all is well." Sophocles' Œdipus, like Dostoevsky's Kirilov, thus gives the recipe for the absurd victory. Ancient wisdom confirms modern heroism.

One does not discover the absurd without being tempted to write a manual of happiness. "What! by such narrow ways—?" There is but one world, however. Happiness and the absurd are two sons of the same earth. They are inseparable. It would be a mistake to say that happiness necessarily springs from the absurd discovery. It happens as well that the feeling of the absurd springs from happiness. "I conclude that all is well," says Œdipus, and that remark is sacred. It echoes in the wild and limited universe of man. It teaches that all is not, has not been, exhausted. It drives out of this world a god who had come into it with dissatisfaction and a preference for futile sufferings. It makes of fate a human matter, which must be settled among men.

All Sisyphus' silent joy is contained therein. His fate belongs to him. His rock is his thing. Likewise, the absurd man, when he contemplates his torment, silences all the idols. In the universe restored to its silence, the myriad wondering little voices of the earth rise up. Unconscious, secret calls, invitations from all the faces, they are the necessary reverse and price of victory. There is no sun without shadow, and it is essential to know the night. The absurd man says yes and his effort will henceforth be unceasing. If there is a personal fate, there is no higher destiny, or at least there is but one which he concludes is inevitable and despicable. For the rest, he knows himself to be the master of his days. At that subtle moment when man glances backward over his life, Sisyphus returning toward his rock, in that slight pivoting he contemplates that series of unrelated actions which becomes his fate, created by him, combined under his memory's eye and soon sealed by his death. Thus, convinced of the wholly human origin of all that is human, a blind man eager to see who knows that the night has no end, he is still on the go. The rock is still rolling.

I leave Sisyphus at the foot of the mountain! One always finds one's burden again. But Sisyphus teaches the higher fidelity that negates the gods and raises rocks. He too concludes that all is well. This universe henceforth without a master seems to him neither sterile nor futile. Each atom of that stone, each mineral flake of that night-filled mountain, in itself forms a world. The struggle itself toward the heights is enough to fill a man's heart. One must imagine Sisyphus happy.

HOWARD KUSHNER

—

Meriwether Lewis and Abraham Lincoln

LATE ONE NOVEMBER
afternoon in 1893, while hunting in a canyon in the outskirts of San
Diego, Edward Grenville discovered the body of a neatly dressed
young man. The dead man's outstretched right hand held a revolver.
When the coroner later examined the corpse, he "found that one car-
tridge had been exploded, and a hole in the right temple showed where
the bullet had gone." The victim's pockets contained "a silver watch,
twenty cents in change, a tin-type picture of the young man, and a pocket-

---

*Howard Kushner is a professor of History at San Diego State University.
This piece, from his highly respected 1989 study of suicide,* Self-Destruction
in the Promised Land, *questions why two famous and familiar characters,
both with suicidal tendencies, would choose opposite fates.*

book containing visiting cards bearing the name 'M. E. White.'" White's pockets also yielded a library card and a slip of paper with the names of several local firms. Alongside each name White had written notations such as "come again," and "favorable." Mr. W. E. Howard, whose name appeared on the list, identified White's body as that of a man who had applied unsuccessfully for work at two o'clock on the day of the suicide. Howard "remembered that the applicant was slightly cross-eyed." The coroner concluded that "from the condition of his hands and the fact that shorthand writing was in his papers, he [White] was unused to hard work."

Max White was only one of many suicides reported by American newspapers in 1893. Often the press and other experts tied what they perceived as an increase in the incidence of suicide to the Depression of 1893, the most severe economic downturn in America's experience until that time. Several months before White's death, the editors of *The San Diego Union*, fearing a suicide epidemic, published a long editorial warning that "suicide has become so frequent as to attract little attention. Day after day the rehearsal of these crimes goes on in the daily press, and" *The Union* feared, "the horror, which such acts should produce, is giving way to indifference, or a morbid condition of the public mind which accepts self-murder as excusable and the natural outgrowth of modern conditions of life."

The suicide of nineteen-year-old Max White seemed to confirm this assessment. During the previous three years, White, a native of Hungary, had lived periodically at his uncle Samuel Fox's ranch in rural San Diego County. At other times, he rented a room in San Diego while he searched for permanent employment. For a brief period White appears to have been employed as a baker. Despondent over his inability to find work, White purchased a pistol with which he intended to kill himself if he did not secure a position by 7 November. White recorded his final thoughts in a diary found in his possession:

An indescribable feeling agitates me as regarding the position I am in hopes of receiving. The suspense is painful to me. If I should unfortunately be refused I should feel it to be my death warrant. I pray to God Almighty that I be given the place, as hunger and death stare me in the face. As for me, I feel so wretched and despair at the slightest ill-fortune.

My God, how willingly would I that I should not be. The misfortune of being brought into this world! I must think of Sam [Samuel I. Fox] for all he has done for me. I can really never really repay for what he has done for me. Ah, I would rather have remained in the dominion of an emperor and become his minion than to be in this land of the free and suffer.

Ah, you false friends, who with your mouth claimed your friendship and with your hands withheld it! My curse upon you. May you ever feel misfortune blighting your whole career. My hatred is indescribable against you.

DURING THE PERIOD when Max White took his life, a French moral statistician named Emile Durkheim (1858-1917) began writing a volume that purported to explain why people like White were particularly vulnerable to suicide. Durkheim's 1897 study, *Suicide: A Study in Sociology,* lent scientific credence to the analysis offered by the editorial writers of *The San Diego Union:* modern life was the killer. Although Durkheim outlined four major types of suicide—egoistic, altruistic, anomic, and fatalistic—his study was concerned mainly with what he asserted to be the statistically verifiable increase in egoistic and anomic suicides, which seemed to mirror Max White's experience.

Anomie, Durkheim explained, "throws open the door to disillusionment and consequently to disappointment." Durkheim's description of the notes left by anomic suicides matched White's proclamation: "very many expressed primarily irritation and exasperated weariness. Sometimes they contain blasphemies, violent recriminations against life in general, sometimes threats and accusations against a particular person whom the responsibility for the suicide's unhappiness is imputed." The typical anomic, Durkheim found, was "a man abruptly cast down below his accustomed status [who] cannot avoid exasperation at feeling a situation escape him of which he thought himself the master, and his exasperation naturally revolts against the cause, whether real or imaginary, to which he attributes his ruin." Such a man has two options. "If he recognizes himself as to blame for the catastrophe, he takes it out on himself; otherwise, on someone else. In the former case there will be only suicide; in the later suicide may be preceded by homicide or by some other violent outburst."

Like the editorial writers of *The San Diego Union*, and unlike Max White, Durkheim denied that factors such as unemployment were themselves responsible for individual suicides: "If . . . industrial or financial crises increase suicides, this is not because they cause poverty, since crises of prosperity have the same result; it is because they are crises, that is, disturbances of the collective order." The breakdown of moral order, not its particular manifestation, was the culprit. Modern urban society tended to free people from traditional restraints, and this social disintegration formed the basis for egoistic suicide. "When a society is disturbed by some painful crisis or by beneficent but abrupt transitions, it is momentarily incapable of exercising this [moral] influence; thence come the sudden rise in the curve of suicides." For Durkheim, "egoism" and "anomy" were "regular and specific factor[s] in suicide in our modern societies; one of the springs from which the annual contingent feeds."

When Durkheim's book appeared, a Viennese neurologist was on the verge of developing a new hypothesis for the etiology of hysteria that soon would become the foundation for modern psychoanalytic psychiatry. If Durkheim's *Suicide* is the starting point for most modern sociological investigations, Sigmund Freud's writings, particularly *Mourning and Melancholia* (1917), have become the classic texts for psychoanalytic discussions of suicide.

In contrast to Durkheim, Freud (1856-1939) would have located the etiology of Max White's suicide in intrapsychic conflicts. According to the logic of Freud's analysis, the complaints of the nineteen-year-old White, even if grounded in some verifiable external problem such as unemployment, would seem too exaggerated to take at face value. For Freud, suicide was an extension of melancholic (depressive) behavior. Like melancholics, the suicidal exhibited "profoundly painful dejection, cessation of interest in the outside world, loss of the capacity to love, inhibition of all activity, and a lowering of the self-regarding feelings to a degree that finds utterance in self-reproaches and self-revilings, and culminates in a delusional expectation of punishment."

Drawing an analogy to mourning, Freud found that both melancholics and mourners experienced the loss of a loved one. Unlike the mourner, for whom "it is the world which has become poor and empty," Freud suggested that the melancholic appears to have lost "the ego itself." A melancholic displays "an extraordinary diminution in his self-regard" and "he reproaches himself, vilifies himself and expects to be cast out and punished." The melancholic, like the suicide, gives up "the instinct which compels every living thing to cling to life." These feelings of self-hatred, which often take the form of public display, resulted, Freud explained, from repressed anger at a deserting love object that melancholics have displaced onto themselves. Thus Freud suggested that suicide always contains an earlier repressed desire to kill someone else: "no neurotic harbors thoughts of suicide which he has not turned back upon himself from murderous impulses against others."

Max White seemed to fit into Freud's characterization. On the one hand, White confided in his diary that he "despair[ed] at the slightest ill-fortune." He articulated a simultaneous wish to kill and be killed. He condemned his imagined enemies with vehement bitterness: "May you ever feel misfortune blighting your whole career," and he announced his own self-destructive response to rejections that had yet to take place: "If I should unfortunately be refused I should feel it to be my death warrant." On the other hand, White's admission of despair was coupled with his expressed desire for "domination," with admissions of low self-esteem and laments that he had ever been born. And, as Freud might have predicted, White had experienced traumatic losses.

—

WHITE'S DIARY AND suicide note provided ample evidence of his profound sense of unresolved loss. Testimony at his inquest revealed that White's mother had died when he was a child (some time before his twelfth birthday) and that when he was thirteen, young Max was sent by his father from his native Hungary to live with his maternal uncle in San Diego. Although White had many legitimate complaints, including his inability to find employment, his diary also was filled with exaggerated ramblings about imagined enemies. He suspected conspiracies involving people with whom he had only a casual acquaintance. And he coupled his own suicide with threats of revenge against those he imagined had plotted his unhappy fate.

Both Durkheim and Freud would have agreed that, as in White's case, suicide is often accompanied by a combination of unresolved grief, an exaggerated belief in the hopelessness of one's condition, fear of conspiracies by others, and a wish for revenge. Both connected this behavior to loss. For Durkheim, the loss resulted from an individual's social and cultural alienation; for Freud, the loss resulted from disconnection from one's self. What neither explained to anyone's satisfaction was why the type of loss that they described did not always result in suicide.

Two case studies, those of Meriwether Lewis and of Abraham Lincoln, speak to this issue. Both of these men experienced extreme loss; both reacted to it in ways that parallel Max White's response. But Lewis killed himself and Lincoln did not. These two examples illustrate that suicidal behavior is both strategic and self-destructive. That is, anger, grief, a sense of hopelessness, risk-taking, and even threatening suicide ought to be viewed as strategies that individuals and groups adopt to help them master the social disorganization and ego disintegration that loss both brings about and exacerbates. We will look at these examples.

All strategies for dealing with loss, as Freud suggested, are reflective of mourning. What is crucial is not the material fact of loss itself but the success or failure of available strategies for "mourning." Lewis and Lincoln serve as compelling examples of the proposition that the success or failure of these strategies depends upon a confluence of historical possibilities and personal experience as both connect with psychological and constitutional factors.

Although neither Lewis nor Lincoln were "typical" Americans, their responses to loss are illustrative of the cultural bounds that inform suicidal behavior. The fact that both of these examples are taken from exceptional life histories does not diminish the argument, but rather magnifies it. I selected late eighteenth and nineteenth-century rather than contemporary cases to demonstrate the importance of histor- ical perspective for a psychocultural approach to suicide. Nevertheless, I employ historical examples here to shed light on the causes of suicide rather than to explain their significance in historical context.

The Suicide of Meriwether Lewis

IN NOVEMBER 1809 newspapers throughout the United States reported the startling news that Meriwether Lewis, the thirty-five-year- old governor of Upper Louisiana Territory and the hero of the Lewis and Clark Expedition, had committed suicide in a rude country inn in southcentral Tennessee.

Three years earlier on 12 September 1806, Lewis, William Clark, and their "corps of discovery" had received a heroes' welcome as they reentered St. Louis, Missouri, after traversing the North American continent along the Missouri River over the Rockies to the Columbia's mouth at the Pacific and back again. At thirty-three, Lewis was a national hero without equal in the young republic.

Rewarded with the governorship of Upper Louisiana Territory, Lewis arrived in St. Louis in March 1808 to assume his new duties. He soon discovered that it had been easier to guide forty-one men across a hostile continent than to satisfy the divergent demands converging on his executive office. The governor's authority and popularity were continually undercut by his chief assistant, Territorial Secretary Frederick Bates. Appointed to his position a month before Lewis's nomination, Bates administered the territory for over a year while Lewis procrastinated in the East. Lewis's early decisions to reverse some of Bates's Indian policies and to remove some of the secretary's appointees created tension between the two men. Mutual resentment grew into personal hostility, to the point where a duel was averted only by the intervention of Clark, now commander-in-chief of the territorial militia. Being not without influence and friends, Bates used both to circulate reports alleging the governor's incompetence. Moreover, Lewis's authoritarian manner undercut the initial popularity of his appointment in both St. Louis and Washington. Failing to establish a local political base, Lewis managed the territorial government like an army corps, lending credence to Bates's charge that he was "altogether military, and he never can . . . succeed in any other profession."

The War Department seemed no better satisfied with the governor. Secretary of War William Eustis refused to honor the payment of various sums that Lewis had authorized without prior approval from the federal government, claiming that the governor had used public funds to support private commercial ventures. Adding to Lewis's personal financial plight were his extensive land speculations in and around St. Louis. These purchases created obligation that amounted to almost three times his annual salary, and by the fall of 1809 Lewis began selling off his holdings to cover his increasingly large debts. His plight was so extreme that he was forced to borrow money from Clark to pay a $49.00 medical bill; during his final months in St. Louis, he relied on loans from friends to meet daily expenses. The actions of the War

Department pushed him to the verge of bankruptcy.

The consequences of these political and financial troubles spilled over into Lewis's personal life. Desiring to bring his widowed mother Mary Marks from Virginia to live with him in St. Louis, he purchased land upon which he planned to build a residence for his mother and himself, but the project failed when the property had to be sold to satisfy his debts. Depressed and angry, his political and personal integrity severely damaged, Lewis resolved to go to Washington to confront the secretary of war and the new president, James Madison. On 4 September 1809, having given power of attorney to his closest associates, he left St. Louis.

On 11 September on the Mississippi south of St. Louis, the governor apparently for the first time in his life wrote a last will and testament, leaving his entire estate to his mother. Lewis planned to go by river to New Orleans and then by sea to the nation's capital. While on route he reportedly made two attempts to kill himself. When he arrived at Fort Pickering near Memphis on 15 September, the commanding officer, Captain Gilbert C. Russell, found Lewis to be intoxicated and "in a state of mental derangement." Uncertain that the governor was emotionally fit to travel, Russell insisted that he rest at Fort Pickering until he recovered. Remaining there for two weeks, Lewis promised "never to drink any more spirits or use snuff again."

Although Lewis's condition seemed to improve, he altered his plans and decided to travel overland to Washington. The British, he feared, might waylay him if he sailed from New Orleans. On 29 September he departed with James Neelly, the federal agent for the Chickasaw nation who was traveling to Nashville. Lewis's personal servant John Pernier and Neelly's slave Tom accompanied them. Soon Lewis began drinking heavily and he acted so strange that Neelly decided that the party should rest for two days. By 8 October they reached the Tennessee River. The following day two of their horses escaped. Lewis and the two servants went ahead, agreeing to wait for

Neelly at the first dwelling inhabited by whites, while he searched for the missing horses.

Lewis, Pernier, and Tom reached the homestead of Robert Grinder about sunset on the tenth. Grinder's Stand was a frequent resting place for travelers along the Nachez Trace. Grinder was away, but his wife took the party in and fed them supper. During and after dinner Lewis appeared incoherent and Mrs. Grinder remembered he was extremely agitated. Lewis retired to the room reserved for guests, while the servants stayed in the barn. Mrs. Grinder, her daughter, and their servants slept in the main house. According to Neelly, who arrived the next morning, Mrs. Grinder informed him that about three o'clock in the morning, "she heard two pistols fire off in the Governor's room." She immediately awakened the servants, who found that Lewis "had shot himself in the head with one pistol, and a little below the breast with the other." Lewis, still alive, reportedly looked up at his servant Pernier and said, "I have done the business my good Servant give me some water." A short time later he died.

In early Spring 1811, an ornithologist, Alexander Wilson, who was cataloguing birds for his *American Ornithology*, stopped at Grinder's Stand and interviewed Mrs. Grinder about the circumstances of Lewis's death. According to Wilson, Mrs. Grinder, "considerably alarmed" by Lewis's behavior, could not sleep and sat in the kitchen next to Lewis's room listening to him "walking backwards and forwards . . . for several hours talking aloud . . . like a lawyer." She then heard a pistol fire "and something heavy fall to the floor" and the words "Oh Lord." Immediately, "she heard another pistol" and a few minutes later outside the kitchen door Lewis called out, "O madam! give me some water and heal my wounds!" The walls of the Grinder's cabin were made of unplastered logs and the terrified woman watched through the cracks as Lewis staggered outside, "crawled for some distance, and raised himself by the side of a tree." Lewis returned to his room and again approached the kitchen door, wanting water. Mrs. Grinder waited petrified until daybreak when she roused the servants, who found Lewis "lying on the bed." The governor "uncovered his side, and showed them where the bullet had entered; a piece of his forehead was blown off, and had exposed his brains, without having bled much." Lewis "begged they take a rifle and blow out his brains." His last words, according to Wilson's report, were "I am no coward; but I am so strong, so hard to die."

Although he was not a witness to the act, Captain Russell at Jefferson's request recounted what he had learned about the circumstances of Lewis's death. While Russell's version varied in details from Mrs. Grinder's, his conclusion confirmed hers. After everyone had retired, Lewis had loaded his pistols and "discharged one against his forehead without much effect." Then, "he discharged the other against his breast where the ball entered and passing downward thro' his body came out low near the backbone." He then staggered to Mrs. Grinder's door asking for water, but "her husband being absent and and having heard the report of pistols she was greatly alarmed and made no answer." When day broke, Lewis's servant found him "sitting up in his bed . . . busily engaged in cutting himself [with his razor] from head to foot." Before he died, Lewis said he wanted to kill himself and "to deprive his enemies the pleasure and honor of doing it."

What led Lewis to take his life? As we have seen, by the early nineteenth century most Americans connected suicide with insanity or at the very least severe emotional distress. And like other diseases, suicide was assumed to result from a combination of constitutional and environmental factors.

Thomas Jefferson, who had known Lewis since Lewis's childhood, attributed the suicide to "a constitutional disposition" to "depressions of the mind" that was "inherited by him from his father." The pressures of urban life, Jefferson believed, exacerbated these tendencies. Whenever Lewis lived in a city, Jefferson noted, he exhibited symptoms of depression. The move to St. Louis in 1808 fit this pattern. "Lewis had from early life been subject to hypochondriac affections," Jefferson wrote. "While he lived with me in Washington, I observed at times sensible depressions of mind. During his Western expedition the constant exertion . . . suspended these distressing affections; but," Jefferson concluded, "after his establishment in sedentary occupations they returned upon him with redoubled vigor."

When he learned of Lewis's suicide, his expedition collaborator William Clark proclaimed, "O! I fear the weight of his mind has overcome him." Lewis's friend, the artist Charles Willson Peale, wrote to his son that Lewis had taken his life because "he had been sometime past in bad health and showed evident signs of disarrangement, & that having drawn bills for the payment of public services, which were protested because no specific funds had been provided, this mortification completed his despair." Lewis's enemy, Louisiana Territorial Secretary Frederick Bates, whose actions others claimed had driven Lewis from office, likewise attributed the suicide to insanity. "Gov. Lewis," wrote Bates, "on his way to Washington became *insane*." "Mental derangement," Bates insisted, was at the root of both Lewis's "political miscarriages" and his subsequent suicide.

The national press affirmed these explanations. Although Lewis recently had experienced severe financial and political reverses, *The National Intelligencer* rejected the possibility that these "alone, could have produced such deplorable consequences." Rather, it connected Lewis's suicide to physical deterioration: "Governor Lewis [was] . . . very weak, from a recent illness at Natchez, and showed signs of mental derangement." Like the *Intelligencer*, newspapers throughout the country, reflecting the popular belief that suicide was connected with illness, reported Lewis's death with no hint of condemnation. *The Nashville Clarion* reported that Lewis "had been under influence of a deranging malady for about six weeks" prior to his suicide. *The Missouri Gazette* explained that Lewis had "been of late very much afflicted with fever, which never failed of depriving him of his reason; to this cause we may ascribe the fatal catastrophe!"

A Life History

MERIWETHER LEWIS WAS born on 14 August 1774 at Locust Hill, the family estate in Albemarle County, Virginia, about seven miles west of Charlottesville. He was the first son and second child of William Lewis (born ca. 1748) and Lucy Meriwether (born 1752). His sister Jane was born in 1770 and his brother Reuben in 1777. When Meriwether was not quite two years old, his father left home to join the revolutionary forces fighting in Virginia and, so far as we know, did not return until late October or early November 1779.

Children tend to view absent parents in contradictory ways. They feel abandoned and resentful but simultaneously somehow responsible for the absence, believing that the parent left because of something the child did or wished to do. Children harbor these ambivalent feelings in part because of their inability to separate fantasies from actual events. A child may view his or her father as a competitor for the affections and time of the mother. Unconsciously and often consciously the child wishes the rival would disappear. Of course it also desires that the rival not disappear. When the father does go away, the child imagines that its own wishes could have caused this event and—at some level—sees itself as responsible. To avoid the overwhelming guilt for such episodes, the child simultaneously externalizes these feelings and blames the absent parent for having abandoned him or her.

Added to this general phenomenon is the idealization of fathers who go off to war and whose return from battle shatters the child's heroic vision. There is of course nothing pathological about any of this; the circumstances are rather ordinary; most children adjust to them by one means or another. However, when an absent parent fails to return, the conflict for the child can be extreme. In Lewis's case the trauma was heightened by the fact that the syndrome repeated itself twice, each time with more permanent consequences. In November 1779, when Meriwether was not quite five, his father returned from the war and soon thereafter died of pneumonia. On 14 November 1779 he was buried on the wife's family estate at Cloverfield. How Meriwether reacted to these events we can only imagine. Yet it would not be in the least farfetched to suppose that the father who returned after a three-year absence had not measured up to Meriwether's idealized expectations, and that the ambivalences and rivalries that are so common in these cases revived. William Lewis's death would thus have been viewed by his son as both the fulfillment of his own unconscious wishes and as the final abandonment and punishment of the son for those wishes.

Moreover, the circumstances of the father's death suggest that these same wartime conditions restricted Meriwether's opportunity to participate fully in rituals of mourning. In May 1780, less than six months after her husband died, Lucy Meriwether married Captain John Marks. It was inevitable that the five-and-a-half-year-old boy would feel ambivalent about his stepfather. In contrast to William Lewis, who died while still in service of his country, Mark had been forced by poor health to retire from the revolutionary army in 1781. He immediately moved his new family from Virginia to his speculative landholdings along the Broad River in Georgia. Thus Meriwether was forced to leave not only his home but also the site of his father's grave. The following years brought the birth of two more siblings, John Hastings and Mary Marks, adding no doubt to the boy's already uncertain relationship with his new father. In any case, by 1785 eleven-year-old Meriwether was sent back to Virginia to live with his maternal uncles, Nicholas and William D. Meriwether. Whether he felt deserted or betrayed by his mother is impossible to determine. In 1791 Captain Marks died, leaving Meriwether fatherless again. Marks's death had the effect of returning Meriwether's mother to Virginia and placing him at the head of the household. Thus at the age of seventeen he had lost and replaced both his father and stepfather. For the remainder of his life he would maintain an extremely close relationship with his mother—so close, in fact, that his biographers concluded that Lewis never married because no women he ever met measured up to his vision of Lucy Marks.

The pattern of Lewis's life suggests that these events troubled him intensely. All people develop strategies for coping with the stresses and contradictions of their lives. Although none of Lewis's strategies were unusual in themselves, in combination and interaction they are revealing. Moreover, the intensity with which they formed the patterns in his life is consistent with the case histories of those who take, or attempt to take, their own lives: a repeated failure to establish lasting interpersonal relations, extreme risk-taking, and a compulsive desire for self-punishment.

Like suicide itself, these modes of behavior are symptomatic of deeper conflicts and they should be viewed less as evidence of "mental disease" than as attempts to master underlying psychological conflicts. The repetition of these modes of behavior could be viewed as a ritualistic attempt to purge—once and for all—the guilt that informs the life of the incomplete mourner.

As a young man, Lewis was constantly in search of the ideal woman, falling in and out of love quickly and often. In each instance he discovered a reason or created a situation that made the continuation or culmination of the romantic relationship impossible. As Donald Jackson notes, "Lewis's search for a wife was dogged and inexplicitly futile." Lewis never married, but he seemed always on the verge of matrimony. As a twenty-year-old soldier during the Whiskey Rebellion he wrote his mother from Pittsburgh that he would be bringing home "an insurgent girl . . . bearing the title of Mrs. Lewis." He didn't. When he was Jefferson's personal secretary and during the months before his departure on the expedition, he pursued several women and decided he might marry his cousin Maria Wood. He named the north fork of the Missouri River after her, but when he returned, his ardor cooled and Maria soon married another. Lewis then fell in love with a mysterious Miss "C," whom he described as rich and beautiful. When Clark announced his own engagement to Julie Hancock, Lewis wrote that he had definitely made up his mind to marry Miss "C," but after meeting Letitia Brackenridge at the Hancock home, he told his brother Reuben that he meant to marry her instead. That notion, like all the others, was soon abandoned.

Past experience, object relations theory suggests, made Lewis cautious in forming close emotional relationships in which he might find himself once again abandoned as his father had abandoned him. He unconsciously made the association between his ambiguous pursuit of women and incomplete mourning when he wrote (and underlined!) in 1807 after another failed love affair that he was "now *a perfect widower with respect to love.*" Throughout his life Lewis created idealized visions of women that served the purpose of avoiding marriage, thus saving himself from feared future desertion by a love object.

Moreover, Lewis had great difficulty maintaining many of his personal relationships, including those with his mentor Jefferson and his close friend Amos Stoddard. The only exceptions to this pattern seem to have occurred during the expedition, when risk-taking, the second derivative of his personality conflict, predominated. This connection between avoiding love and risk-taking was presented, though unintentionally, by Bakeless, who excused Lewis's inability to form lasting relationships with women in this fashion: "What, after all, is a woman, compared to solitude in the wilderness, Indians, the bright face of danger, the high adventure of the Rockies, canoes in foaming rapids, a grizzly hunt, or sword blades flashing in the sun, a flag that flutters over steel-tipped columns, the cadenced tramp of doughboys at your back, and polished brass and bugles, calling, calling; and rifles crashing smartly to 'Present'?"

What indeed? All Lewis's friends and all his biographers have agreed that he was an extreme risk-taker. From earliest childhood he gambled with his life. Jefferson recalled that when Lewis was only eight years old, "he habitually went out in the dead of night alone . . . to hunt." Jefferson noted Lewis's compulsive pursuit of danger even at this young age: "no season or circumstance could obstruct his purposes, plunging thro' the winter's snows and frozen streams in pursuit of his object." Lewis's biographers repeat the many stories of his boyhood bravado. One of his schoolmates remembered him in his early teens as having an "obstinacy in pursuing . . . trifles" and "a martial temper; great steadiness of purpose, self-possession, and undaunted courage." Lewis's personal stiffness, "almost without flexibility," recalled to his classmate "a very strong resemblance to Buonaparte."

This pattern continued throughout Lewis's early army career, including his reckless challenge of a superior officer to a duel in 1795. His reputation as one who invited rather than avoided danger followed him to Washington. Attorney General Levi Lincoln, fearing Lewis's impulsiveness, urged Jefferson to modify the guidelines for the expedition: "From my ideas of Capt. Lewis he will be much more likely, in case of difficulty, to push too far, than to recede too soon. Would it not be well," Lincoln suggested, "to change the term, 'certain destruction' into probable destruction & to add—that these dangers are never to be encountered, which vigilance precaution & attention can secure against, at a reasonable expense." Lewis's actions during the transcontinental explorations demonstrated both his extraordinary courage and his excessive inclination to gamble with his life. While no one ever doubted Clark's personal bravery, "Lewis had most of the narrow escapes."

Placing one's life in constant danger is, as we have seen, a common trait of suicidal personalities. We can look at Lewis's excessive and repetitive risk-taking as repeated attempts to purge recurring self-destructive urges. That is why he seemed the least troubled when he was in the greatest danger.

The third and in Lewis's case ultimate strategy was self-punishment. Suicide is of course the most extreme form of self-affliction, but Lewis also pursued other slower means, especially hard drink. The evidence of his addiction to alcohol appears as early as his twentieth year, when Lewis, though ultimately found innocent, was court-martialed for drunkenness and "conduct unbecoming an officer." Evidence from contemporary sources supports the view that he was a confirmed alcoholic. Jefferson, for example, noted that he "was much afflicted & habitually so with hypochondria. This was probably increased by the habit [intemperance] into which he had fallen & the painful reflections that would necessarily produce in a mind like his." Gilbert Russell was convinced that Lewis's "untimely death may be attributed solely to the free use he made of liquor." Lewis admitted his dependence to Gilbert and promised to reform. Yet by all accounts he was drinking heavily before and after his arrival at Grinder's Stand. Only during the expedition does he seem to have lived without liquor.

Lewis's actions as governor of Upper Louisiana Territory—including his suspicions of a conspiracy to damage his reputation and to remove him from office—are consistent with a deep-seated wish for punishment. Given to fits of temper, he was portrayed by one not-unbiased observer as behaving "like an overgrown baby[;] he began to think that everybody about the House must regulate their conduct by his caprices."

From a psychological point of view, Lewis's suicide, then, was not merely a means of dying, but a grisly final self-punishment, even a self-execution. The reports about the manner of his death suggest that Lewis inflicted upon himself a punishment much worse than the "enemies" whom he imagined as desiring "the pleasure and the honor of doing it."

A final thread in Lewis's psychological life remains dangling. It is impossible to ignore the important role that his relationship with and feelings toward his mother played in his life. The ambivalent child's wish to replace his father became a possibility early, and the fantasy grew into reality during his teenage years when his stepfather died and circumstances placed Meriwether at the head of his household. Lewis's inability to find a suitable mate, though marriage remained a central goal of his life and a topic of his letters, cannot be dismissed. Until the end of his days, he depended closely and constantly on his mother. While none of this is unusual, nor is it pathological, this relationship remained the anchor in his world of failed strategies.

His difficulties in St. Louis, however, made it impossible for Lewis finally to bring his mother under his own roof. This fact added to his despondency. His announced plan of action was to return to Washington to redeem himself, with a visit to his mother en route. He took all his worldly possessions with him, indicating that he did not intend to return to the West. Perhaps his impending reunion with his mother, with Jefferson, President Madison, and Secretary of War Eustis (father figures?) troubled him. Would they reject him as a failure? Would they judge him as his life indicates he judged himself? In any case, the will he prepared a few days after departing from St. Louis left his estate to his mother. Only then did Lewis twice attempt, and fail, to take his life. He drank incessantly. Inexplicably, he altered his route, taking the more dangerous overland trail. Finally he succeeded in killing himself; though not before calling out for aid to another mother who was too frightened to answer his pleas and ignored his cries for help.

Different societies and different eras have dealt with death, mourning, and suicide in different ways; but to the extent that any society or set of circumstances restricts the mourning ritual for any of its members, one would expect to find evidence of alternative individual or social strategies that attempt to deal with earlier repressed loss. Because the death of parents and siblings was more common in the late eighteenth or early nineteenth-century America than it is today, we might suppose that people of Lewis's generation would not react to loss in the same way that we do. In fact, as recent studies have shown, during the early colonial period children generally were not separated from the mourning process and death rituals involved the participation of the entire community. This is what makes Lewis's response so useful for our purposes. He seems to have responded to loss in a manner that appears to have been atypical of his generation, and this suggests that social parameters combined with constitutional and psychological problems to inform his behavior. The circumstances of the Revolutionary War restricted young Meriwether's mourning his father's death. His mother's remarriage and subsequent migration to Georgia exacerbated this loss. Although he was a life-long depressive and alcoholic, historical circumstance in the form of the Lewis and Clark expedition provided a successful strategy—at least while it lasted—for Lewis to deal with his incomplete mourning.

Suicide emerges as an alternative of last resort for the incomplete mourner when other strategies prove either insufficient or unavailable. The life of Meriwether Lewis is suggestive of incomplete mourning, and a fuller understanding of his death should lead us to a more complete picture of his life. Admittedly, Lewis's suicide provides a sketch rather than a complete picture of how cultural and historical factors interact with psychological and organic factors in suicidal behavior... Now I want to explore more fully the relationship between loss and subsequent suicidal behavior by examining a successful strategy: the case of an individual who experienced severe early loss, but who nevertheless did not commit suicide.

The Strategy of Abraham Lincoln

ALL LOSS, AS the case of Meriwether Lewis illustrates, calls forth personal strategies and socially defined rituals. It is the failure of these strategies that can eventually lead to suicide. Even suicide is not necessarily a denial of life. As Robert Jay Lifton explains, suicide often includes an attempt to live on, if only in the memory of those left behind. We shall examine Lincoln's early years from this point of view.

The main argument here is that the goal of Lincoln's well-known depressive behavior was to avoid self-destruction. As we shall see, his actions prior to 1842 fit this pattern. A threatened suicide in 1841 served as an extreme and partially successful attempt to purge the guilt, anger, and fears of desertion brought on by severe early loss and incomplete mourning.

Lincoln was born in Kentucky in 1809, the same year that Meriwether Lewis killed himself. Among Abraham Lincoln's earliest memories was the death of his infant brother Thomas when Abraham was between two and three years old. Thomas was buried in a small grave within sight of the family cabin. In 1816, when Abraham was seven, his father Thomas, his mother Nancy Hanks, and his nine-year-old sister Sarah moved to Little Pigeon Creek in Spencer County, Indiana. Soon they were joined by Nancy's uncle, Thomas Sparrow, his wife Elizabeth, and Nancy's illegitimate nineteen-year-old cousin, Dennis Hanks. Thomas Lincoln and his family lived in a one-room cabin, while the Sparrows and young Hanks lived close by in an even more primitive lean-to.

In September 1818 Thomas Sparrow and his wife Elizabeth contracted brucellosis, a disease transmitted from cow's milk, and within a week both died. As her aunt and uncle lay dying, thirty-five-year-old Nancy Hanks Lincoln realized that she had contracted early signs of the illness. She called her children, Abraham, now nine, and Sarah, eleven, to her bedside. To her son, Nancy reportedly said, "I am going away from you, Abraham, and I shall not return. I know that you will be a good boy that you will be kind to Sarah and to your father." Nancy Lincoln died on 5 October 1818, one week after her uncle Thomas Sparrow. Abraham had watched his mother go through the course of the "milk sickness" in their one-room cabin and now he helped his father fashion a rude coffin. Father and son hauled it to a burial plot 1500 feet south of the cabin site, where a neighbor conducted a brief interment service.

The next several years were bleak ones for Thomas Lincoln

and his children. Young Sarah took over the duties of her mother until her father married the widow Sarah Bush Johnston of Elizabeth Town, Kentucky, a year later. Sarah Johnston moved into the already crowded Lincoln cabin with her three children, Elizabeth, twelve, John D., ten, and Matilda, eight.

Lincoln's relationship with his new stepmother seems to have been untroubled and affectionate—indeed, it remained closer than his relationship with his father. Charles B. Strozier writes that "Nowhere does Lincoln ever say anything good about Thomas—a reticence that contrasts strikingly with his openly expressed idealization of Nancy and his deep affection for Sarah." The portrait Lincoln left of his father in an 1848 letter to a relative is curt and unflattering: "Owing to my father being left an orphan at the age of six years, in poverty, and in a new country, he became a wholly uneducated man; which I suppose is the reason why . . . I can say nothing more that would interest you at all." All evidence indicates that Lincoln shared William H. Herndon's characterization of Thomas Lincoln's "utter laziness and want of energy," which Herndon attributed to Thomas's loss of potency. In 1851 Lincoln declined to visit Thomas, then on his deathbed, because, he wrote to his stepbrother John D. Johnston, "Say to him that if we could meet now, it is doubtful whether it would not be more painful than pleasant." At times Lincoln seems to have had the fantasy that Thomas Lincoln was not actually his father and that his mother Nancy Hanks was the illegitimate descendent of aristocratic Virginia planters.

In any case, with his mother's death, Lincoln transferred his familial affections even more intensely to his sister Sarah. Her death at twenty-one during childbirth in January 1828 devastated the nineteen-year-old youth: "He sat down on the door of the smoke house and buried his face in his hands. The tears slowly trickled from between his bony fingers and his gaunt frame shook with sobs." One who remembered Lincoln in the years immediately following Sarah's death pictured him as "witty and sad and thoughtful by turns." His sister's death, according to Louis Warren, "left lasting marks deep within his mind and spirit, and he endured long periods of melancholic brooding and depression."

Hearing of more promising opportunities in central Illinois, Thomas Lincoln led his family to a settlement about ten miles west of Decatur in the winter of 1830-1831. Within a year the Lincoln family moved to Coles County, Illinois, and twenty-two-year-old Abraham left his father's house to settle ultimately in New Salem along the Sangamon River where he worked as a clerk in a general store. Within six months Lincoln was an unsuccessful Whig candidate for the state legislature. In the middle of the campaign Lincoln served briefly as a militia captain in the Blackhawk War. By 1833 he was appointed as postmaster; he was a respected member of the community and a joint owner with William F. Berry of a general store. Even though that venture failed in 1834, twenty-five-year-old Abraham Lincoln was elected to the state legislature at Vandalia. Thus, in a relatively short period Lincoln had achieved what he had admitted candidly in 1832 was one of his primary motives for seeking political office: "Every man is said to have his peculiar ambition. Whether it be true or not, I can say for one that I have no other so great as that of being truly esteemed by my fellow men, by rendering myself worthy of their esteem. How far I shall succeed in gratifying this ambition, is yet to be developed."

Electoral success, however, did not remove his recurrent depressive (or as he called them "hypochondria") episodes. The death of his friend Ann Rutledge in 1835 brought back memories of his earlier losses. Lincoln had become friends with Ann when he had first arrived in New Salem and had boarded at her father's tavern. No evidence exists to substantiate Herndon's claim that Lincoln and Ann were engaged. Lincoln's well-documented fears of rejection by women during this period suggests that he had sought out Ann's company because she was engaged and therefore Lincoln could maintain a friendship with her without the danger of commitment. Even after Ann broke off her engagement with

John MacNamar, it is unlikely, because of Lincoln's internal conflicts, that he would have suggested marriage. On the other hand, it cannot be doubted that he suffered greatly from her death. Lincoln's excessive public mourning at Ann Rutledge's death suggests to Robert V. Bruce "that the long repressed grief at the loss of his mother may have broken out again to swell Lincoln's grief at the similar death of Ann."

All the women for whom Lincoln had cared most intensely had died. This fact provides an important context for understanding Lincoln's seemingly bizarre courtship of Mary Owens, which began in 1836, a little more than a year after Ann's death. Mary Owens, who lived in Kentucky, had met Lincoln briefly during an 1833 visit to her older sister, Mrs. Bennett Abell, in New Salem. Three years later Mrs. Abell suggested that she would bring Mary Owens back from Kentucky if Lincoln were interested in marrying her. Lincoln consented, but when Mary arrived, Lincoln's actions and words transformed his proposal into an offer no young woman could accept.

In December 1836 Lincoln left for the legislative session meeting at the capitol in Vandalia. His letters to Mary Owens were filled with ambiguous messages. Although these were couched in terms of his continuing commitment to marriage, they seemed aimed at least unconsciously at obtaining a release from his promise. For instance, he wrote in December that "things I cannot account for, have conspired and have gotten my spirits so low, that I feel I would rather be any place in the world but here." he told Mary that he had "not been pleased since I left you." Yet he did not take the next step. Instead he ended, "This letter is so dry and stupid that I am ashamed to send it, but with my present feelings I can not do any better."

Instead of returning to New Salem when the legislative session ended, Lincoln traveled to Springfield where he decided to settle. In May he wrote Mary that although he was "often thinking about what we said of your coming to live in Springfield. I am afraid you would not be satisfied." He informed her at great length and detail the unpleasant living conditions that awaited her if she joined him. "My opinion," Lincoln offered, "is that you had better not do it." But, he promised, if she were inclined to insist on accepting his earlier offer of marriage, he would "most positively abide by it."

If Mary Owens had not by then totally abandoned any ideas of marriage, Lincoln's letter of August must have provided the final reasons for that: "I want at this particular time, more than anything else, to do right with you, and if I *knew* it would be doing right, as I rather suspect it would, to let you alone, I would do it." It was up to her, Lincoln suggested, to make the next move: "And for the purpose of making the matter as plain as possible, I now say, that you can drop the subject, dismiss your thoughts (if you ever had any) from me forever, and leave this letter unanswered, without calling forth one accusing murmur from me." One cannot imagine how Mary Owens ever could have accepted Lincoln's "proposal." Certainly, politician and orator that he was, it is difficult to believe that Lincoln expected that Owens would have held him to his commitment. His closing lines could not be misunderstood: "If it suits you best not to answer this—farewell—a long life and merry one attend you."

Nevertheless, one cannot read these letters without also sensing the pain that he felt. Lincoln was attracted to the idea of marrying Mary Owens, yet he maintained a genuine conscious fear that he could make no woman happy. This was no doubt a projection of his unconscious anxiety that previous experiences would be repeated; that Mary Owens, like the other women he had loved, would desert him. Later Lincoln related his relationship with Owens to others in a humorous context; but humor, particularly Lincoln's, often obscured deeper ambivalences and harms. When he told Eliza Browning in 1838 that "when I beheld her [Owens], I could not for my life avoid thinking of my mother," Lincoln was revealing more of his inner conflicts than his caricature of Mary suggests.

Lincoln unquestionably suffered from the loss of those he

loved most intensely. His fear of further losses was acute—particularly when it came to women. It manifested itself in a reluctance to form attachments that surpassed nineteenth-century-frontier conventions of male shyness. In January 1841 Lincoln, not quite thirty-two, began a six-month-long severe episode of depression that included a threat to take his own life.

The Strategy of Depression

LINCOLN CHARACTERIZED HIS behavior as "a discreditable exhibition of myself in the way of hypochondriaism." His actions led his friends "to remove all razors, knives, pistols, etc. from his room and presence," because they feared "that he might commit suicide." They described his behavior variously as "crazy as a loon," "deranged," and "that he had two Cat fits and a Duck fit." He described himself as "the most miserable man living. If what I feel were equally distributed to the whole human family, there would not be one cheerful face on earth." Lincoln wrote to a close friend that he could not go on living: "To remain as I am is impossible; I must die or be better." Scholars generally agree with Strozier that although Lincoln was "subject to depression throughout his life," this was "his most severe bout."

The precipitating incident was the threat of still another loss. Two important events preceded Lincoln's suicidal behavior. On 1 January 1841, Lincoln's most intimate friend, Joshua Speed, with whom Lincoln had shared a bed for the past four years, sold his store in preparation for leaving town to marry a woman in the neighboring state of Kentucky. On the same day, Lincoln broke his engagement to marry his fiancée, Mary Todd.

One scholar, who studied these events intensively, concluded that the suicidal behavior resulted almost entirely from the broken engagement: "It is clear from his later references . . . to his ensuing emotional chaos, that Lincoln underwent misery of no mild variety as a result, not merely of his own indecision and instability, but also his awareness that he was the cause of an injury . . . no less severe and humiliating than his own." Other investigators, however, have found Speed's imminent departure as the primary anxiety-producing element. Speed was so concerned about his friend's condition (and apparently so aware of his role in producing it) that he deferred his plans to leave for Kentucky for almost six months. Speed's father's death late that spring made his remaining in Springfield impossible. Concluding that Lincoln was "emotionally unfit to be alone," Speed took him to Kentucky where Lincoln lived with Speed and his family for the next several months. At the end of the summer, Speed returned to Springfield with Lincoln, where he remained until December 1841.

Having deferred his plans for almost a year, Joshua Speed finally married Fanny Henning in February 1842. Prior to the wedding Lincoln and Speed exchanged a series of letters in which Lincoln revealed quite explicitly his own anxieties about the connection between love and death. Speed had written that he feared for Fanny's health and, ultimately, for her life. "Why Speed," Lincoln replied, "if you did not love her, although you might not wish her death, you would most calmly be resigned to it." Then Lincoln added, "Perhaps this point is no longer a question with you, . . . [but] you must pardon me. You know the Hell I have suffered on that point." With Speed's assurance that married life was far from miserable, Lincoln resumed his relationship with the jilted Mary Todd and on 4 November 1942 they were married. Lincoln was thirty-three.

Although Lincoln would experience other depressive or melancholic episodes during his life, none reached the intensity of his experience of 1841. A clinician encountering Lincoln in the early months of 1841 would have taken seriously both Lincoln's threats and his friends' judgments that he was a candidate for suicide. Lincoln's life history prior to 1841 provides compelling support for such a view.

In Lincoln's case, those toward whom he had felt the closest—his mother, his sister, and Ann Rutledge—all had deserted him by dying. His only brother died at the age of two or three and perhaps because of these events, Lincoln proved unable to form any positive attachment to his father. Lincoln's experience made him anxious about desertion by those (especially women) with whom he formed close relationships. His behavior toward Mary Owens provides a graphic example of these ambivalent feelings. When Joshua Speed, the closest friend he ever made, decided to leave Springfield (and Lincoln) to move to Kentucky to marry Fanny Henning, it was not surprising that Lincoln, feeling deserted by Speed, recalled his earlier losses and in panic deserted Mary Todd before she too might desert him.

In 1841, during the period when he contemplated suicide, Lincoln told Speed that "he had 'done nothing to make any human being remember that he had lived.'" Suicide can be a form of revenge, like the child's threat to run away so it will be missed by those who have done it harm. In short, suicide may be imagined as a way of living on in other people's memories just as the lost object lives on in the memory of the potential suicide. After death, the suicide fantasizes, he too will become mourned (remembered). Abraham Lincoln's suicide threats fit this pattern.

Speed's sensitive response to his friend's cry for help provided Lincoln with crucial therapeutic support. Although he continued to experience depressive episodes, Lincoln made no other threats to end his life. Like Meriwether Lewis, however, Lincoln remained troubled by the severe loss he had experienced and like Lewis he pursued strategies to alleviate his incomplete mourning. Unlike Lewis's, Lincoln's strategies proved to be sufficient, yet death and dying remained one of his central concerns. Throughout the rest of his life Lincoln mourned the early losses he had suffered and he continually seemed in search of an adequate way to resolve the guilt, anger, and anxiety that still accompanied them. What some writers have portrayed as Lincoln's obsession with death may be understood also as Lincoln's attempt to come to terms with these early losses.

Unlike Lewis, Lincoln seemed to have had a genuine opportunity to grieve both publicly and privately for the early losses he suffered. Like many of his literate nineteenth-century contemporaries, Lincoln rejected the existence of an afterlife. One result, suggests Robert Bruce, was that Lincoln adopted the emerging "romanticism of death," which moved the survivor rather than the departed to the center of mourning rituals. This reaction to death tended to downplay traditional communitarian participation in favor of private rites confined to family members. For isolated frontier families like Lincoln's, the ideology of romanticized death often was reinforced by physical isolation. Thus, as death came to mean more to survivors, the privacy of mourning rituals exacerbated loss, anger, and guilt.

Lincoln's romanticizing of death was evident in his repeated anxiety that those with whom he was closest were likely to die. He wrote to Speed in 1842 that "the death scenes of those we love are surely painful enough; but these we are prepared to, and expect to see." Moreover, he feared that his death was imminent. Two "romantic" poems about death illustrate his response to these issues. The first was written by William Knox, a Scot who died in 1825 at the age of thirty-three, and the other by Lincoln himself.

In October 1844 Lincoln visited the graves of his mother and sister. This was Lincoln's first trip in fifteen years to "the neighborhood. . . where my mother and only sister were buried." The experience recalled a poem that he had "seen . . . once before, about fifteen years ago," the author and title of which he did not learn until he was president. Knox's "Mortality" portrays life "Like a swift-fleeting meteor, a fast-flying cloud,/a flash of lightening, a break in the waves." "I would give all I am worth, and go in debt," Lincoln wrote enclosing a copy to the editor of the *Quincy Whig* in 1846, "to be able to write so fine a piece as I think that is." Most scholars concur with Bruce's assessment that the poem "possessed Lincoln's mind throughout his adult life" with an "extraordinary . . . duration and intensity." Lincoln's first contact with the poem was in 1831 when he was twenty-two. Later he kept a newspaper clipping reproduction of the poem in his pocket until he had memorized it. In 1850 Lincoln read Knox's lines as a eulogy on the death of President Zachary Taylor. He quoted it to his relatives and to his fellow circuit-riding lawyers in the 1850s. One of them recalled Lincoln often "sitting before the fire . . . with the saddest expression I have ever seen in a human being's eyes." On these occasions, the companion remembered, Lincoln invariably would recite Knox's "Mortality." Toward the end of his life Lincoln explained that the poem "is my almost constant companion; indeed, I may say it is continually present with me, as it crosses my mind whenever I have relief from anxiety."

Lincoln's extraordinary attachment to this poem went beyond its expression of the brevity of life. The poem's most compelling images meshed with Lincoln's personal experiences and fantasies about the death of a young woman—mother, sister, fiancée:

> *The maid on whose cheek, on whose brow, in whose eye,*
> *Shone beauty and pleasure, her triumphs are by.*
> *And the memory of those that beloved her and praised,*
> *Are alike from the minds of the living erased.*

At one level Lincoln's fascination with the piece rests upon its romantic portrayal of death and its refusal to seek relief from loss in an afterlife. However, it is less certain that Lincoln agreed with the poet's insistence that the goal of life is to "rest in the grave":

> *So the multitude goes, like the flower or the weed,*
> *That withers away to let others succeed;*
> *So the multitude comes, even those we behold,*
> *To repeat every tale that has ever been told.*

Lincoln's obsession with Knox's poem should not be confused with his endorsement of its sentiments. Rather its repetition may indicate Lincoln's search for an alternative meaning for his losses. although the central theme speaks of the need to accept "the death we are shirking," Lincoln's own life history suggests less than total resignation to an end "To the thoughts we are thinking, . . . To the life we are clinging."

Lincoln's poem, "My Childhood-Home I See Again," was inspired by the same graveside visit that recalled Knox's "Mortality." Written from 1844 to 1846, "My Childhood-Home" implies a different response to Knox's opening and closing lines, "Oh! why should the spirit of mortal be proud?" Although Lincoln was saddened by the memories his visit recalled, he discovered also that "still, as memory crowds my brain,/ There's pleasure in it too." If there were no actual life after death, "memory" might substitute:

> O Memory! thou midway world
> 'Twixt earth and paradise
> Where things decayed and loved one lost
> In dreamy shadows rise,

Memory and Ambition

LINCOLN'S DESIRE, AS he had confided to Speed during the depressive episode of 1841, was "to connect his name with the events transpiring in his day and generation, and so impress himself upon them as to link his name with something that would redound to the interest of his fellow man." That, he informed Speed, "was what he desired to live for." If there were no heaven, the only life after death, the only meaning for having lived would be in the memories one left behind. To live after death one's deeds must be truly memorable. Lincoln's recent biographers all have found him to be extremely ambitious. Along with Bruce, they tie Lincoln's "almost obsessive ambition" to his fear of his own death: "Lincoln found the total annihilation of the self an intolerable prospect." Thus, Bruce finds, he "turned to the idea of survival by proxy in the minds of others. . . . Lincoln's antidote for numb despair was the concept of immortality through remembrance." "Lincoln's ambition," argues Dwight Anderson, "was rooted in what can only be described as an obsession about death. . . . Ambition provided the means by which immortality could be attained." Lincoln's goal was "to win immortality... [and] to live on in the memory of subsequent generations."

Although these same biographers' value judgements differ as to the quality of Lincoln's ambition, they concur with Strozier's evaluation that "Lincoln's driving ambition" was tied to his shame about his own father's "dull . . . character." His fantasy that Thomas Lincoln was not his biological father, that he was descended on his mother's side from Virginia aristocracy, is similar to a common childhood regressive and nostalgic fantasy, which Otto Rank linked to all heroic mythic constructs:

> the substitutions of both parents, or of the father alone, by more exalted personages—the discovery will be made that these new and highborn parents are invested throughout with the qualities which are derived from real memories of the true lowly parents. . . . The entire endeavor . . . is merely the expression of the child's longing for the vanished happy time, when his father still appeared to be the strongest and greatest man, and the mother seemed the dearest and most beautiful woman.

By the time Lincoln was nine years old he had learned that his father Thomas could not protect him from loss, and subsequent events suggest that Lincoln might have found some solace in such a childhood fantasy.

According to Anderson this translates into Lincoln's conscious desire to transform the fantasy into reality by becoming father of
himself and, ultimately, father of his country by replacing the
Constitution of the Founding Fathers with the Declaration of
Independence. Quoting Ernest Becker, Anderson compares Lincoln to
the child who "wants to conquer death by becoming the *father of himself*, the creator and sustainer of his own life." One does not have to go
as far as Anderson to conclude that Lincoln's incomplete mourning led
him to hope that fame rather than faith would bring life everlasting.
Rather than viewing Lincoln's ambitions to live in memory after death
as a pathological response to the events of his early life, one might conceive of Lincoln's solution as therapeutic.

Lincoln's desires mesh with what Becker describes as the wish
for "heroism" that springs from "the denial of death." The wish to be a
hero, according to Becker, derives from the fear that after death one will
be forgotten. Those that suffer the greatest from this anxiety are those
who already have suffered desertion in their lives. Heroism shares with
suicide a fantasy of remembrance. In both we uncover a wish to transcend death. The most heroic act that one can imagine of course is to
sacrifice one's life for social good—an act that Durkheim labeled "altruistic suicide."

Lincoln, thanks to accident and design, achieved his goal to
live on in the memory of others. Before he died he realized that he
had approached the heroic, the self-made vision of national paternity.
Those who knew him well in the 1860s attested to Lincoln's accep-
tance of death; some suggested that he welcomed it; others assert that
Lincoln continually risked his own safety. To the extent that these
latter analyses are accurate, one might conclude that Lincoln's strategies
for dealing with his early loss never surrendered all of their suicidal
content. Unique historical circumstances allowed Lincoln to deal
with his depressive disorders on the national stage. Unlike many
others who have experienced incomplete mourning, Lincoln's strategy

allowed him to live out his fantasies and for the most part to transform his self-destructive urges into socially acceptable behavior.

Conclusion

The life history of Abraham Lincoln provides an example of why the experience of severe early loss does not automatically result in a suicide. To put it another way, although loss often may bring on suicidal behavior, the aim of that behavior is not necessarily self-destruction, rather it is a search for a strategy to deal with guilt, anger, and the desire for revenge so that life can continue. Completed or "successful" suicide occurs only when alternative strategies fail.

The issues raised by the self-destructive behavior of both Meriwether Lewis and Abraham Lincoln are emblematic of the psycho-cultural etiology of suicide in America. The strategies each man pursued, while typical of suicidal behavior, were nevertheless shaped by personal circumstances and by the possibilities offered in the larger world that each inhabited. The larger world was, of course, the historically specific world of late eighteenth- and early nineteenth-century America. Thus, the early and subsequent losses that Lewis and Lincoln sustained did not make suicide inevitable; rather it led each man to seek strategies whose possibilities of success were to a great extent determined by forces beyond his control.

VIRGINIA WOOLF

The Waves

I

F I COULD believe," said Rhoda, "that I should grow old in pursuit and change, I should be rid of my fear: nothing persists. One moment does not lead to another. The door opens and the tiger leaps. You did not see me come. I circled round the chairs to avoid the horror of the spring. I am afraid of you all. I am afraid of the shock of sensation that leaps upon me, because I cannot deal with it as you do—I cannot make one moment merge in the

---

Virginia Woolf's innovative novelistic style reached its pinnacle with The Waves, *which employs the stream-of-consciousness narratives of six characters to tell the story of their lives. In this excerpt, Rhoda, the most precarious of the six, reflects on the nature of her fears. Woolf, author of* Mrs. Dalloway *and* To the Lighthouse, *struggled with debilitating mental illness all her life. She drowned herself in the River Ouse at the age of 59.*

next. To me they are all violent, all separate; and if I fall under the shock of the leap of the moment you will be on me, tearing me to pieces. I have no end in view. I do not know how to run minute to minute and hour to hour, solving them by some natural force until they make the whole and indivisible mass that you call life. Because you have an end in view—one person, is it, to sit beside, an idea is it, your beauty is it? I do not know—your days and hours pass like the boughs of forest trees and the smooth green of forest rides to a hound running on the scent. But there is no single scent, no single body for me to follow. And I have no face. I am like the foam that races over the beach or the moonlight that falls arrowlike here on a tin can, here on a spike of the mailed sea holly, or a bone or a half-eaten boat. I am whirled down caverns, and flap like paper against endless corridors, and must press my hand against the wall to draw myself back.

LANGSTON HUGHES

Suicide's Note

THE CALM,
Cool face of the river
Asked me for a kiss.

Langston Hughes, a leading poet of the Harlem Renaissance of the 1920s, was notable for directness and simplicity. "Suicide's Note," no exception, is from the recently rereleased Selected Poems.

GUSTAVE FLAUBERT

—

Madame Bovary

S

HE ASKED HERSELF as she walked along, "What am I going to say? How shall I begin?" And as she went on she recognized the thickets, the trees, the sea-rushes on the hill, the château yonder. All the sensations of her first tenderness came back to her, and her poor aching heart opened out amorously. A warm wind blew in her face; the melting snow fell drop by drop from the buds to the grass.

From the 1850s to 1880, French novelist Gustave Flaubert produced masterpiece after masterpiece. Among them: Salammbô, L'Education Sentimentale, *and* A Simple Heart. *This excerpt, from* Madame Bovary, *tells of one of the most famous and distressing suicides in the history of literature.*

She entered, as she used to, through the small park-gate. Then came to the avenue bordered by a double row of dense lime trees. They were swaying their long whispering branches to and fro. The dogs in their kennels all barked, and the noise of their voices resounded, but brought out no one.

She went up the large straight staircase with wooden balusters that led to the corridor paved with dusty flags, into which several doors in a row opened, as in a monastery or an inn. His was at the top, right at the end, on the left. When she placed her fingers on the lock her strength suddenly deserted her. She was afraid, almost wished he would not be there, though this was her only hope, her last chance of salvation. She collected her thoughts for one moment, and, strengthening herself by the feeling of present necessity, went in.

He was in front of the fire, both his feet on the mantelpiece, smoking a pipe.

"What! it is you!" he said, getting up hurriedly.

"Yes, it is I, Rodolphe. I should like to ask your advice." And, despite all her efforts, it was impossible for her to open her lips.

"You have not changed; you are charming as ever!"

"Oh," she replied bitterly, "they are poor charms since you disdained them."

Then he began a long explanation of his conduct, excusing himself in vague terms, in default of being able to invent better.

She yielded to his words, still more to his voice and the sight of him, so that she pretended to believe, or perhaps believed, in the pretext he gave for their rupture; this was a secret on which depended the honor, the very life of a third person.

"No matter!" she said, looking at him sadly. "I have suffered much."

He replied philosophically—

"Such is life!"

"Has life," Emma went on, "been good to you at least, since our separation?"

"Oh, neither good nor bad."

"Perhaps it would have been better never to have parted."

"Yes, perhaps."

"You think so?" she said, drawing nearer, and she sighed. "Oh, Rodolphe! if you but knew! I loved you so!"

It was then that she took his hand, and they remained some time, their fingers intertwined, like that first day at the Show. With a gesture of pride he struggled against this emotion. But sinking upon his breast she said to him—

"How did you think I could live without you? One cannot lose the habit of happiness. I was desolate. I thought I should die. I will tell you about all that and you will see. And you—you fled from me!"

For, all the three years, he had carefully avoided her in consequence of that natural cowardice that characterizes the stronger sex. Emma went on with dainty little nods, more coaxing than an amorous kitten—

"You love others, confess it! Oh, I understand them, dear! I excuse them. You probably seduced them as you seduced me. You are indeed a man; you have everything to make one love you. But we'll begin again, won't we? We will love one another. See! I am laughing; I am happy! Oh, speak!"

And she was charming to see, with her eyes, in which trembled a tear, like the rain of a storm in a blue corolla.

He had drawn her upon his knees, and with the back of his hand was caressing her smooth hair, where in the twilight was mirrored like a golden arrow one last ray of the sun. She bent down her brow; at last he kissed her on the eyelids quite gently with the tips of his lips.

"Why, you have been crying! What for?"

She burst into tears. Rodolphe thought this was an outburst of her love. As she did not speak, he took this silence for a last remnant of resistance, and then he cried out—

"Oh, forgive me! You are the only one who pleases me. I am imbecile and cruel. I love you. I will love you always. What is it? Tell me!" He was kneeling by her.

"Well, I am ruined, Rodolphe! You must lend me three thousand francs."

"But—but—" said he, getting up slowly, while his face assumed a grave expression.

"You know," she went on quickly, "that my husband had placed his whole fortune at a notary's. He ran away. So we borrowed; the patients don't pay us. Moreover, the settling of the estate is not yet done; we shall have the money later on. But today, for want of three thousand francs, we are to be sold up. It is to be at once, this very moment, and, counting upon your friendship, I have come to you."

"Ah!" thought Rodolphe, turning very pale, "that was what she came for." At last he said with a calm air—

"Dear madame, I have not got them."

He did not lie. If he had had them, he would, no doubt, have given them, although it is generally disagreeable to do such fine things: a demand for money being, of all the winds that blow upon love, the coldest and most destructive.

First she looked at him for some moments.

"You have not got them!" she repeated several times. "You have not got them! I ought to have spared myself this last shame. You never loved me. You are no better than the others."

She was betraying, ruining herself.

Rodolphe interrupted her, declaring he was "hard up" himself.

"Ah! I pity you," said Emma. "Yes—very much."

And fixing her eyes upon an embossed carabine that shone

against its panoply. "But when one is so poor one doesn't have silver on the butt of one's gun. One doesn't buy a clock inlaid with tortoiseshell," she went, pointing to a buhl timepiece, "nor silver-gilt whistles for one's whips," and she touched them, "nor charms for one's watch. Oh, he wants for nothing! even to a liqueur-stand in his room! For you love yourself; you live well. You have a château, farms, woods; you go hunting; you travel to Paris. Why, if it were but that," she cried, taking up two studs from the mantelpiece, "but the least of these trifles, one can get money for them. Oh, I do not want them; keep them!"

And she threw the two links away from her, their gold chain breaking as it struck against the wall.

"But I! I would have given you everything. I would have sold all, worked for you with my hands, I would have begged on the highroads for a smile, for a look, to hear you say 'Thanks!' And you sit there quietly in your armchair, as if you had not made me suffer enough already! But for you, and you know it, I might have lived happily. What made you do it? Was it a bet? Yet you loved me— you said so. And but a moment since—Ah! it would have been better to have driven me away. My hands are hot with your kisses, and there is the spot on the carpet where at my knees you swore an eternity of love! You made me believe you; for two years you held me in the most magnificent, the sweetest dream! Eh! Our plans for the journey, do you remember? Oh, your letter! it tore my heart! And then when I come back to him—to him, rich, happy, free—to implore the help the first stranger would give, a suppliant, and bringing back to him all my tenderness, he repulses me because it would cost him three thousand francs!"

"I haven't got them," replied Rodolphe, with that perfect calm with which resigned rage covers itself as with a shield.

She went out. The walls trembled, the ceiling was crushing her, and she passed back through the long alley, stumbling against the heaps of dead leaves scattered by the wind. At last she reached the ha-ha hedge in front of the gate; she broke her nails against the lock in her haste to open it. Then a hundred steps farther on, breathless, almost falling, she stopped. And now turning around, she once more saw the impassive château, with the park, the gardens, the three courts, and all the windows of the façade.

She remained lost in stupor, and having no more consciousness of herself than through the beating of her arteries, that she seemed to hear bursting forth like a deafening music filling all the fields. The earth beneath her feet was more yielding than the sea, and the furrows seemed to her immense brown waves breaking into foam. Everything in her head, of memories, ideas, went off at once like a thousand pieces of fireworks. She saw her father, Lheureux's closet, their room at home, another landscape. Madness was coming upon her; she grew afraid, and managed to recover herself, in a confused way, it is true, for she did not in the least remember the cause of the terrible condition she was in, that is to say, the question of money. She suffered only in her love, and felt her soul passing from her in this memory, as wounded men, dying, feel their life ebb from their bleeding wounds.

Night was falling, crows were flying about.

Suddenly it seemed to her that fiery spheres were exploding in the air like fulminating balls when they strike, and were whirling, whirling, to melt at last upon the snow between the branches of the trees. In the midst of each of them appeared the face of Rodolphe. They multiplied and drew near her, penetrating her. It all disappeared; she recognized the lights of the houses that shone through the fog.

Now her situation, like an abyss, rose up before her. She was panting as if her heart would burst. Then in an ecstasy of heroism, that made her almost joyous, she ran down the hill, crossed the cow-plank, the footpath, the alley, the market, and reached the chemist's shop. She was about to enter, but at the sound of the bell some one might come, and slipping in by the gate, holding her breath, feeling her way along the walls, she went as far as the door of the kitchen, where a candle stuck on the stove was burning. Justin in his shirt-sleeves was carrying out a dish.

"Ah! they are dining! I will wait."

He returned; she tapped at the window. He went out.

"The key! the one for upstairs where he keeps the——"

"What?"

And he looked at her, astonished at the pallor of her face, that stood out white against the black background of the night. She seemed to him extraordinarily beautiful and majestic as a phantom. Without understanding what she wanted, he had the presentiment of something terrible.

But she went on quickly in a low voice, in a sweet, melting voice, "I want it; give it to me."

As the partition wall was thin, they could hear the clatter of the forks on the plates in the dining-room.

She pretended that she wanted to kill the rats that kept her from sleeping.

"I must tell master."

"No, stay!" Then with an indifferent air, "Oh, it's not worth while; I'll tell him presently. Come, light me upstairs."

She entered the corridor into which the laboratory door opened. Against the wall was a key labelled *Capharnaüm*.

"Justin!" called the druggist impatiently.

"Let us go up."

And he followed her. The key turned in the lock, and she went straight to the third shelf, so well did her memory guide her, seized the blue jar, tore out the cork, plunged her hand and withdrawing it full of white powder, she began eating it.

"Stop!" he cried, rushing at her.

"Hush! some one will come."

He was in despair, was calling out.

"Say nothing, or all the blame will fall on your master."

Then she went home, suddenly calmed, and with something of the serenity of one that had performed a duty.

WHEN CHARLES, DISTRACTED by the news of the distraint, returned home, Emma had just gone out. He cried aloud, wept, fainted, but she did not return. Where could she be? He sent Félicité to Homais, to Monsieur Tuvache, to Lheureux, to the "Lion d'Or," everywhere, and in the intervals of his agony he saw his reputation destroyed, their fortune lost. Berthe's future ruined. By what?—Not a word! He waited till six in the evening. At last, unable to bear it any longer, and fancying she had gone to Rouen, he set out along the highroad, walked a mile, met no one, again waited, and returned home. She had come back.

"What was the matter? Why? Explain to me."

She sat down at her writing-table and wrote a letter, which she sealed slowly, adding the date and the hour. Then she said in a solemn tone—

"You are to read it tomorrow; till then, I pray you, do not ask me a single question. No, not one!"

"But—"

"Oh, leave me!"

She lay down full length on her bed. A bitter taste that she felt in her mouth awakened her. She saw Charles, and again closed her eyes.

She was studying herself curiously, to see if she were not suffering. But no! nothing as yet. She heard the ticking of the clock, the crackling of the fire, and Charles breathing as he stood upright by her bed.

"Ah! it is but a little thing, death!" she thought. "I shall fall asleep and all will be over."

She drank a mouthful of water and turned to the wall. The

frightful taste of ink continued.

"I am thirsty; oh! so thirsty," she sighed.

"What is it?" said Charles, who was handing her a glass.

"It is nothing! Open the window; I am choking."

She was seized with a sickness so sudden that she had hardly time to draw out her handkerchief from under the pillow.

"Take it away," she said quickly; "throw it away."

He spoke to her; she did not answer. She lay motionless, afraid that the slightest movement might make her vomit. But she felt an icy cold creeping from her feet to her heart.

"Ah! it is beginning," she murmured.

She turned her head from side to side with a gentle movement full of agony, while constantly opening her mouth as if something very heavy were weighing upon her tongue. At eight o'clock the vomiting began again.

Charles noticed that at the bottom of the basin there was a sort of white sediment sticking to the sides of the porcelain.

"This is extraordinary—very singular," he repeated.

But she said in a firm voice, "No, you are mistaken."

Then gently, and almost as caressing her, he passed his hand over her stomach. She uttered a sharp cry. He fell back terror-stricken.

Then she began to groan, faintly at first. Her shoulders were shaken by a strong shuddering, and she was growing paler than the sheets in which her clenched fingers buried themselves. Her unequal pulse was now almost imperceptible.

Drops of sweat oozed from her bluish face, that seemed as if rigid in the exhalations of a metallic vapor. Her teeth chattered, her dilated eyes looked vaguely about her, and to all questions she replied only with a shake of the head; she even smiled once or twice. Gradually, her moaning grew louder; a hollow shriek burst from her; she pretended she was better and that she would get up presently. But she was seized with convulsions and cried out—

"Ah! my God! It is horrible!"

He threw himself on his knees by her bed.

"Tell me! what have you eaten? Answer, for heaven's sake!"

And he looked at her with a tenderness in his eyes such as she had never seen.

"Well, there—there!" she said in a faint voice. He flew to the writing-table, tore open the seal, and read aloud: "Accuse no one." He stopped, passed his hands across his eyes, and read it over again.

"What! help—help!"

He could only keep repeating the word: "Poisoned! poisoned!" Félicité ran to Homais, who proclaimed it in the market-place; Madame Lefrançois heard it at the "Lion d'Or"; some got up to go and tell their neighbors, and all night the village was on the alert.

Distraught, faltering, reeling, Charles wandered about the room. He knocked against the furniture, tore his hair, and the chemist had never believed that there could be so terrible a sight.

He went home to write to Monsieur Canivet and to Doctor Larivière. He lost his head, and made more than fifteen rough copies. Hippolyte went to Neufchâtel, and Justin so spurred Bovary's horse that he left it foundered and three parts dead by the hill at Bois-Guillaume.

Charles tried to look up his medical dictionary, but could not read it; the lines were dancing.

"Be calm," said the druggist; "we have only to administer a powerful antidote. What is the poison?"

Charles showed him the letter. It was arsenic.

"Very well," said Homais, "we must make an analysis."

For he knew that in cases of poisoning an analysis must be made; and the other, who did not understand, answered—

"Oh, do anything! save her!"

Then going back to her, he sank upon the carpet, and lay there with his head leaning against the edge of her bed, sobbing.

"Don't cry," she said to him. "Soon I shall not trouble you any more."

"Why was it? Who drove you to it?"

She replied. "It had to be, my dear!"

"Weren't you happy? Is it my fault? I did all I could!"

"Yes, that is true—you are good—you."

And she passed her hand slowly over his hair. The sweetness of this sensation deepened his sadness; he felt his whole being dissolving in despair at the thought that he must lose her, just when she was confessing more love for him than ever. And he could think of nothing; he did not know, he did not dare; the urgent need for some immediate resolution gave the finishing stroke to the turmoil of his mind.

So she had done, she thought, with all the treachery and meanness, and numberless desires that had tortured her. She hated no one now; a twilight dimness was settling upon her thoughts, and, of all earthly noises, Emma heard none but the intermittent lamentations of this poor heart, sweet and indistinct like the echo of a symphony dying away.

"Bring me the child," she said, raising herself on her elbow.

"You are not worse, are you?" asked Charles.

"No, no!"

The child, serious, and still half-asleep, was carried in on the servant's arm in her long white nightgown, from which her bare feet peeped out. She looked wonderingly at the disordered room, and half-closed her eyes, dazzled by the candles burning on the table. They reminded her, no doubt, of the morning of New Year's day and Mid-Lent, when thus awakened early by candlelight she came to her mother's bed to fetch her presents, for she began saying—

"But where is it, mamma?" And as everybody was silent, "But

I can't see my little stocking."

Félicité held her over the bed while she still kept looking towards the mantelpiece.

"Has nurse taken it?" she asked.

And at this name, that carried her back to the memory of her adulteries and her calamities, Madame Bovary turned away her head, as at the loathing of another bitterer poison that rose to her mouth. But Berthe remained perched on the bed.

"Oh, how big your eyes are, mamma! How pale you are! how hot you are!"

Her mother looked at her.

"I am frightened!" cried the child, recoiling.

Emma took her hand to kiss it; the child struggled.

"That will do. Take her away," cried Charles, who was sobbing in the alcove.

Then the symptoms ceased for a moment; she seemed less agitated; and at every insignificant word, at every respiration a little more easy, he regained hope. At last, when Canivet came in, he threw himself into his arms.

"Ah! it is you. Thanks! You are good! But she is better. See! look at her."

His colleague was by no means of this opinion, and, as he said of himself, "never beating about the bush," he prescribed an emetic in order to empty the stomach completely.

She soon began vomiting blood. Her lips became drawn. Her limbs were convulsed, her whole body covered with brown spots, and her pulse slipped beneath the fingers like a stretched thread, like a harp-string nearly breaking.

After this she began to scream horribly. She cursed the poison, railed at it, and implored it to be quick, and thrust away with her stiff-ened arms everything that Charles, in more agony than herself, tried to make her drink. He stood up, his handkerchief to his lips, with a rattling sound in his throat, weeping, and choked by sobs that shook his whole body. Félicité was running hither and thither in the room. Homais, motionless, uttered great sighs; and Monsieur Canivet, always retaining his self-command, nevertheless began to feel uneasy.

"The devil! yet she has been purged, and from the moment that the cause ceases—"

"The effect must cease," said Homais, "that is evident."

"Oh, save her!" cried Bovary.

And without listening to the chemist, who was still venturing the hypothesis, "It is perhaps a salutary paroxysm," Canivet was about to administer some theriac, when they heard the cracking of a whip; all the windows rattled, and a post-chaise drawn by three horses abreast, up to their ears in mud, drove at a gallop round the corner of the market. It was Doctor Larivière.

The apparition of a god would not have caused more commotion. Bovary raised his hands; Canivet stopped short; and Homais pulled off his skull-cap long before the doctor had come in.

He belonged to that great school of surgery begotten of Bichat, to that generation, now extinct, of philosophical practitioners, who, loving their art with a fanatical love, exercised it with enthusiasm and wisdom. Every one in his hospital trembled when he was angry; and his students so revered him that they tried, as soon as they were themselves in practice, to imitate him as much as possible. So that in all the towns about they were found wearing his long wadded merino overcoat and black frock-coat, whose buttoned cuffs slightly covered his brawny hands—very beautiful hands, and that never knew gloves, as though to be more ready to plunge into suffering. Disdainful of honors, of titles, and of academies, like one of the old Knight-Hospitallers, generous, fatherly to the poor, and practicing virtue without believing in it, he would almost have passed for a saint if the keenness of his intellect had not caused him to be feared as a demon. His glance, more penetrating than his bistouries, looked straight into your soul, and dissected every lie athwart all assertions and all reticences. And thus he went along, full of that debonair majesty that is given by the consciousness of great talent, of fortune, and of forty years of a laborious and irreproachable life.

He frowned as soon as he had passed the door when he saw the cadaverous face of Emma stretched out on her back with her mouth open. Then, while apparently listening to Canivet, he rubbed his fingers up and down beneath his nostrils, and repeated—

"Good! good!"

But he made a slow gesture with his shoulders. Bovary watched him; they looked at one another; and this man, accustomed as he was to the sight of pain, could not keep back a tear that fell on his shirt-frill.

He tried to take Canivet into the next room. Charles followed him.

"She is very ill, isn't she? If we put on sinapisms? Anything! Oh, think of something, you who have saved so many!"

Charles caught him in both his arms, and gazed at him wildly, imploringly, half-fainting against his breast.

"Come, my poor fellow, courage! There is nothing more to be done."

And Doctor Larivière turned away.

"You are going?"

"I will come back."

He went out only to give an order to the coachman, with Monsieur Canivet, who did not care either to have Emma die under his hands.

The chemist rejoined them on the Place. He could not by temperament keep away from celebrities, so he begged Monsieur Larivière to do him the signal honor of accepting some breakfast.

He sent quickly to the "Lion d'Or" for some pigeons; to the butcher's for all the cutlets that were to be had; to Tuvache for cream; and to Lestiboudois for eggs; and the druggist himself aided in the preparations, while Madame Homais was saying as she pulled together the strings of her jacket—

"You must excuse us, sir, for in this poor place, when one hasn't been told the night before——"

"Wine glasses!" whispered Homais.

"If only we were in town, we could fall back upon stuffed trotters."

"Be quiet! Sit down, doctor!"

He thought fit, after the first few mouthfuls, to give some details as to the catastrophe.

"We first had a feeling of siccity in the pharynx, then intolerable pains at the epigastrium, super-purgation, coma."

"But how did she poison herself?"

"I don't know, doctor, and I don't even know where she can have procured the arsenious acid."

Justin, who was just bringing in a pile of plates, began to tremble.

"What's the matter?" said the chemist.

At this question the young man dropped the whole lot on the ground with a crash.

"Imbecile!" cried Homais, "awkward lout! blockhead! confounded ass!"

But suddenly controlling himself—

"I wished, doctor, to make an analysis, and *primo* I delicately introduced a tube——"

"You would have done better," said the physician, "to introduce your fingers into her throat."

His colleague was silent, having just before privately received a severe lecture about his emetic, so that this good Canivet, so arrogant and so verbose at the time of the club-foot, was today very modest. He smiled without ceasing in an approving manner.

Homais dilated in Amphytrionic pride, and the affecting thought of Bovary vaguely contributed to his pleasure by a kind of egotistic reflex upon himself. Then the presence of the doctor transported him. He displayed his erudition, cited pell-mell cantharides, upas, the manchineel, vipers.

"I have even read that various persons have found themselves under toxicological symptoms, and, as it were, thunder-stricken by black-pudding that had been subjected to a too vehement fumigation. At least, this was stated in a very fine report drawn up by one of our pharmaceutical chiefs, one of our masters, the illustrious Cadet de Gassicourt!"

Madame Homais reappeared, carrying one of those shaky machines that are heated with spirits of wine; for Homais liked to make his coffee at table, having, moreover, torrefied it, pulverized it, and mixed it himself.

"*Saccharum*, doctor?" said he, offering the sugar.

Then he had all his children brought down, anxious to have the physician's opinion on their constitutions.

At last Monsieur Larivière was about to leave, when Madame Homais asked for a consultation about her husband. He was making his blood too thick by going to sleep every evening after dinner.

"Oh, it isn't his blood that's too thick," said the physician.

And, smiling a little at his unnoticed joke, the doctor opened the door. But the chemist's shop was full of people; he had the greatest difficulty in getting rid of Monsieur Tuvache, who feared his spouse would get inflammation of the lungs, because she was in the habit of spitting on the ashes; then of Monsieur Binet, who sometimes experienced sudden attacks of great hunger; and of Madame Caron, who suffered from tinglings; of Lheureux, who had vertigo; of Lestiboudois, who had rheumatism; and of Madame Lefrançois, who had heartburn. At last the three horses started; and it was the general opinion that he had not shown himself at all obliging.

Public attention was distracted by the appearance of Monsieur Bournisien, who was going across the market with the holy oil.

Homais, as was due to his principles, compared priests to ravens attracted by the odor of death. The sight of an ecclesiastic was personally disagreeable to him, for the cassock made him think of the shroud, and he detested the one from some fear of the other.

Nevertheless, not shrinking from what he called his mission, he returned to Bovary's in company with Canivet, whom Monsieur Larivière, before leaving, had strongly urged to make this visit; and he would, but for his wife's objections, have taken his two sons with him, in order to accustom them to great occasions; that this might be a lesson, an example, a solemn picture, that should remain in their heads later on.

The room when they went in was full of mournful solemnity. On the work-table, covered over with a white cloth, there were five or six small balls of cotton in a silver dish, near a large crucifix between two lighted candles.

Emma, her chin sunken upon her breast, had her eyes inordinately wide open, and her poor hands wandered over the sheets with that hideous and soft movement of the dying, that seems as if they wanted already to cover themselves with the shroud. Pale as a statue and with eyes red as fire, Charles, not weeping, stood opposite her at the foot of the bed, while the priest, bending one knee, was muttering words in a low voice.

She turned her face slowly, and seemed to fill with joy on seeing suddenly the violet stole, no doubt finding again, in the midst of a temporary lull in her pain, the lost voluptuousness of her first mystical transports, with the visions of eternal beatitude that were beginning.

The priest rose to take the crucifix; then she stretched forward her neck as one who is athirst, and gluing her lips to the body of the Man-God, she pressed upon it with all her expiring strength the fullest kiss of love that she had ever given. Then he recited the *Misereatur* and the *Indulgentiam*, dipped his right thumb in the oil, and began to give extreme unction. First, upon the eyes, that had so coveted all worldly pomp; then upon the nostrils, that had been greedy of the warm breeze and amorous odors; then upon the mouth, that had uttered lies, that had curled with pride and cried out in lewdness; then upon the hands that had delighted in sensual touches; and finally upon the soles of the feet, so swift of yore, when she was running to satisfy her desires, and that would now walk no more.

The curé wiped his fingers, threw the bit of cotton dipped in oil into the fire, and came and sat down by the dying woman, to tell her that she must now blend her sufferings with those of Jesus Christ and abandon herself to the divine mercy.

Finishing his exhortations, he tried to place in her hand a blessed candle, symbol of the celestial glory with which she was soon to be surrounded. Emma, too weak, could not close her fingers, and the taper, but for Monsieur Bournisien would have fallen to the ground.

However, she was not quite so pale, and her face had an expression of serenity as if the sacrament had cured her.

The priest did not fail to point this out; he even explained to Bovary that the Lord sometimes prolonged the life of persons when he thought it meet for their salvation; and Charles remembered the day when, so near death, she had received the communion. Perhaps there was no need to despair, he thought.

In fact, she looked around her slowly, as one awakening from a dream; then in a distinct voice she asked for her looking-glass, and remained some time bending over it, until the big tears fell from her eyes. Then she turned away her head with a sigh and fell back upon the pillows.

Her chest soon began panting rapidly; the whole of her tongue protruded from her mouth; her eyes, as they rolled, grew paler, like the two globes of a lamp that is going out, so that one might have thought her already dead but for the fearful laboring of her ribs, shaken by violent breathing, as if the soul were struggling to free itself. Félicité knelt down before the crucifix, and the druggist himself slightly bent his knees, while Monsieur Canivet looked out vaguely at the Place. Bournisien had again begun to pray, his face bowed against the edge of the bed, his long black cassock trailing behind him in the room. Charles was on the other side, on his knees, his arms outstretched towards Emma. He had taken her hands and pressed them, shuddering at every beat of her heart, as at the shaking of a falling ruin. As the death-rattle became stronger the priest prayed faster; his prayers mingled with the stifled sobs of Bovary, and sometimes all seemed lost in the muffled murmur of the Latin syllables that tolled like a passing bell.

Suddenly on the pavement was heard a loud noise of clogs and the clattering of a stick; and a voice rose—a raucous voice—that sang—

"Maids in the warmth of a summer day
Dream of love and of love alway."

Emma raised herself like a galvanized corpse, her hair undone, her eyes fixed, staring.

"Where the sickle blades have been,
Nannette, gathering ears of corn,
Passes bending down, my queen,
To the earth where they were born."

"The blind man!" she cried. And Emma began to laugh, an atrocious, frantic, despairing laugh, thinking she saw the hideous face of the poor wretch that stood out against the eternal night like a menace.

"The wind is strong this summer day,
Her petticoat has flown away."

She fell back upon the mattress in a convulsion. They all drew near. She was dead.

CYNTHIA OZICK

—

Primo Levi's Suicide Note

PRIMO LEVI, AN Italian
Jewish chemist from Turin, was liberated from Auschwitz by a Soviet
military unit in January of 1945, when he was twenty-five, and from
that moment of reprieve (*Moments of Reprieve* was one of his titles)
until shortly before his death in April of 1987, he went on recalling,
examining, reasoning, recording—telling the ghastly tale—in book
after book. That he saw himself as a possessed scribe of the German
hell, we know from the epigraph to his final volume, *The Drowned and
the Saved*—familiar lines taken from "The Rime of the Ancient Mariner"

Novelist and essayist Cynthia Ozick is the author of Art and Ardor *and*
Metaphor and Memory. *In this 1988 piece, she examines the writer
Primo Levi's unusual suicide note—his last novel.*

and newly startling to a merely literary reader, for whom the words of Coleridge's poem have never before rung out with such an antimetaphorical contemporary demand, or seemed so cruel:

Since then, at an uncertain hour,
That agony returns,
And till my ghastly tale is told
This heart within me burns.

SEIZED BY THE survivor's heart, this stanza no longer answers to the status of Lyrical Ballad, and still less to the English Department's quintessential Romantic text redolent of the supernatural; it is all deadly self-portrait. In the haven of an Italian spring—forty years after setting down the somber narrative called in Italian "If This Be a Man" and published in English as *Survival in Auschwitz*—Primo Levi hurled himself into the well of a spiral staircase four stories deep, just outside the door of the flat he was born in, where he had been living with his wife and aged ailing mother. Suicide. The composition of the late Lager manuscript was complete, the heart burned out; there was no more to tell.

There was no more to tell. That, of course, is an assumption nobody can justify, and nobody perhaps ought to dare to make. Suicide is one of the mysteries of the human will, with or without a farewell note to explain it. And it remains to be seen whether *The Drowned and the Saved* is, after all, a sort of suicide note.

Levi, to be sure, is not the first writer of high distinction to survive hell and to suggest, by a self-willed death, that hell in fact did not end when the chimneys closed down, but was simply freshening for a second run—Auschwitz being the first hell, and post-Auschwitz the second; and if "survival" is the thing in question, then it isn't the "survivor" whose powers of continuation are worth marveling at, but hell itself. The victim who has escaped being murdered will sometimes contrive to finish the job, not because he is attached to death—never this—but because death is under the governance of hell, and it is in the nature of hell to go on and on: inescapability is its rule, No Exit its sign. "The injury cannot be healed," Primo Levi writes in *The Drowned and the Saved*; "it extends through time, and the Furies, in whose existence we are forced to believe...perpetuate the tormentor's work by denying peace to the tormented."

Tadeusz Borowski, for instance, author of *This Way for the Gas, Ladies and Gentlemen*, eluded the gas at both Auschwitz and Dachau from 1943-1945; in Warsaw, in 1951, not yet thirty, three days before the birth of his daughter, he turned on the household gas. Suicide. The poet Celan: a suicide. The Austrian-born philosopher Hans Mayer—another suicide—who later became Jean Améry by scrambling his name into a French anagram, was in Auschwitz together with Primo Levi, though the two never chanced on one another. Before his capture and deportation, Améry had been in the Belgian resistance and was subjected to Gestapo torture. After the war, Améry and Levi corresponded about their experiences. Levi esteemed Améry, appeared to understand him, but evidently could not like him— because, he says, Améry was a man who "traded blows." "A gigantic Polish criminal," Levi recounts, "punches [Améry] in the face over some trifle; he, not because of an animallike reaction but because of a reasoned revolt against the perverted world of the Lager, returns the blow as best he can." "'Hurting all over from the blows, I was satisfied with myself,'" Levi quotes Améry; but for himself, Levi asserts,

> "trading punches" is an experience I do not have, as far
> back as I can go in memory; nor can I say I regret not
> having it . . . go[ing] down onto the battlefield . . . was
> and is beyond my reach. I admire it, but I must point out

that this choice, protracted throughout his post-Auschwitz existence led [Améry] to such severity and intransigence as to make him incapable of finding joy in life, indeed of living. Those who "trade blows" with the entire world achieve dignity but pay a very high price for it because they are sure to be defeated.

REMARKABLY, LEVI CONCLUDES: "Améry's suicide, which took place in Salzburg in 1978 [i.e. nine years before Levi's leap into the stairwell], like other suicides allows for a nebula of explanations, but, in hindsight, that episode of defying the Pole offers one interpretation of it."

This observation—that the rage of resentment is somehow linked to self-destruction—is, in the perplexing shadow of Levi's own suicide, enigmatic enough, and bears returning to. For the moment it may be useful to consider that Primo Levi's reputation—rather, the grave and noble voice that sounds and summons through his pages—has been consummately free of rage, resentment, violent feelings, or any overt drive to "trade blows." The voice has been one of pristine sanity and discernment. Levi has been unwilling to serve either as preacher or as elegist. He has avoided polemics; he has shrunk from being counted as one of those message-bearers "whom I view with distrust: the prophet, the bard, the soothsayer. That I am not." Instead, he has offered himself as a singular witness—singular because he was "privileged" to survive as a laboratory slave, meaning that German convenience, at least temporarily, was met more through the exploitation of his training as a chemist than it would have been through his immediate annihilation as a Jew; and, from our own point of view, because of his clarity and selflessness as a writer. It is selfless to eschew freely running emotion, sermonizing, the catharsis of anger, when these so plainly plead their case before an unprecedentedly loathsome record of criminals and their crimes. Levi has kept his distance from blaming, scolding, insisting, vilifying, lamenting, crying out. His method has been to describe—meticulously, analytically, clarifyingly. He has been a Darwin of the death camps: not the Virgil of the German hell but its scientific investigator.

Levi himself recognizes that he has been particularly attended to for this quality of detachment. "From my trade," he affirms in *The Drowned and the Saved*,

> I contracted a habit that can be variously judged and defined at will as human or inhuman—the habit of never remaining indifferent to the individuals that chance brings before me. They are human beings but also "samples," specimens in a sealed envelope to be identified, analyzed, and weighed. Now, the sample book that Auschwitz had placed before me was rich, varied, and strange, made up of friends, neutrals, and enemies, yet in any case food for my curiosity, which some people, then and later, have judged to be detached. . . . I know that this "naturalistic" attitude does not derive only or necessarily from chemistry, but in my case it did come from chemistry.

—

THE DROWNED AND *the Saved* is a book of catching-up after decades of abstaining. It is a book of blows returned by a pen on fire. The surrender to fury in these burning chapters does not swallow up their exactness—the scientist's truthful lens is not dissolved—but Levi in the violated voice of this last completed work lets fly a biblical ululation that its predecessors withheld: *thy brother's blood cries up from the ground.* I do not mean that Levi has literally set down those words; but he has, at long last, unleashed their clamor.

And what of the predecessor-volumes? What of their lucid calm, absence of hatred, magisterial equanimity, unaroused detachment? Readers have not misconstrued Levi's tone, at least not until now. *The Drowned and the Saved* makes it seem likely that the restraint of forty years was undertaken out of a consistent adherence to an elevated *idée fixe*, possibly to a self-deception: a picture of how a civilized man ought to conduct himself when he is documenting savagery. The result was the world's consensus: a man somehow set apart from retaliatory passion. A man who would not trade punches. A transparency; a pure spirit. A vessel of clear water.

I spoke earlier of creeping fuses, mutedness, the slow accretion of an insurmountable pressure. "The Furies . . . perpetuate the tormentor's work by denying peace to the tormented." But all that was subterranean. Then came the suicide. Consider now an image drawn from Primo Levi's calling. Into a vessel of clear water—tranquil, innocuous—drop an unaccustomed ingredient: a lump of potassium, say, an alkali metal that reacts with water so violently that the hydrogen gas given off by the process will erupt into instant combustion. One moment, a beaker of unperturbed transparency. The next moment, a convulsion: self-destruction.

The unaccustomed ingredient, for Levi, was rage. "Suicide," he reflects in *The Drowned and the Saved*—which may be seen, perhaps and after all, as the bitterest of suicide notes—"is an act of man and not of the animal. It is a meditated act, a noninstinctive, unnatural choice." In the Lager, where human beings were driven to become animals, there were almost no suicides at all. Améry, Borowski, Celan, and ultimately Levi did not destroy themselves until some time after they were released. Levi waited more than forty years; and he did not become a suicide until he let passion in, and returned the blows. If he is right about Améry—that Améry's willingness to trade punches is the key to his suicide—then he has deciphered for us his own suicide as well.

What we know now—we did not know it before *The Drowned and the Saved*—is that at bottom Levi could not believe in himself as a vessel of clear water standing serenely apart. It was not detachment. It was dormancy, it was latency, it was potentiality; it was inoperativeness. He was always conscious of how near to hand the potassium was. I grieve that he equated rage—the rage that speaks for mercifulness—with self-destruction. A flawed formula. It seems to me it would not have been a mistake—and could not have been misinterpreted—if all of Primo Levi's books touching on the German hell had been as vehement, and as pointed, as the last, the most remarkable.

PRIMO LEVI

—

Shame

CERTAIN FIXED
IMAGE has been proposed innumerable times, consecrated by literature and poetry, and picked up by the cinema: "the quiet after the
storm," when all hearts rejoice. "To be freed from pain/is delightful for
us." The disease runs its course and health returns. To deliver us from
imprisonment "our boys," the liberators, arrive just in time, with wav-
ing flags; the soldier returns and again finds his family and peace.

Judging by the stories told by many who came back and from my

---

Primo Levi was a chemist, novelist, and essayist, known particularly for Survival in
Auschwitz *and* The Reawakening, *memoirs of his holocaust survival. Levi died
in his home in Turin, Italy, in 1987; many were surprised when doctors labeled it an
"apparent suicide." "Shame" is from his last novel,* The Drowned and the Saved.

own memories, Leopardi the pessimist stretched the truth in this representation; despite himself, he showed himself to be an optimist. In the majority of cases, the hour of liberation was neither joyful nor lighthearted. For most it occurred against a tragic background of destruction, slaughter, and suffering. Just as they felt they were again becoming men, that is, responsible, the sorrows of men returned: the sorrow of the dispersed or lost family; the universal suffering all around; their own exhaustion, which seemed definitive, past cure; the problems of a life to begin all over again amid the rubble, often alone. Not "pleasure the son of misery," but misery the son of misery. Leaving pain behind was a delight for only a few fortunate beings, or only for a few instants, or for very simple souls; almost always it coincided with a phase of anguish.

Anguish is known to everyone, even children, and everyone knows that it is often blank, undifferentiated. Rarely does it carry a clearly written label that also contains its motivation; any label it does have is often mendacious. One can believe or declare oneself to be anguished for one reason and be so due to something totally different. One can think that one is suffering at facing the future and instead be suffering because of one's past; one can think that one is suffering for others, out of pity, out of compassion, and instead be suffering for one's own reasons, more or less profound, more or less avowable and avowed, sometimes so deep that only the specialist, the analyst of souls, knows how to exhume them.

Naturally, I dare not maintain that the movie script I referred to before is false in every case. Many liberations were experienced with full, authentic joy—above all by combatants, both military and political, who at that moment saw the aspirations of their militancy and their lives realized, and also on the part of those who had suffered less and for less time, or only in their own person and not because of their family, friends, or loved ones. And besides, luckily, human beings are not all the same: there are among us those who have the virtue and the privilege of extracting, isolating those instants of happiness, of enjoying them fully, as though they were extracting pure gold from dross. And finally, among the testimonies, written or spoken, some are unconsciously stylized, in which convention prevails over genuine memory: "Whoever is freed from slavery rejoices. I too was liberated, hence I too rejoice over it. In all films, all novels, just as in *Fidelio*, the shattering of the chains is a moment of solemn or fervid jubilation, and so was mine." This is a specific case of that drifting of memory I mentioned in the first chapter, and which is accentuated with the passing of years and the piling up of the experiences of others, true or presumed, on one's own. But anyone who, purportedly or by temperament, shuns rhetoric, usually speaks in a different voice. This, for example, is how, on the last page of his memoir, *Eyewitness Auschwitz: Three Years in the Gas Chambers*, Filip Müller, whose experience was much more terrible than mine, describes his liberation:

> Although it may seem incredible, I had a complete letdown or depression. That moment, on which for three years all my thoughts and secret desires were concentrated, did not awaken happiness or any other feeling in me. I let myself fall from my pallet and crawled to the door. Once outside I tried vainly to go further, then I simply lay down on the ground in the woods and fell asleep.

I NOW REREAD the passage from my own book, *The Reawakening*, which was published in Italy only in 1963, although I had written these words as early as 1947. In it is a description of the first Russian soldiers facing our Lager packed with corpses and dying prisoners.

> They did not greet us, nor smile; they seemed oppressed, not only by pity but also by a confused

restraint which sealed their mouths, and kept their eyes fastened on the funereal scene. It was the same shame which we knew so well, which submerged us after the selections, and every time we had to witness or undergo an outrage: the shame that the Germans never knew, the shame which the just man experiences when confronted by a crime committed by another, and he feels remorse because of its existence, because of its having been irrevocably introduced into the world of existing things, and because his will has proven nonexistent or feeble and was incapable of putting up a good defense.

I do not think that there is anything I need erase or correct, but there is something I must add. That many (including me) experienced "shame," that is, a feeling of guilt during the imprisonment and afterward, is an ascertained fact confirmed by numerous testimonies. It may seem absurd, but it is a fact. I will try to interpret it myself and to comment on the interpretations of others.

As I mentioned at the start, the vague discomfort which accompanied liberation was not precisely shame, but it was perceived as such. Why? There are various possible explanations.

I will exclude certain exceptional cases: the prisoners who, almost all of them political, had the strength and opportunity to act within the Lager in defense of and to the advantage of their companions. We, the almost total majority of common prisoners, did not know about them and did not even suspect their existence, and logically so: due to obvious political and police necessity (the Political Section of Auschwitz was simply a branch of the Gestapo) they were forced to operate secretly, not only where the Germans were concerned but in regard to everyone. In Auschwitz, the concentrationary empire which in my time was constituted by 95 percent Jews, this political network was embryonic; I witnessed only one episode that should have led me to sense something had I not been crushed by the everyday travail.

Around May 1944 our almost innocuous *Kapo* was replaced, and the newcomer proved to be a fearsome individual. All *Kapos* gave beatings: this was an obvious part of their duties, their more or less accepted language. After all, it was the only language that everyone in that perpetual Babel could truly understand. In its various nuances it was understood as an incitement to work, a warning or punishment, and in the hierarchy of suffering it had a low rank. Now, the new *Kapo* gave his beatings in a different way, in a convulsive, malicious, perverse way: on the nose, the shin, the genitals. He beat to hurt, to cause suffering and humiliation. Not even, as with many others, out of blind racial hatred, but with the obvious intention of inflicting pain, indiscriminately, and without pretext, on all his subjects. Probably he was a mental case, but clearly under those conditions the indulgence that we today consider obligatory toward such sick people would have been out of place. I spoke about it with a colleague, a Jewish Croatian Communist: What should we do? How to protect ourselves? How to act collectively? He gave me a strange smile and simply said: "You'll see, he won't last long." In fact, the beater vanished within a week. But years later, during a meeting of survivors, I found out that some political prisoners attached to the Work Office inside the camp had the terrifying power of switching the registration numbers on the lists of prisoners to be gassed. Anyone who had the ability and will to act in this way, to oppose in this or other ways the machine of the Lager, was beyond the reach of "shame"—or at least the shame of which I am speaking, because perhaps he experiences something else.

Equally protected must have been Sivadjan, a silent and tranquil man whom I mentioned in passing in *Survival in Auschwitz*, in the chapter "The Canto of Ulysses," and about whom I discovered on that same occasion that he had brought explosives into the camp to foment a possible insurrection.

In my opinion, the feeling of shame or guilt that coincided with reacquired freedom was extremely composite: it contained diverse elements, and in diverse proportions for each individual. It must be remembered that each of us, both objectively and subjectively, lived the Lager in his own way.

Coming out of the darkness, one suffered because of the reacquired consciousness of having been diminished. Not by our will, cowardice, or fault, yet nevertheless we had lived for months and years at an animal level: our days had been encumbered from dawn to dusk by hunger, fatigue, cold, and fear, and any space for reflection, reasoning, experiencing emotions was wiped out. We endured filth, promiscuity, and destitution, suffering much less than we would have suffered such things in normal life, because our moral yardstick had changed. Furthermore, all of us had stolen: in the kitchen, the factory, the camp, in short, "from the others," from the opposing side, but it was theft nevertheless. Some (few) had fallen so low as to steal bread from their own companions. We had not only forgotten our country and our culture, but also our family, our past, the future we imagined for ourselves, because, like animals, we were confined to the present moment. Only at rare intervals did we come out of this condition of leveling, during the very few Sundays of rest, the fleeting minutes before falling asleep, or the fury of the air raids, but these were painful moments precisely because they gave us the opportunity to measure our diminishment from the outside.

I believe that it was precisely this turning to look back at the "perilous water" that gave rise to so many suicides after (sometimes immediately after) Liberation. It was in any case a critical moment which coincided with a flood of rethinking and depression. By contrast, all historians of the Lager—and also of the Soviet camps—agree in pointing out that cases of suicide *during* imprisonment were rare. Several explanations of this fact have been put forward; for my part I offer three, which are not mutually exclusive.

First of all, suicide is an act of a man and not of the animal. It is a meditated act, a noninstinctive, unnatural choice, and in the Lager there were few opportunities to choose: people lived precisely like enslaved animals that sometimes let themselves die but do not kill themselves.

Secondly, "there were other things to think about," as the saying goes. The day was dense: one had to think about satisfying hunger, in some way elude fatigue and cold, avoid the blows. Precisely because of the constant imminence of death there was no time to concentrate on the idea of death. Svevo's remark in *Confessions of Zeno*, when he ruthlessly describes his father's agony, has the rawness of truth: "When one is dying, one is much too busy to think about death. All one's organism is devoted to breathing."

Thirdly, in the majority of cases, suicide is born from a feeling of guilt that no punishment has attenuated; now, the harshness of imprisonment was perceived as punishment, and the feeling of guilt (if there is punishment, there must have been guilt) was relegated to the background, only to re-emerge after the Liberation. In other words, there was no need to punish oneself by suicide because of a (true or presumed) guilt: one was already expiating it by one's daily suffering.

What guilt? When all was over, the awareness emerged that we had not done anything, or not enough, against the system into which we had been absorbed. About the failed resistance in the Lagers, or, more accurately, in some Lagers, too much has been said, too superficially, above all by people who had altogether different crimes to account for. Anyone who made the attempt knows that there existed situations, collective or personal, in which active resistance was possible, and others, much more frequent, in which it was not. It is known that, especially in 1941, millions of Soviet military prisoners fell into German hands. They were young, generally well nourished and robust; they had military and political training, and often they formed organic units with soldiers with the rank of corporal and up, noncommissioned officers, and officers. They hated the Germans who had invaded their country, and yet they rarely resisted. Malnutrition, despoilment, and other physical discomforts, which it is so easy and economically advantageous to provoke and at which the Nazis were masters, are rapidly destructive and paralyze before destroying, all the more so when they are preceded by years of segregation, humiliation, maltreatment, forced migration, laceration of family ties, rupture of contact with the rest of the world—that is to say, the situation of the bulk of the prisoners who had landed in Auschwitz after the introductory hell of the ghettos or the collection camps.

Therefore, on a rational plane, there should not have been much to be ashamed of, but shame persisted nevertheless, especially for the few bright examples of those who had the strength and possibility to resist. I spoke about this in the chapter "The Last" in *Survival in Auschwitz*, where I described the public hanging of a resistor before a terrified and apathetic crowd of prisoners. This is a thought that then just barely grazed us, but that returned "afterward": you too could have, you certainly should have. And this is a judgment that the survivor believes he sees in the eyes of those (especially the young) who listen to his stories and judge with facile hindsight, or who perhaps feel cruelly repelled. Consciously or not, he feels accused and judged, compelled to justify and defend himself.

GRAHAM GREENE

—

The Heart of the Matter

I T GRIPS ME," Scobie said, "like a vice."

"And what do you do then?"

"Why nothing. I stay as still as I can until the pain goes."

"How long does it last?"

"It's difficult to tell, but I don't think more than a minute."

The stethoscope followed like a ritual. Indeed there was some-

---

British novelist Graham Greene's characters usually tread the thin line between good and evil, engaged in a desperate struggle against their own darker selves. Greene himself seems to have been drawn to suicide until he converted to Catholicism at age twenty-one. The Heart of the Matter, *written in 1948, is considered one of his masterpieces, along with* The Power and the Glory *and* The Third Man.

thing clerical in all that Dr. Travis did: an earnestness, almost a reverence. Perhaps because he was young he treated the body with great respect; when he rapped the chest he did it slowly, carefully, with his ear bowed close as though he really expected somebody or something to rap back. Latin words came softly on his tongue as though in the Mass— *sternum* instead of *pacem*.

"And then," Scobie said, "there's the sleeplessness."

The young man sat back behind his desk and tapped with an indelible pencil; there was a mauve smear at the corner of his mouth which seemed to indicate that sometimes—off guard—he sucked it. "That's probably nerves," Dr. Travis said, "apprehension of pain. Unimportant."

"It's important to me. Can't you give me something to take? I'm all right when once I get to sleep, but I lie awake for hours, waiting. . . Sometimes I'm hardly fit for work. And a policeman, you know, needs his wits."

"Of course," Dr. Travis said. "I'll soon settle you. Evipan's the stuff for you." It was as easy as all that. "Now for the pain—" he began his tap, tap, tap, with the pencil. He said, "It's impossible to be certain, of course . . . I want you to note carefully the circumstances of every attack . . . what seems to bring it on. Then it will be quite possible to regulate it, avoid it almost entirely."

"But what's wrong?"

Dr. Travis said, "There are some words that always shock the layman. I wish we could call cancer by a symbol like H_2O. People wouldn't be nearly so disturbed. It's the same with the word angina."

"You think it's angina?"

"It has all the characteristics. But men live for years with angina—even work in reason. We have to see exactly how much you can do."

"Should I tell my wife?"

"There's no point in not telling her. I'm afraid this might mean—retirement."

"Is that all?"

"You may die of a lot of things before angina gets you—given care."

"On the other hand I suppose it could happen any day?"

"I can't guarantee anything, Major Scobie. I'm not even absolutely satisfied that this is angina."

"I'll speak to the Commissioner then on the quiet. I don't want to alarm my wife until we are certain."

"If I were you, I'd tell her what I've said. It will prepare her. But tell her you may live for years with care."

"And the sleeplessness?"

"This will make you sleep."

Sitting in the car with the little package on the seat beside him, he thought, I have only now to choose the date. He didn't start his car for quite a while; he was touched by a feeling of awe as if he had in fact been given his death sentence by the doctor. His eyes dwelt on the neat blob of sealing-wax like a dried wound. He thought, I have still got to be careful, so careful. If possible no one must even suspect. It was not only the question of his life insurance: the happiness of others had to be protected. It was not so easy to forget a suicide as a middle-aged man's death from angina.

He unsealed the package and studied the directions. He had no knowledge of what a fatal dose might be, but surely if he took ten times the correct amount he would be safe. That meant every night for nine nights removing a dose and keeping it secretly for use on the tenth night. More evidence must be invented in his diary which had to be written right up to the end—November 12. He must make engagements for the following week. In his behaviour there must be no hint of farewells. This was the worst crime a Catholic could commit—it must be a perfect one.

First the Commissioner . . . He drove down towards the police station and stopped his car outside the church. The solemnity of the crime lay over his mind almost like happiness; it was action at last—he had fumbled and muddled too long. He put the package for safekeeping into his pocket and went in, carrying his death. An old mammy was lighting a candle before the Virgin's statue; another sat with her market basket beside her and her hands folded staring up at the altar. Otherwise the church was empty. Scobie sat down at the back: he had no inclination to pray—what was the good? If one was a Catholic, one had all the answers: no prayer was effective in a state of mortal sin, but he watched the other two with sad envy. They were still inhabitants of the country he had left. This was what human love had done to him— it had robbed him of love for eternity. It was no use pretending as a young man might that the price was worth while.

If he couldn't pray he could at least talk, sitting there at the back, as far as he could get from Golgotha. He said, O God, I am the only guilty one because I've known the answers all the time. I've preferred to give you pain rather than give pain to Helen or my wife because I can't observe your suffering. I can only imagine it. But there are limits to what I can do to you—or them. I can't desert either of them while I'm alive, but I can die and remove myself from their blood stream. They are ill with me and I can cure them. And you too, God— you are ill with me. I can't go on, month after month, insulting you. I can't face coming up to the altar at Christmas—your birthday feast— and taking your body and blood for the sake of a life. I can't do that. You'll be better off if you lose me once and for all. I know what I'm doing. I'm not pleading for mercy. I am going to damn myself, whatever that means. I've longed for peace and I'm never going to know peace again. But you'll be at peace when I am out of your reach. It will be no use then sweeping the floor to find me or searching for me over the mountains. You'll be able to forget me, God, for eternity. One hand clasped the package in his pocket like a promise.

No one can speak a monologue for long alone—another voice will always make itself heard; every monologue sooner or later becomes a discussion. So now he couldn't keep the other voice silent; it spoke from the cave of his body; it was as if the sacrament which had lodged there for his damnation gave tongue. You say you love me, and yet you'll do this to me—rob me of you forever. I made you with love. I've wept your tears. I've saved you from more than you will ever know; I planted in you this longing for peace only so that one day I could satisfy your longing and watch your happiness. And now you push me away, you put me out of your reach. There are no capital letters to separate us when we talk together. I am not Thou but simply you, when you speak to me; I am humble as any other beggar. Can't you trust me as you'd trust a faithful dog? I have been faithful to you for two thousand years. All you have to do now is ring a bell, go into a box, confess . . . the repentance is already there, straining at your heart. It's not repentance you lack, just a few simple actions: to go up to the Nissen hut and say good-bye. Or if you must, continue rejecting me but without lies any more. Go to your house and say good-bye to your wife and live with your mistress. If you live you will come back to me sooner or later. One of them will suffer, but can't you trust me to see that the suffering isn't too great?

The voice was silent in the cave and his own voice replied hopelessly: No, I don't trust you. I've never trusted you. If you made me, you made this feeling of responsibility that I've always carried about like a sack of bricks. I'm not a policeman for nothing—responsible for order, for seeing justice is done. There was no other profession for a man of my kind. I can't shift my responsibility to you. If I could, I would be someone else. I can't make one of them suffer so as to save myself. I'm responsible and I'll see it through the only way I can. A sick man's death means to them only a short suffering—everybody has to die. We are all of us resigned to death: it's life we aren't resigned to.

So long as you live, the voice said, I have hope. There's no human hopelessness like the hopelessness of God. Can't you just go on, as you are doing now? the voiced pleaded, lowering the terms every time it spoke like a dealer in a market. It explained: there are worse acts. But no, he said, no. That's impossible. I won't go on insulting you at your own altar. You see it's an *impasse*, God, an *impasse*, he said, clutching the package in his pocket. He got up and turned his back on the altar and went out. Only when he saw his face in the driving mirror did he realize that his eyes were bruised with suppressed tears. He drove towards the police station and the Commissioner.

NOVEMBER 3. *Yesterday I told the Commissioner that angina had been diagnosed and that I should retire as soon as a successor could be found. Temperature at 2 p.m. 91°. Much better night as the result of Evipan.*

November 4. Went with Louise to 7:30 Mass but as pain threatened to return did not wait for Communion. In the evening told Louise that I should have to retire before end of tour. Did not mention but spoke of strained heart. Another good night as a result of Evipan. Temperature at 2 p.m. 89°.

November 5. Lamp thefts in Wellington Street. Spent long morning at Azikawe's store checking story of fire in storeroom. Temperature at 2 p.m. 90°. Drove Louise to Club for library night.

November 6-10. First time I've failed to keep up daily entries. Pain has become more frequent and unwilling to take on any extra exertion. Like a vice. Lasts about a minute. Liable to come on if I walk more than half a mile. Last night or two I have slept badly in spite of Evipan, I think from the apprehension of pain.

November 11. Saw Travis again. There seems to be no doubt now that it is angina. Told Louise tonight, but also that with care I may live for years. Discussed with Commissioner an early passage home. In any case

*can't go for another month as too many cases I want to see through the courts
in the next week or two. Agreed to dine with Fellowes on the 13th,
Commissioner on the 14th. Temperature at 2 p.m. 88°.*

SCOBIE LAID DOWN his pen and wiped his wrist on the blotting
paper. It was just six o'clock on November 12 and Louise was out at
the beach. His brain was clear, but the nerves tingled from his shoulder
to his wrist. He thought: I have come to the end. What years had
passed since he walked up through the rain to the Nissen hut, while
the sirens wailed: the moment of happiness. It was time to die after so
many years.

But there were still deceptions to be practised, just as though
he were going to live through the night, good-byes to be said with only
himself knowing that they were good-byes. He walked very slowly
up the hill in case he was observed—wasn't he a sick man?—and
turned off by the Nissens. He couldn't just die without some word—
what word? O God, he prayed, let it be the right word, but when he
knocked there was no reply, no words at all. Perhaps she was at the
beach with Bagster.

The door was not locked and he went in. Years had passed in
his brain, but here time had stood still. It might have been the same bottle of gin from which the boy had stolen—how long ago? The junior
official's chairs stood stiffly around, as though on a film set: he
couldn't believe they had ever moved, any more than the pouf presented by—was it Mrs. Carter? On the bed the pillows had not been
shaken after the siesta, and he laid his hand on the warm mould of a
skull. O God, he prayed, I'm going away from all of you forever: let
her come back in time: let me see her once more, but the hot day cooled
around him and nobody came. At 6:30 Louise would be back from
the beach. He couldn't wait any longer.

I must leave some kind of a message, he thought, and perhaps before I have written it she will have come. He felt a constriction in his breast worse than any pain he had ever invented to Travis. I shall never touch her again. I shall leave her mouth to others for the next twenty years. Most lovers deceived themselves with the idea of an eternal union beyond the grave, but he knew all the answers: he went to an eternity of deprivation. He looked for paper and couldn't find so much as a torn envelope; he thought he saw a writing-case, but it was the stamp-album that he unearthed, and opening it at random for no particular reason, he felt fate throw another shaft, for he remembered that particular stamp and how it came to be stained with gin. She will have to tear it out, he thought, but that won't matter: she had told him that you can't see where a stamp has been torn out. There was no scrap of paper even in his pockets, and in a sudden rush of jealousy he lifted up the little green image of George V and wrote in ink beneath it: *I love you.* She can't take that out, he thought with cruelty and disappointment, that's indelible. For a moment he felt as though he had laid a mine for an enemy, but this was no enemy. Wasn't he clearing himself out of her path like a piece of dangerous wreckage? He shut the door behind him and walked slowly down the hill—she might yet come. Everything he did now was for the last time—an odd sensation. He would never come this way again, and five minutes later taking a new bottle of gin from his cupboard, he thought: I shall never open another bottle. The actions which could be repeated became fewer and fewer. Presently there would be only one unrepeatable action left, the act of swallowing. He stood with the gin bottle poised and thought: then Hell will begin, and they'll be safe from me, Helen, Louise, and You.

At dinner he talked deliberately of the week to come; he blamed himself for accepting Fellowes's invitation and explained that dinner with the Commissioner the next day was unavoidable—there was much to discuss.

"Is there no hope, Ticki, that after a rest, a long rest . . . ?"

"It wouldn't be fair to carry on—to them or you. I might break down at any moment."

"It's really retirement?"

"Yes."

She began to discuss where they were to live. He felt tired to death, and it needed all his will to show interest in this fictitious village or that, in the kind of house he knew they would never inhabit. "I don't want a suburb," Louise said. "What I'd really like would be a weather-board house in Kent, so that one can get up to town quite easily."

He said, "Of course it will depend on what we can afford. My pension won't be very large."

"I shall work," Louise said. "It will be easy in wartime."

"I hope we shall be able to manage without that."

"I wouldn't mind."

Bed-time came, and he felt a terrible unwillingness to let her go. There was nothing to do when she had once gone but die. He didn't know how to keep her—they had talked about all the subjects they had in common. He said, "I shall sit here a while. Perhaps I shall feel sleepy if I stay up half an hour longer. I don't want to take the Evipan if I can help it."

"I'm very tired after the beach. I'll be off."

When she's gone, he thought, I shall be alone forever. His heart beat and he was held in the nausea of an awful unreality. I can't believe that I'm going to do this. Presently I shall get up and go to bed, and life will begin again. Nothing, nobody, can force me to die. Though the voice was no longer speaking from the cave of his belly, it was as though fingers touched him, signalled their mute messages of distress, tried to hold him . . .

"What is it, Ticki? You look ill. Come to bed too."

"I wouldn't sleep," he said obstinately.

"Is there nothing I can do?" Louise asked. "Dear, I'd do anything . . ." Her love was like a death sentence.

"There's nothing dear," he said. "I mustn't keep you up." But so soon as she turned towards the stairs he spoke again. "Read me something," he said, "you got a new book today. Read me something."

"You wouldn't like it, Ticki. It's poetry."

"Never mind. It may send me to sleep." He hardly listened while she read. People said you couldn't love two women, but what was this emotion if it were not love? This hungry absorption of what he was never going to see again? The greying hair, the line of nerves upon the face, the thickening body held him as her beauty never had. She hadn't put on her mosquito-boots, and her slippers were badly in need of mending. It isn't beauty that we love, he thought, it's failure— the failure to stay young forever, the failure of nerves, the failure of the body. Beauty is like success: we can't love it for long. He felt a terrible desire to protect—but that's what I'm going to do, I am going to protect her from myself forever. Some words she was reading momentarily caught his attention:

We are all falling. This hand's falling too—
all have this falling sickness none withstands.

And yet there's always One whose gentle hands
this universal falling can't fall through.

THEY SOUNDED LIKE truth, but he rejected them—comfort can come too easily. He thought, those hands will never hold my fall: I slip between the fingers, I'm greased with falsehood, treachery. Trust was a dead language of which he had forgotten the grammar.

"Dear, you are half asleep."

"For a moment."

"I'll go up now. Don't stay long. Perhaps you won't need your

Evipan tonight."

He watched her go. The lizard lay still upon the wall. Before she had reached the stairs he called her back. "Say good night, Louise, before you go. You may be asleep."

She kissed him perfunctorily on the forehead and he gave her hand a casual caress. There must be nothing strange on this last night, and nothing she would remember with regret. "Good night, Louise. You know I love you," he said with careful lightness.

"Of course and I love you."

"Yes. Good night, Louise."

"Good night, Ticki." It was the best he could do with safety.

As soon as he heard the door close, he took out the cigarette carton in which he kept the ten doses of Evipan. He added two more doses for greater certainty—to have exceeded by two doses in ten days could not, surely, be regarded as suspicious. After that he took a long drink of whisky and sat still and waited for courage with the tablets in the palm of his hand. Now, he thought, I am absolutely alone: this was freezing-point.

But he was wrong. Solitude itself has a voice. It said to him, Throw away those tablets. You'll never be able to collect enough again. You'll be saved. Give up play-acting. Mount the stairs to bed and have a good night's sleep. In the morning you'll be woken by your boy, and you'll drive down to the police station for a day's ordinary work. The voice dwelt on the word "ordinary" as it might have dwelt on the word "happy" or "peaceful."

"No," Scobie said aloud, "no." He pushed the tablets in his mouth six at a time, and drank them down in two draughts. Then he opened his diary and wrote against November 12, *Called on H. R., out; temperature at 2 p.m.* and broke abruptly off as though at that moment he had been gripped by the final pain. Afterwards he sat bolt upright and waited what seemed a long while for any indication at all of approaching death; he had no idea how it would come to him. He tried to pray, but the Hail Mary evaded his memory, and he was aware of his heartbeats like a clock striking the hour. He tried out an act of contrition, but when he reached, "I am sorry and beg pardon;" a cloud formed over the door and drifted down over the whole room and he couldn't remember what it was that he had to be sorry for. He had to hold himself upright with both hands, but he had forgotten the reason why he so held himself. Somewhere far away he thought he heard the sounds of rain. "A storm," he said aloud, "there's going to be a storm," as the clouds grew, and he tried to get up to close the windows. "Ali," he called, "Ali." It seemed to him as though someone outside the room were seeking him, calling him, and he made a last effort to indicate that he was here. He got to his feet and heard the hammer of his heart beating out a reply. He had a message to convey, but the darkness and the storm drove it back within the case of his breast, and all the time outside the house, outside the world that drummed like hammer blows within his ear, someone wandered, seeking to get in, someone appealing for help, someone in need of him. And automatically at the call of need, at the cry of a victim, Scobie strung himself to act. He dredged his consciousness up from an infinite distance in order to make some reply. He said aloud, "Dear God, I love. . ." but the effort was too great and he did not feel his body when it struck the floor or hear the small tinkle of the medal as it span like a coin under the ice-box—the saint whose name nobody could remember.

DOROTHY PARKER

—

Résumé

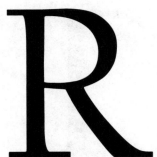AZORS PAIN YOU;
Rivers are damp;
Acids stain you;
And drugs cause cramp.
Guns aren't lawful;
Nooses give;
Gas smells awful;
You might as well live.

After attempting suicide twice, poet, critic, and incorrigible social satirist Dorothy Parker decided that there were no adequate ways to kill oneself. "Résumé" is her elegy to those failed attempts. The sharp tone of this poem is not unusual from Parker, who was often dubbed "the wittiest woman in America."

EMILE DURKHEIM

—

Suicide and Psychopathic States

HERE ARE TWO sorts
of extra-social causes to which one may, *a priori*, attribute an influence
on the suicide-rate; they are organic-psychic dispositions and the nature
of the physical environment. In the individual constitution, or at least in
that of a significant class of individuals, it is possible that there might
exist an inclination, varying in intensity from country to country, which
directly leads man to suicide; on the other hand, the action of climate, temperature, etc., on the organism, might indirectly have the same effects.

---

*Emile Durkheim was the first scholar to study society using the methods of
science—hence, the first sociologist. This excerpt is from his controversial
1897 work,* Suicide: A Study in Sociology, *in which he argues that
suicide rates directly reflect social stability.*

Under no circumstances can the hypothesis be dismissed unconsidered. We shall examine these two sets of factors successively, to see whether they play any part in the phenomenon under study and if so, what.

I

THE ANNUAL RATE of certain diseases is relatively stable for a given society though varying perceptibly from one people to another. Among these is insanity. Accordingly, if a manifestation of insanity were reasonably to be supposed in every voluntary death, our problem would be solved; suicide would be a purely individual affliction.

This thesis is supported by a considerable number of alienated. According to Esquirol: "Suicide shows all the characteristics of mental alienation." —"A man attempts self-destruction only in delirium and suicides are mentally alienated." From this principle he concluded that suicide, being involuntary, should not be punished by law. Falret and Moreau de Tours use almost the same terms. The latter, to be sure, in the same passage where he states his doctrine, makes a remark which should subject it to suspicion: "Should suicide be regarded in all cases as the result of mental alienation? Without wishing to dispose here of this difficult question, let us say generally that one is instinctively the more inclined to the affirmative, the deeper the study of insanity which he has made, the greater the experience and the greater the number of insane persons whom he has examined." In 1845 Dr. Bourdin, in a brochure which at one time created a stir in the medical world, had enunciated the same opinion even more unreservedly.

This theory may be and has been defended in two different ways. Suicide itself is either called a disease in itself, *sui generis*, a specific form of insanity; or it is regarded, not as a distinct species, but simply an event involved in one or several varieties of insanity, and not to be found in sane persons. The former is Bourdin's theory. Esquirol is the chief authority holding the other view. "From what has preceded," he writes, "suicide may be seen to be for us only a phenomenon resulting from many different causes and appears under many different forms; and it is clear that this phenomena is not characteristic of a disease. From considering suicide as a disease *sui generis*, general propositions have been set up which are benefiting by experience."

The second of these two methods of proving suicide to be a manifestation of insanity is the less rigorous and conclusive, since because of it negative experiences are impossible. A complete inventory of all cases of suicide cannot indeed be made, nor the influence of mental alienation shown in each. Only single examples can be cited which, however numerous, cannot support a scientific generalization; even though contrary examples were not affirmed, there would always be possibility of their existence. The other proof, however, if obtainable, would be conclusive. If suicide can be shown to be a mental disease with its own characteristics and distinct evolution, the question is settled; every suicide is a madman.

But does suicidal insanity exist?

I I

SINCE THE SUICIDAL tendency is naturally special and definite if it constitutes a sort of insanity, this can be only a form of partial insanity, limited to a single act. To be considered a delirium it must bear solely on this one object; for, if there were several, the delirium could no more be defined by one of them than by the others. In traditional terminology of mental pathology these restricted deliria are called monomanias. A monomaniac is a sick person whose mentality is perfectly healthy in all respects but one; he has a single flaw, usually localized. At times, for example, he has an unreasonable and absurd desire to drink or steal or use abusive language; but all his other acts and all his other thoughts are strictly correct. Therefore, if there is a suicidal mania it can only be a monomania and has indeed been usually so-called.

On the other hand, if this special variety of disease called monomania is admitted, it is clear why one readily includes suicide among them. The character of these kinds of afflictions, according to the definition just given, is that they imply no essential disturbance of intellectual functions. The basis of mental life is the same in the mono-maniac and the sane person; only, in the former, a specific psychic state is prominently detached from this common basis. In short, monomania is merely one extreme emotion in the order of impulses, one false idea in the order of representations, but of such intensity as to obsess the mind and completely enslave it. Thus, ambition, from being normal, becomes morbid and a monomania of grandeur when it assumes such proportions that all other cerebral functions seem paralyzed by it. A somewhat violent emotional and disturbing mental equilibrium is therefor enough to cause the monomania to appear. Now suicides generally seem influenced by some abnormal passion, whether its energy is abruptly expended or gradually developed; it may thus even appear reasonable that some such force is always necessary to offset the fundamental instinct of self-preservation. Moreover, many suicides are completely indistinguishable from other men except by the particular act of self-destruction, and there is therefore no reason to impute a general delirium to them. This is the reasoning by which suicide, under the appellation of monomania, has been considered a manifestation of insanity.

But, do monomanias exist? For a long time this was not ques-tioned; alienists one and all concurred without discussion in the theory of partial deliria. It was not only thought confirmed by clinical observa-tion but regarded as corollary to the findings of psychologists. The human intelligence was suppose to consist of distinct faculties and sep-arate powers which usually function cooperatively but may act sepa-rately; thus it seemed natural that they might be separately affected by disease. Since human intelligence may be manifested without volition and emotion without intelligence, why might there not be affections of the intelligence or will without disturbances of the emotions and *vice versa?* Applied to the specialized forms of these faculties, the same principle led to the theory that a lesion may exclusively affect an impulse, or action or an isolated idea.

Today however this opinion has been universally discarded. The non-existence of monomanias cannot indeed be proved from direct observation, but not a single incontestable example of their exis-tence can be cited. Clinical experience has never been able to observe a diseased mental impulse in a state of pure isolation; whenever there is a lesion of one faculty the others are also attacked, and if these concomitant lesions have not been observed by the believers in monomania, it is only because of poorly conducted observations. "For example," writes Falret,"take an insane person obsessed by religious ideas who would be classified among religious monomaniacs. He declares himself divinely inspired; entrusted with a heavenly mission he brings a new religion to the world. . . . This idea will be said to be wholly insane; yet he reasons like other men except for this series of religious thoughts. Question him more carefully, however, and other morbid ideas will soon be discovered; for instance, you will find a tendency to pride parallel to religious ideas. He believes himself called upon to reform not only religion but also to reform society; perhaps he will also imagine the highest sort of destiny reserved for himself. . . . If you have not discovered tendencies to pride in this patient, you will encounter ideas of humility or tendencies to fear. Preoccupied with religious ideas he will believe himself lost, destined to perish, etc." All of these forms of delirium will, of course, not usually be met with combined in a single person, but such are those most commonly found in association; if not existing all the same moment in the illness they will be found in more or less quick succession.

Finally, apart from these special manifestations, there always exists in these supposed monomaniacs a general state of the whole mental life which is fundamental to the disease and of which these delirious ideas are merely the outer and momentary expression. Its essential character is an excessive exaltation or deep depression or general perversion. There is, especially, a lack of equilibrium and coordination in both thought and action. The patient reasons, but with lacunas in his ideas; he acts, not absurdly, but without sequence. It is incorrect then to say that insanity constitutes a part, and a restricted part of his mental life; as soon as it penetrates the understanding it really invades it.

Moreover, the principle underlying the hypothesis of monomania contradicts the actual data of science. The old theory of the faculties has few defenders left. The different sorts of conscious activity are no longer regarded as separate forces, disunited, and combined only in the depths of a metaphysical substance, but as interdependent functions; thus one cannot suffer lesion without the others being affected. This interpenetration is even closer in mental life than in the rest of the organism; for psychic functions have no organs sufficiently distinct from one another for one to be affected without the others. Their distribution among the different regions of the brain is not well defined, as appears from the readiness with which its different parts mutually replace each other, if one of them is prevented from fulfilling its task. They are too completely interconnected for insanity to attack certain of them without injury to the others. With yet greater reason it is totally impossible for insanity to alter a single idea or emotion without psychic life being radically changed. For representations and impulses have no separate existence, they are not so many little substances, spiritual atoms, constituting the mind by their combinations. They are merely extreme manifestations of the general state of the centers of consciousness from which they derive and which they express. Thus they cannot be morbid without this state itself being vitiated.

But if mental flaws cannot be localized, there are not, there cannot be monomanias properly so-called. The apparently local disturbances given this name always derive from a more extensive perturbation, they are not diseases themselves, but particular and secondary manifestations of more general diseases. If then there are no monomanias there cannot be a suicidal monomania and, consequently, suicide is not a distinct form of insanity.

III

IT REMAINS POSSIBLE, however, that suicide may occur only in a state of insanity. If it is not by itself a special form of insanity, there are no forms of insanity in connection with which it may not appear. It is only an episodic syndrome of them, but one of frequent occurrence. Perhaps this frequency indicates that suicide never occurs in a state of sanity, and that it indicates mental alienation with certainty.

The conclusion would be hasty. For though certain acts of the insane are peculiar to them and characteristic of insanity, others are common to them and to normal persons, though assuming a special form in the case of the insane. There is no reason, *a priori*, to place suicide in the first of the two categories. To be sure, alienists state that most of the suicides known to them show all the indications of mental alienation, but this evidence could not settle the questions for the reviews of such cases are much too summary. Besides, any general law could be drawn from so narrowly specialized an experience. From the suicides they have known, who were, of course, insane, no conclusion can be drawn as to those not observed, who moreover, are much more numerous.

The only methodical procedure consists of classifying according-
ing to their essential characteristics the suicides committed by insane
persons, thus forming the principal types of insane suicide, and thus
trying to learn whether all cases of voluntary death can be included
under these systematically arranged groups. In other words, to learn
whether suicide is an act peculiar to the insane one must fix the forms
it assumes in mental alienation and discover whether these are the only
ones assumed by it.

In general, specialists have paid little heed to classifying the
suicides of the insane. The four following types, however, probably
include the most important varieties. The essential elements of the clas-
sification are borrowed from Jousset and Moreau de Tours.

1. *Maniacal suicide.*—This is due to hallucinations or delirious perceptions. The patient kills himself to escape from an imaginary danger or disgrace, or to obey a mysterious order from on high,
etc. But the motives of such suicide and its manner of evolution
reflect the general characteristics of the disease from which it
derives—namely, mania. The quality characteristic of this condition
is its extreme mobility. The most varied and even conflicting ideas
and feelings succeed each other with intense rapidity in the maniac's
consciousness. It is a constant whirlwind. One state of mind is indirectly replaced by another. Such, too, are the motives of maniacal
suicide; they appear, disappear, or change with amazing speed. The
hallucination or delirium which suggests suicide suddenly occurs;
the attempt follows; then instantly the scene changes, and if the
attempt fails it is not resumed, at least, for the moment. If it is later
repeated it will be for another motive. The most trivial incident may
cause these sudden transformations. One such patient, wishing to
kill himself, had leaped into a river—one that was generally shallow.
He was seeking a place where submersion was possible when a cus-
toms officer, suspecting his intention, took aim and threatened to fire

if he did not leave the water. The man went peaceably home at once, no longer thinking of self-destruction.

2. *Melancholy suicide.*—This is connected with a general state of extreme depression and exaggerated sadness, causing the patient no longer to realize sanely the bonds which connect him with people and things about him. Pleasures no longer attract; he sees everything as through a dark cloud. Life seems to him boring or painful. As these feelings are chronic, so are the ideas of suicide; they are very fixed and their broad determining motives are always essentially the same. A young girl, daughter of healthy parents, having spent her childhood in the country, has to leave at about the age of fourteen, to finish her education. From that moment she contracts an extreme disgust, a definite desire for solitude and soon an invincible desire to die. "She is motionless for hours, her eyes on the ground, her breast laboring, like someone fearing a threatening occurrence. Firmly resolved to throw herself into the river, she seeks the remotest places to prevent any rescue." However, as she finally realizes that the act she contemplates is a crime she temporarily renounces it. But after a year the inclination to suicide returns more forcefully and attempts recur in quick succession.

Hallucination and delirious thoughts often associate themselves with this general despair and lead directly to suicide. However, they are not mobile like those just observed among maniacs. On the contrary they are fixed, like the general state they come from. The fears by which the patient is haunted, his self-reproaches, the grief he feels are always the same. If then this sort of suicide is determined like its predecessor by imaginary reasons, it is distinct by its chronic character. And it is very tenacious. Patents of this category prepare their means of self-destruction calmly; in the pursuit of their purpose they even display incredible persistence and, at times, cleverness. Nothing less resembles this consistent state of mind than the maniac's constant instability. In the latter, passing impulses without durable cause; in the former, a persistent condition linked with the patient's general character.

3. *Obsessive suicide.*—In this case, suicide is caused by no motive, real or imaginary, but solely by the fixed idea of death which, without clear reason, has taken complete possession of the patient's mind. He is obsessed by the desire to kill himself, though he perfectly knows he has no reasonable motive for doing so. It is an instinctive need beyond the control of reflection and reasoning, like the needs to steal, to kill, to commit arson, supposed to constitute other varieties of monomania. As the patient realizes the absurdity of his wish he tries at first to resist it. But throughout this resistance he is sad, depressed, with a constantly increasing anxiety oppressing the pit of his stomach. Hence, this sort of suicide has sometimes been called *anxiety-suicide.* Here is the confession once made by a patient to Brierre de Boismont, which perfectly describes the condition: "I am employed in a business house. I perform my regular duties satisfactorily but like an automaton, and when spoken to, the words sound to me as though echoing in a void. My greatest torment is the thought of suicide, from which I am never free. I have been the victim of this impulse for a year; at first it was insignificant; then for about the last two months it has pursued me everywhere, *yet I have no reason to kill myself* . . . . My health is good; no one in my family has been similarly afflicted; I have had no financial losses, my income is adequate and permits me the pleasures of people of my age." But as soon as the patient has decided to give up the struggle and to kill himself, anxiety ceases and calm returns. If the attempt fails it is sometimes sufficient, though unsuccessful, to quench temporarily the morbid desire. It is as though the patient had voided this impulse.

4. *Impulsive or automatic suicide.*—It is as unmotivated as the preceding; it has no cause either in reality or in the patient's imagination. Only, instead of being produced by a fixed idea obsessing the mind for a shorter or longer period and only gradually affecting the

will, it results from an abrupt and immediately irresistible impulse. In a twinkling of an eye it appears in full force and excites the act, or at least its beginning. This abruptness recalls what has been mentioned above in connection with mania; only the maniacal suicide has always some reason, however irrational. It is connected with the patient's delirious conceptions. Here on the contrary the suicidal tendency appears and is effective in truly automatic fashion, not preceded by any intellectual antecedent. The sight of a knife, a walk by the edge of a precipice, etc. engender the suicidal idea instantaneously and its execution follows so swiftly that patients often have no idea of what has taken place. "A man is quietly talking with his friends; suddenly he leaps, clears a parapet and falls into the water. Rescued immediately and asked for the motives of his behavior, he knows nothing of them, he has yielded to an irresistible force." "The strange thing is," another says, "that I can't remember how I climbed the casement and my controlling idea at the time; for I had no thought of killing myself, or, at least I have no memory of such a thought today." To a lesser degree, patients feel the impulse growing and manage to escape the fascination of the mortal instrument by fleeing from it immediately.

In short, all suicides of the insane are either devoid of any motive or determined by purely imaginary motives. Now, many voluntary deaths fall into neither category; the majority have motives, and motives not unfounded in reality. Not every suicide can therefore be considered insane, without doing violence to language. Of all the suicides just characterized, that which may appear hardest to detect of those observed among the sane is melancholy suicide; for very often the normal person who kills himself is also in a state of dejection and depression like the mentally alienated. But an essential difference between them always exists in that the state of the former and its resultant act are not without an objective cause, whereas in the latter they are wholly unrelated to external circumstances. In short, the suicides of the insane differ from others as illusions and hallucinations differ from normal perceptions and automatic impulses from deliberate acts. It is true that there is a gradual shading from the former to the latter; but if that sufficed to identify them one would also, generally speaking, have to confuse health with sickness, since the latter is but a variety of the former. Even if it were proved that the average man never kills himself and that only those do so who show certain anomalies, this would still not justify considering insanity a necessary condition of suicide; for an insane person is not simply a man who thinks or acts somewhat differently from the average.

Thus, suicide has been so closely associated with insanity only by arbitrarily restricting the meaning of the words. "That man does not kill himself," Esquirol exclaims, "who, obeying only noble and generous sentiments, throws himself into certain peril, exposes himself to inevitable death, and willingly sacrifices his life in obedience to the laws, to keep pledged faith, for his country's safety." He cites the examples of Decius, of Assas, etc. Falret likewise refuses to consider Curtius, Codrus or Aristodemus as suicides. Bourdin excepts in this manner all voluntary deaths inspired not only by religious faith or political conviction but even by lofty affection. But we know that the nature of the motives immediately causing suicide cannot be used to define it, nor consequently to distinguish it from what it is not. All cases of death resulting from an act of the patient himself with full knowledge of the inevitable results, whatever their purpose, are too essentially similar to be assigned to separate classes. Whatever their cause, they can only be species of a single genus; and to distinguish among them, one must have other criteria than the victim's more or less doubtful purpose. This leaves at least a group of suicides unconnected with insanity. Once exceptions are admitted, it is hard to stop. For there is only a gradual shading between deaths inspired by usually generous feelings and those from less lofty motives. An imperceptible gradation leads from one class to the other. If then the former are suicides, there is no reason for not giving the same name to the latter.

There are therefore suicides, and numerous ones at that, not connected with insanity. They are doubly identifiable as being deliberate and as springing from representations involved in this deliberation which are not purely hallucinatory. This often debated question may therefore be solved without requiring reference to the problem of freedom. To learn whether all suicides are insane, we have not asked whether or not they act freely; we have based ourselves solely on the empirical characteristics observable in the various sorts of voluntary death.

WILLIAM SHAKESPEARE

—

Hamlet

R EENTER OPHELIA

Laertes. "O heat, dry up my brains! Tears seven times salt,
Burn out the sense and virtue of mine eye!
By heaven, thy madness shall be paid by weight,
Till our scale turn the beam. O rose of May
Dear maid, kind sister, sweet Ophelia!
O heavens! Is't possible, a young maid's wits
Should be as mortal as an old man's life?
Nature is fine in love and where 'tis fine,

William Shakespeare's Hamlet *tells a tale of murder, jealousy, revenge, and
madness. In this excerpt, we meet Ophelia, the beautiful, heartbroken fiancée of
Hamlet, shortly before and after she ends her life.*

It sends some precious instance of itself
After the thing it loves.
>> *Ophelia.* [*Sings*]
>>>> *They bore him barefac'd on the bier;*
>>>>> *Hey non nonny, nonny, hey nonny;*
>>>> *And in his grave rain'd many a tear.*—
Fare you well, my dove!
>> *Laertes.* Hadst thou thy wits, and didst persuade revenge,
>> It could not move thus.
>> *Ophelia.* [*Sings*] You must sing *Down a-down, and you call him a-*
down-a. O how the wheel becomes it! It is the false steward that stole
his master's daughter.
>> *Laertes.* This nothing's more than matter.
>> *Ophelia.* There's rosemary, that's for remembrance;
pray, love, remember: and there is pansies, that's for thoughts.
>> *Laertes.* A document in madness, thoughts and re-
membrance fitted.
>> *Ophelia.* There's fennel for you, and columbines; there's rue for
you; and here's some for me. We may call it herb of grace o' Sundays.
O, you must wear your rue with a difference. There's a daisy. I would
give you some violets, but they withered all when my father died.
They say he made a good end,—
>> [*Sings*] *For bonny sweet Robin is all my joy.*
>> *Laertes.* Thought and affliction, passion, hell itself,
She turns to favour and to prettiness.
>> *Ophelia.* [*Sings*] *And will he not come again?*
>> *And will he not come again?*
>>> *No, no, he is dead;*
>>> *Go to thy death-bed;*
>>> *He never will come again.*
>> *His beard was white as snow,*
>> *All flaxen was his poll.*

He is gone, he is gone,
And we cast away moan;
God ha' mercy on his soul!
And of all Christian souls, I pray God. God be wi' ye.
   Laertes. Do you see this, O God? *Exit* OPHELIA
   King. Laertes, I must commune with your grief,
Or you deny me right. Go but apart,
Make choice of whom your wisest friends you will,
And they shall hear and judge 'twixt you and me.
If by direct or by collateral hand
They find us touch'd, we will our kingdom give,
Our crown, our life, and all that we call ours,
To you in satisfaction; but if not,
Be you content to lend your patience to us,
And we shall jointly labour with your soul
To give it due content.
   Laertes.   Let this be so.
His means of death, his obscure burial—
No trophy, sword, nor hatchment o'er his bones,
No noble rite nor formal ostentation—
Cry to be heard, as 'twere from heaven to earth,
That I must call't in question.
   King.   So you shall;
And where the offence is let the great axe fall.
I pray you, go with me.   *[Exeunt.*

      —

Enter QUEEN
   King. How now, sweet queen!
   Queen. One woe doth tread upon another's heel,
So fast they follow. Your sister's drown'd, Laertes.
   Laertes. Drown'd! O, where?
   Queen. There is a willow grows aslant a brook,

That shows his hoar leaves in the glassy stream.
There with fantastic garlands did she come
Of crow-flowers, nettles, daisies, and long purples
That liberal shepherds give a grosser name,
But our cold maids do dead men's fingers call them.
There, on the pendent boughs her coronet weeds
Clambering to hang, an envious sliver broke;
When down her weedy trophies, and herself
Fell in the weeping brook. Her clothes spread wide,
And, mermaid-like, awhile they bore her up:
Which time she chanted snatches of old tunes,
As one incapable of her own distress
Or like a creature native and indued
Unto that element. But long it could not be
Till that her garments, heavy with their drink,
Pull'd the poor wretch from her melodious lay
To muddy death.
      Laertes.   Alas, then, she is drown'd?
      Queen. Drown'd, drown'd.
      Laertes. Too much of water hast thou, poor Ophelia,
And therefore I forbid my tears. But yet
It is our trick; nature her custom holds,
Let shame say what it will. When these are gone,
The woman will be out. Adieu, my lord.
I have a speech of fire, that fain would blaze,
But that this folly douts it.   *[Exit.*
      King.   Let's follow, Gertrude:
How much I had to do to calm his rage!
Now fear I this will give it start again;
Therefore let's follow.   *[Exeunt.*

EMILY DICKINSON

—

After Great Pain

FTER GREAT PAIN,
a formal feeling comes—
The Nerves sit ceremonious, like Tombs—
The stiff Heart questions was it He, that bore,
And Yesterday, or Centuries before?

---

*Emily Dickinson wrote over eighteen hundred poems, but only seven were
published during her lifetime. By the 1860s, when she was in her
thirties, Dickinson had withdrawn from society, often talking to visitors through
closed doors or from the top of a flight of stairs. For Dickinson, the simplest
acts or moments of life were universal symbols; this is revealed in her short but
unsimple poems, such as "After Great Pain."*

The Feet, mechanical, go round—
Of Ground, or Air, or Ought—
A Wooden way
Regardless grown,
A Quartz contentment, like a stone—

This is the Hour of Lead—
Remembered, if outlived,
As Freezing persons, recollect the Snow—
First—Chill—then Stupor—then the letting go—

JOHN DONNE

Biathanatos

BEZA, A MAN as eminent and illustrious, in the full glory and Noone of Learning, as others were in the dawning, and Morning, when any, the least sparkle was notorious, confesseth of himself, that only for the anguish of a Scurffe, which over-ranne his head, he had once drown'd himselfe from the Miller's bridge in Paris, if his Uncle by chance had not then come that way; I have often such a sickly inclination. And, whether it be, because I had my first breeding and conversation with men of supressed and afflicted Religion, accustomed to the despite of death, and

---

Seventeenth-century poet and clergyman John Donne wrote Biathanatos *in 1608, a period of poverty and severe marital distress. It was never published in his lifetime, most likely due to its unorthodox reasoning on the nature of suicide and mortal sin.*

hungry of an imagin'd Martyrdome; Or that the common Enemie find that doore worst locked against him in mee; Or that there bee a perplexitie and flexibility in the doctrine it selfe; Or because my Conscience ever assures me, that no rebellious grudging at Gods gifts, nor other sinfull concurrence accompanies these thoughts in me, or that a brave scorn, or that a faint cowardliness beget it, whensoever any affliction assails me, mee thinks I have the keyes of my prison in mine owne hand, and no remedy presents it selfe so soone to my heart, as mine own sword. Often Meditation of this hath wonne me to a charitable interpretation of their action, who dy so: and provoked me a little to watch and exagitate their reasons, which pronounce so peremptory judgements upon them.

A devout and godly man, hath guided us well, and rectified our uncharitablenesse in such cases, by this remembrace, [Scis lapsum etc. *Thou knowest this mans fall, but thou knowest not his wrastling; which perchance was such, that almost his very fall is justified and accepted of God.*] For, to this end, saith one, [*God hath appointed us tentations, that we might have some excuse for our sinnes, when he calls us to account.*]

An uncharitable mis-interpreter unthriftily demolishes his own house, and repaires not another. He loseth without any gaine or profit to any. And, as Tertullian comparing and making equall, him which provokes another, and him who will be provoked by another, sayes, [*There is no difference, but that the provoker offended first, And that is nothing, because in evill there is no respect of Order or Prioritie.*] So wee may soone become as ill as any offendor, if we offend in a severe increpation of the fact. For, Climachus in his Ladder of Paradise, places these two steps very neere one another, when hee sayes, [*Though in the world it were possible for thee, to escape all defiling by actuall sinne, yet by judging and condemning those who are defiled, thou art defiled.*] In this thou are defiled, as *Basil* notes, [*That in comparing others sinnes, thou canst not avoid excusing thine owne*] Especially this is done, if thy zeale be too fervent in the reprehension of others: For, as in most other Accidents, so in this also, Sinne hath the nature of Poyson, that [*It enters easiest, and works fastest upon cholerique constitutions.*] It is good counsell of the Pharises stiled, [*Ne judices proximum, donec ad ejus locum pertingas.*] Feele and wrastle with such tentations as he hath done, and thy zeale will be tamer. For, [*Therefore* (saith the Apostle) *it became Christ to be like us, that he might be mercifull.*] If therefore after a Christian protestation of an innocent purpose herein, And after a submission of all which is said, not only to every Christian Church, but to every Christian man, and after an entreaty, that the Reader will follow this advice of Tabaeus, [*Qui litigant, sint ambo in conspectu tuo mali et rei,*] and trust neither me, nor the adverse part, but the Reasons, there be any scandall in this enterprise of mine, it is Taken, not Given. And though I know, that the malitious prejudged man, and the lazy affectors of ignorance, will use the same calumnies and obtrectations toward me, (for the voyce and sound of the Snake and Goose is all one) yet because I thought, that as in the poole of *Bethsaida*, there was no health till the water was troubled, so the best way to finde the truth in this matter, was to debate and vexe it, (for [We must as well dispute de veritate, *as* pro veritate,]) I abstained not for feare of mis-interpretation from this undertaking. Our stomachs are not now so tender, and queasie, after so long feeding upon solid Divinity, nor we so umbragious and startling, having been so long enlightened in Gods pathes, that wee should thinke any truth strange to us, or relapse into that childish age, in which a Councell in France forbad *Aristotles Metaphysiques*, and punished with Excommunication the excribing, reading, or having that booke.

Contemplative and bookish men, must of necessitie be more quarrelsome than others, because they contend not about matter of fact, nor can determine their controversies by any certaine witnesses, nor judges. But as long as they goe towards peace, that is Truth, it is no matter which way. The tutelare Angels resisted one another in *Persia*, but neither resisted Gods revealed purpose. *Hierome* and *Gregorie* seem to be of opinion, that *Solomon* is damned; *Ambrose* and *Augustine*, that he is saved: All Fathers, all zealous of Gods glory. At the same time when the *Romane* Church canonized *Becket*, the Schooles of *Paris* disputed whether hee could be saved; both Catholique Judges, and of reverend authoritie. And after so many Ages of a devout and religious celebrating the memory of Saint *Hierome*, *Causaeus* hath spoken so dangerously, that *Campian* saies, hee pronounceth him to be as deepe in hell as the Devill. But in all such intricacies, where both opinions seem equally to conduce to the honor of God, his Justice being as much advanced in the one, as his Mercie in the other, it seemes reasonable to me, that this turne the scales, if on either side there appeare charity towards the poore soul departed. The Church in her Hymnes and Antiphones, doth often salute the Nayles and the Crosse, with Epithets of sweetnesse, and thanks; But the Speare which pierced Christ when he was dead, it ever calles *dirum Mucronem.*

    This pietie, I protest againe, urges me in this discourse; and what infirmity soever my reasons may have, yet I have comfort in Trismegistus Axiome [*Qui pius est, summe Philosophatur.*] And therefore without any disguising, or curious and libellous concealing, I present and object it, to all of candour, and indifferencie, to escape that just taxation, [*Novum malitiæ genus est, et intemperantis, scribere quod occultes.*] For as, when *Ladislaus* tooke occasion of the great schisme, to corrupt the nobility in Rome, and hoped thereby to possesse the towne, to their seven Governours whom they called *Sapientes* they added three more, whom they called *Bonos*, and confided in them; So doe I wish, and as much as I can, effect, that to those many learned and subtile men which have travelled in this point, some charitable and compassionate men might be added.

    If therefore, of Readers, which *Gorionides* observes to be of foure sorts, [Spunges which attract all without distinguishing; Howre-glasses,

which receive and powre out as fast; Bagges which retaine onely the
dregges of the Spices, and let the Wine escape; And Sives, which
retaine the best onely], I finde some of the last sort, I doubt not but they
may bee hereby enlightened. And as the eyes of *Eve*, were opened by
the taste of the Apple, though it bee said before that shee saw the beauty of the tree, So the digesting of this may, though not present faire
objects, yet bring them to see the nakednesse and deformity of their
owne reasons, founded upon a rigorous suspition, and winne them to
be of that temper, which *Chrisostome* commends, [*He which suspects
benignly would faine be deceived, and bee overcome, and is piously glad, when
he findes it to be false, which he did uncharitably suspect.*] And it may have
as much vigour (as one observes of another Author) as the Sunne in
March; it may stirre and dissolve humors, though not expell them; for
that must bee the worke of a stronger power.

 Every branch which is excerpted from other authors, and
engrafted here, is not written for the readers faith, but for illustration
and comparison. Because I undertooke the declaration of such a proposition as was controverted by many, and therefore was drawne to the
citation of many authorities, I was willing to goe all the way with company, and to take light from others, as well in the journey as at the journeys
end. If therefore in multiplicity of not necessary citations there appeare
vanity, or ostentation, or digression my honesty must make my excuse
and compensation, who acknowledge as Pliny doth [*That to chuse
rather to be taken in a theft, than to give every man due,* is obnoxii animi, et
infelicis ingenii.] I did it the rather because scholastique and artificial
men use this way of instructing; and I made account that I was to deal
with such, because I presume that naturall men are at least enough
inclinable of themselves to this doctrine.

 This my way; and my end is to remove scandall. For certainly
God often punisheth a sinner much more severely, because others
have taken occasion of sinning by his fact. If therefore wee did correct

in our selves this easines of being scandalized, how much easier and lighter might we make the punishment of many transgressors! for God in his judgement hath almost made us his assistants, and counsellers, how far he shall punish; and our interpretation of anothers sinne doth often give the measure to Gods Justice or Mercy.

If therefore, since [*disorderly long haire which was pride and wantonnesse in* Absolon, *and squallor and horridnes in* Nebuchodonozor *was vertue and strength in* Samson, *and sanctification in* Samuel,] these severe men will not allow to indifferent things the best construction they are capable of, nor pardon my inclination to do so, they shall pardon me this opinion, that their severity proceeds from a self-guiltines, and give me leave to apply that of *Ennodius,* [*That it was the nature of stiffe wickednesse, to think that of others, which themselves deserve and it is all the comfort the guilty have, not to find any innocent.*]

JORGE LUIS BORGES

Donne's Biathanatos

To De Quincey (my debt to him is so vast that to specify a part of it seems to repudiate or to silence the others) I owe my first knowledge of the *Biathanatos*. It was written at the beginning of the seventeenth century by the great poet John Donne, who left the manuscript to Sir Robert Carr with one stipulation: that it be published or burned. Donne died in 1631; civil war broke out in 1642; in 1644 the poet's eldest son published the old manuscript to save it from burning. The *Biathanatos* is about two hundred

---

Jorge Luis Borges was an Argentinian essayist, novelist, and poet, creator of the compelling metaphor of life as a labyrinth through which one passes, vainly seeking to comprehend existence. This 1954 heretical reading of Donne's heretical Biathanatos *needles the Catholic Church's unrelenting position on suicide.*

pages long; De Quincey (*Writings*, VIII, 336) sums them up as follows: Suicide is one form of homicide; the canonists distinguish voluntary homicide from justifiable homicide; logically, that distinction should also apply to suicide. As not every murderer is an assassin, not every self-murderer is guilty of mortal sin. This is the apparent thesis of the *Biathanatos*; it is stated in the subtitle (*That Self-homicide is not so naturally Sin that it may never be otherwise*), and it is illustrated, or burdened, by a learned catalogue of fabulous or authentic examples: Homer, who had written a thousand things that no one else could understand, and who was said to have hanged himself because he did not understand the riddle of the fisherman; the pelican, symbol of paternal love; and the bees which, as the *Hexameron* of Ambrose declares, kill themselves when they have violated the laws of their king. The catalogue fills three pages and I have observed that it has this show of vanity: it includes obscure examples (Festus, favorite of Domitian, who killed himself to conceal the ravages of a skin disease), and omits others of equally persuasive virtue—Seneca, Themistocles, Cato—which could have seemed too easy.

Epictetus ("Remember the essential thing: the door is open") and Schopenhauer ("Is Hamlet's soliloquy the meditation of a criminal?") have written many pages to vindicate suicide; our inner certainty that those defenders are right causes us to read them carelessly. That is what happened to me with the *Biathanatos* until I noticed, or thought I noticed, an implicit or esoteric plot beneath the apparent one.

We shall never know whether Donne wrote the *Biathanatos* with the deliberate aim of insinuating that hidden plot or whether a pre-figuring of that plot, even if only momentary or crepuscular, called him to the task. I think the second theory is the more probable one; the hypothesis of a book that says *B* in order to say *A*, as in a cryptogram, is artificial, but the thought of a work inspired by an imperfect intuition is not. Hugh Fausset has suggested that Donne planned to culminate his vindication of suicide with suicide. That Donne may have played with such an idea is possible or even probable; that Fausset's suggestion is sufficient to explain the *Biathanatos* is, naturally, ridiculous.

In the third part of the *Biathanatos* Donne considers the voluntary deaths recorded by the Scriptures; to no other does he devote as many pages as to the death of Samson. He begins by establishing that this "exemplary man" is the emblem of Christ and that to the Greeks he seems to have been the archetype of Hercules. Francisco de Vitoria and the Jesuit Gregorio de Valencia did not wish to include him among the suicides. To refute them, Donne quotes the last words Samson said before he wreaked his vengeance: "Let me die with the Philistines" (Judges 16:30). He also refutes the conjecture of St. Augustine, who affirms that in breaking the pillars of the temple Samson was not guilty of the deaths of others or of his own death, but was obeying an inspiration of the Holy Spirit, "like the sword whose blade is guided by the will of the user" (*The City of God* I, 20). After proving that this conjecture is unfounded, Donne closes the chapter with a line by Benito Pererio, which states that Samson, no less in his death than in other acts, was the symbol of Christ.

Inverting the Augustinian thesis, the quietists believed that Samson "killed himself with the Philistines because of the violence of the devil" (*Heterodox Spaniards*, V, 1, 8); Milton (*Samson Agonistes*) vindicated him from the attribution of suicide; Donne, I suspect, saw nothing in that casuistical problem except a sort of metaphor or image. Samson's case did not matter to him—and indeed, why should it—or it mattered only, we shall say, as an "emblem of Christ." Nearly all Old Testament heroes have received that distinction: for St. Paul, Adam is the figure of the One Who was to come; for St. Augustine, Abel represents the Saviour's death, and his brother Seth, the resurrection; for Quevedo, "Job was a prodigious outline of Christ." Donne made use of that trivial analogy to show his reader that it might well be false when said of Samson, but that it was not when said of Christ.

The chapter that speaks directly of Christ is not effusive. It merely invokes two scriptural passages: the phrase "I lay down my life for the sheep" (John 10:15) and the curious expression "he gave up the ghost," which the four Evangelists use to say "died." From those passages, which are confirmed by the verse "No man taketh my life from me, but I lay it down of myself" (John 10:18), Donne infers that the suffering on the Cross did not kill Jesus Christ but that He, in fact, killed Himself with a prodigious and voluntary emission of His soul. Donne wrote that conjecture down in 1608; in 1631 he included it in a sermon he preached, at the point of death, in the chapel of Whitehall Palace.

The avowed purpose of the *Biathanatos* is to palliate suicide; the underlying aim is to indicate that Christ committed suicide. It seems unlikely and even incredible that Donne's only way to reveal this thesis was the use of a verse from St. John and the repetition of the verb *to expire*; no doubt he preferred not to insist on a blasphemous theme. For the Christian the life and death of Christ are the central occurrences in the history of the world. The previous ages prepared the way for those events, and the subsequent centuries reflected them. Before Adam was formed from the dust of the earth, before the firmament separated the waters from the waters, the Father already knew that the Son would die on the Cross, and He created the earth and the heavens as a stage for the Son's future death. Christ died a voluntary death, Donne suggests, implying that the elements and the world and the generations of men and Egypt and Rome and Babylon and Judah were drawn from nothingness to destroy Him. Perhaps iron was created for the nails, thorns for the crown of mockery, and blood and water for the wound. That baroque idea is perceived beneath the *Biathanatos*—the idea of a god who fabricates the universe in order to fabricate his scaffold.

As I reread this essay, I think of the tragic Philipp Batz, who is called Philipp Mainländer in the history of philosophy. Like me, he was an impassioned reader of Schopenhauer, under whose influence (and perhaps under the influence of the Gnostics) he imagined that we are fragments of a God who destroyed Himself at the beginning of time, because He did not wish to exist. Universal history is the obscure agony of those fragments. Mainländer was born in 1841; in 1876 he published his book *Philosophy of the Redemption*. That same year he killed himself.

AMBROSE BIERCE

—

Taking Oneself Off

 PERSON WHO
LOSES heart and hope through a personal bereavement is like a grain
of sand on the seashore complaining that the tide has washed a neighboring grain out of sight. He is worse, for the bereaved grain can not
help itself; it has to be a grain of sand and play the game of tide, win or
lose; whereas he can quit—by watching his opportunity can "quit a
winner." For sometimes we do beat "the man that keeps the table"—
never in the long run, but infrequently and out of small stakes. But this

---

*In 1913, Ambrose Bierce mysteriously disappeared into the wilds of Mexico. The
much respected, saber-tongued journalist was over 70 when he saddled up and rode off.
Some claimed he went there to fight for Pancho Villa; most believed that he simply
went there to die. This column, written around 1890, supports the latter scenario.*

is no time to "cash in" and go, for you can not take your little winning with you. The time to quit is when you have lost a big stake, your foolish hope of eventual success, your fortitude and your love of the game. If you stay in the game, which you are not compelled to do, take your losses in good temper and do not whine about them. They are hard to bear, but that is no reason why you should be.

But we are told with tiresome iteration that we are "put here" for some purpose (not disclosed) and have no right to retire until "summoned"—it may be by small-pox, it may be by the bludgeon of a blackguard, it may be by the kick of a cow; the "summoning" Power (said to be the same as the "putting" Power) has not a nice taste in the choice of messengers. That argument is not worth attention, for it is unsupported by either evidence or anything resembling evidence. "Put here." Indeed! And by the keeper of the table! We were put here by our parents—that is all that anybody knows about it; and they had no authority and probably no intention.

The notion that we have not the right to take our own lives comes of our consciousness that we have not the courage. It is the plea of the coward—his excuse for continuing to live when he has nothing to live for—or his provision against such a time in the future. If he were not egotist as well as coward he would need no excuse. To one who does not regard himself as the center of creation and his sorrows as throes of the universe, life, if not worth living, is also not worth leaving. The ancient philosopher who was asked why he did not die if, as he taught, life was no better than death, replied: "Because death is no better than life." We do not know that either proposition is true, but the matter is not worth considering, for both states are supportable—life despite its pleasures and death despite its repose.

It was Robert G. Ingersoll's opinion that there is rather too little than too much suicide in the world—that people are so cowardly as to live on long after endurance has ceased to be a virtue. This view is but a return to the wisdom of the ancients, in whose splendid civilization suicide has as honorable place as any other courageous, reasonable and unselfish act. Antony, Brutus, Cato, Seneca—these were not of the kind of men to do deeds of cowardice and folly. The smug, self-righteous modern way of looking upon the act as that of a craven or a lunatic is the creation of priests, philistines and women. If courage is manifest in endurance of profitless discomfort it is cowardice to warm oneself when cold, to cure oneself when ill, to drive away mosquitoes, to go in when it rains. The "pursuit of happiness," then, is not an "unalienable right," for it implies avoidance of pain.

No principle is involved in this matter; suicide is justifiable or not, according to circumstances; each case is to be considered on its merits, and he having the act under advisement is sole judge. To his decision, made with whatever light he may chance to have, all honest minds will bow. The appellant has no court to which to take his appeal. Nowhere is a jurisdiction so comprehensive as to embrace the right of condemning the wretched to life.

Suicide is always courageous. We call it courage in a soldier merely to face death—say to lead a forlorn hope—although he has a chance of life and a certainty of "glory." But the suicide does more than face death; he incurs it, and with a certainty, not of glory, but of reproach. If that is not courage we must reform our vocabulary.

True, there may be a higher courage in living than in dying. The courage of the suicide, like that of the pirate, is not incompatible with a selfish disregard of the rights of others—a cruel recreancy to duty and decency. I have been asked: "Do you not think it cowardly for a man to end his life, thereby leaving his family in want?" No, I do not; I think it selfish and cruel. Is not that enough to say of it? Must we distort words from their true meaning in order more effectually to damn the act and cover its author with a greater infamy? A word means something; despite the maunderings of the lexicographers, it does not mean whatever you want it to mean. "Cowardice" means a shrinking from danger, not a shrinking of duty. The writer who allows himself as much liberty in the use of words as he is allowed by the dictionary-maker and by popular consent is a bad writer. He can make no impression on his reader, and would do better service at the ribbon-counter.

The ethics of suicide is not a simple matter; one can not lay down laws of universal application, but each case is to be judged, if judged at all, with a full knowledge of all the circumstances, including the mental and moral make-up of the person taking his own life—an impossible qualification for judgment. One's time, race and religion have much to do with it. Some peoples, like the ancient Romans and the modern Japanese, have considered suicide in certain circumstances honorable and obligatory; among ourselves it is held in disfavor. A man of sense will not give much attention to considerations of this kind, excepting in so far as they affect others, but in judging weak offenders they are to be taken into the account. Speaking generally, I should say that in our time and country the persons here noted (and some others) are justified in removing themselves, and that in some of them it is a duty:

One afflicted with a painful or loathsome and incurable disease.

One who is a heavy burden to his friends, with no prospect of their relief.

One threatened with permanent insanity.

One irreclaimably addicted to drunkenness or some similarly destructive or offensive habit.

One without friends, property, employment or hope.

One who has disgraced himself.

Why do we honor the valiant soldier, sailor, fireman? For obedience to duty? Not at all; that alone—without the peril—seldom elicits remark, never evokes enthusiasm. It is because he faced without flinching the risk of that supreme disaster, or what we feel to be such—death. But look you: the soldier braves the danger of death; the suicide braves death itself! The leader of the forlorn hope may not be struck. The sailor who involuntarily goes down with his ship may be picked up or cast ashore. It is not certain that the wall will topple until the fireman shall have descended with his precious burden. But the suicide—his is the foeman that has never missed a mark, his the sea that gives nothing back; the wall that he mounts bears no man's weight. And his, at the end of it all, is the dishonored grave where the wild ass of public opinion

Stamps o'er his head but can not break his sleep.

LEO TOLSTOY

—

Anna Karenina

THERE, IT IS that girl again! Again I see it all!" said Anna to herself as soon as the carriage started and, rocking slightly, rumbled over the little cobbles of the roadway. Once more the impressions succeeded one another in her brain.

"Now, what was the last thing I thought of that was so good?" She tried to remember. "*Tuttikin, coiffeur?* No, not that. I know—what Yashvin said: the struggle for existence and hate are the only things that

---

Although Leo Tolstoy was a great writer of suicides, he was not in that way inclined. However, his wife, Sophia, was often inspired by her husbands plots to attempt suicide: After Anna Karenina *was completed, she tried to throw herself under a train, and, the day* Master and Man *was sent to the printer, she ran out half-clothed into a blinding snowstorm. She survived all attempts and outlived her husband.*

hold men together. No, it's a useless journey you're making," she men-tally addressed a party of people in a coach and four who were evidently going on an excursion into the country. "And the dog you are taking with you won't help either. You can't get away from yourselves." Glancing in the direction in which Peter was looking, she saw a work-man, almost dead-drunk, his head swaying, being led off by a police-man. "He's found a quicker way," she thought. "Count Vronsky and I did not find our happiness either, though we expected so much." And now for the first time Anna turned the glaring light in which she was seeing everything upon her relations with him, which she had hitherto avoided thinking about. "What did he look for in me? Not love so much as the gratification of his vanity." She remembered his words, the expression of his face, like a faithful setter's, in the early days of their liaison. And everything now confirmed that. "Yes, in him there was triumph over a success for his vanity. Of course there was love too, but the chief element was pride of success. He gloried in me. Now that is past. There is nothing to be proud of—nothing to be proud of, only ashamed. He has taken from me everything he could, and now I am no more use to him. He is tired of me and is trying not to act dishon-ourably towards me. Only yesterday he blurted out that he wants divorce and marriage so as to burn his boats. He loves me, but how? *The zest is gone,*" she said to herself in English. "That fellow wants everyone to admire him, and is very well pleased with himself," she thought, looking at a ruddy-cheeked clerk riding by on a hired horse. "No, there's not the same flavor about me for him now. If I leave him, at the bottom of his heart he will be glad."

This was not surmise—she saw it distinctly in the piercing light which revealed to her now the meaning of life and human relations.

"My love grows more and more passionate and selfish, while his is dying, and that is why we are drifting apart," she went on mus-ing. "And there's no help for it. He is all in all to me, and I demand that he should give himself more and more entirely up to me. And he wants to get farther and farther away from me. Up to the time of our union we were irresistibly drawn together, and now we are irresistibly drawn apart. And nothing can be done to alter it. He says I am insanely jealous and I have kept on telling myself that I am insanely jealous; but it is not true. I am not jealous, but unsatisfied. But..." Her mouth dropped open and she was so agitated by the sudden thought that came to her that she changed her place in the carriage. "If I could be anything but his mistress, passionately caring for nothing but his caresses—but I can't, and I don't want to be anything else. And my desire arouses his disgust, and that excites resentment in me, and it cannot be otherwise. Don't I know that he wouldn't deceive me, that he has no thought of wanting to marry the Princess Sorokin, that he is not in love with Kitty, that he won't be unfaithful to me? I know all that, but it doesn't make it any the easier for me. If he does not love me, but treats me kindly and gently out of a sense of *duty*, and what I want is not there—that would be a thousand times worse than having him hate me. It would be hell! And that is just how it is. He has long ceased to love me. And where love ends, hate begins. I don't know these streets at all. How hilly it is—and houses and houses everywhere.... And in the houses people, and more people... No end to them, and all hating each other. Suppose I think to myself what it is I want to make me happy. Well? I get a divorce, and Alexei Alexandrovich lets me have Seriozha, and I marry Vronsky." Thinking of Karenin she immediately saw him before her with extraordinary vividness—the mild, lifeless, faded eyes, the blue veins in his white hands—heard his intonations and the cracking of his finger joints, and remembering the feeling that had once existed between them, and which had also been called love, she shuddered with revulsion. "Well, I get divorced, and become Vronsky's wife. What then? Will Kitty cease looking at me as she looked at me today? No. And will Seriozha leave off asking and wondering about my two husbands? And is there any new feeling I can imagine between Vronsky and me? Could there be if not happiness, just absence of torment? No, and no again!" she answered herself now without the smallest hesitation. "Impossible! Life is sundering us, and I am the cause of his unhappiness and he of mine, and there's no altering him or me. Every attempt has been made but the screw has been twisted tight.... A beggar-woman with a baby. She thinks she inspires pity. Are we not all flung into the world for no other purpose than to hate each other, and so to torture ourselves and one another? There go some schoolboys, laughing. Seriozha?" she remembered. "I thought, too, that I loved him, and used to be moved by my own tenderness for him. Yet here I have lived without him. I exchanged him for another love, and did not complain so long as the other love satisfied me." And she thought with disgust of what she called the " other love." The clearness with which she saw her own life now, and everyone else's, gave her a sense of pleasure. "So it is with me, and Peter, and Fiodor the coachman, and that tradesman, and all those people who live by the Volga where those advertisements there invite us to go. It is the same everywhere and always," she thought as they drove up to the low building of Nizhny station, and the porters ran to meet her.

" Shall I take a ticket to Obiralovka?" asked Peter.

She had completely forgotten where she was going, and why, and only by a great effort could she understand his question.

"Yes," she said, handing him her purse; and, hanging her little red bag on her arm, she got out of the carriage.

As she made her way through the crowd to the first-class waiting-room she gradually recalled all the details of her situation and the plans between which she was wavering. And again hope and despair in turn, chafing the old sores, lacerated the wounds of her tortured, cruelly throbbing heart. Sitting on the star-shaped couch waiting for her train, she looked with aversion at the people coming in and out. They were all objectionable to her. She thought of how she would arrive at the station and send him a note, of what she would write, and of how he was at this moment complaining to his mother (not understanding her sufferings) of his position, and of how she would enter the room and what she would say to him. Then she thought of how life might still be happy, and how wretchedly she loved and hated him, and how dreadfully her heart was beating.

THE BELL RANG, and some ugly, insolent young men passed by, hurriedly yet mindful of the impression they were creating. Then Peter, in his livery and gaiters, with his dull, animal face also crossed the room to come and see her into the train. The noisy young men fell silent as she passed them on the platform, and one of them whispered some remark about her to his neighbor—something vile, no doubt. Anna climbed the high step of the railway carriage and sat down in an empty compartment on the once white but now dirty seat. Her bag gave a bounce on the cushion and then was still. With a foolish smile Peter raised his gold-braided hat at the window to take leave of her, and an impudent guard slammed the door and pulled down the catch. A misshapen lady wearing a bustle (Anna mentally undressed the woman and was appalled at her hideousness), followed by a girl laughing affectedly, ran past outside the carriage window.

"Katerina Andreevna has everything, *ma tante!*" cried the little girl.

"Even the girl is grotesque and affected," thought Anna. To avoid seeing people she got up quickly and seated herself at the opposite window of the empty compartment. A grimy, deformed-looking peasant in a cap from beneath which tufts of his matted hair stuck out, passed by this window, stooping down to the carriage wheels. "There's something familiar about that deformed peasant," thought Anna. And remembering her dream she walked over to the opposite door, trembling with fright. The guard opened the door to let in a man and his wife.

"Are you getting out?"

Anna made no reply. Neither the guard nor the passengers getting in noticed, under her veil, the terror on her face. She went back to her corner and sat down. The couple took their seats opposite her and cast stealthy curious glances at her dress. Anna found both husband and wife repellent. The husband asked her if she would object if he smoked, evidently not because he wanted to smoke but in order to get into conversation with her. Receiving her permission, he then began speaking to his wife in French of things he wanted to talk about still less than he wanted to smoke. They made inane remarks to one another, entirely for her benefit. Anna saw clearly that they were bored with one another and hated each other. Nor could such miserable creatures be anything else but hated.

The second bell rang, and was followed by the loading of luggage, noise, shouting and laughter. It was so clear to Anna that nobody had any cause for joy that this laughter grated on her painfully, and she longed to stop her ears and shut it out. At last the third bell went, the engine whistled and screeched, the coupling chains gave a jerk, and the husband crossed himself.

"It would be interesting to ask him what meaning he attaches to that," thought Anna, regarding him spitefully. She looked past the lady out of the window at the people standing on the platform who had been seeing the train off and who looked as though they were gliding backwards. With rhythmic jerks over the joints of the rails, the carriage in which Anna sat rattled past the platform, past a brick wall, past the signals and some other carriages. The wheels slid more smoothly and evenly along the rails, making a slight ringing sound. The bright rays of the evening sun shone through the window, and a little breeze played against the blind. Anna forgot her fellow-passengers. Rocked gently by the motion of the train, she inhaled the fresh air and continued the current of her thoughts.

"Where was it I left off? On the reflection that I couldn't conceive a situation in which life would not be a misery, that we were all created in order to suffer, and that we all know this and all try to invent means for deceiving ourselves. But when you see the truth, what are you to do?"

"Reason has been given to man to enable him to escape from his troubles," said the lady in French, obviously pleased with her phrase and mouthing it.

The words fitted in with Anna's thoughts.

"To escape from his troubles," Anna repeated to herself. She glanced at the red-cheeked husband and his thin wife, and saw that the sickly woman considered herself misunderstood, and that the husband was unfaithful to her and encouraged her in that idea of herself. Directing her searchlight upon them, Anna as it were read their history and all the hidden crannies of their souls. But there was nothing of interest, and she resumed her reflections.

"Yes, I am very troubled, and reason was given man that he might escape his troubles. Therefore I must escape. Why not put out the candle when there's nothing more to see, when everything looks obnoxious? But how? Why did that guard run along the footboard? Why do those young men in the next carriage make such a noise? Why do they talk and laugh? Everything is false and evil—all lies and deceit!"

When the train stopped at the station, Anna got out with a crowd of other passengers and shunning them as if they were lepers she stood still on the platform trying to remember why she had come and what it was she had intended doing. Everything that had seemed possible before was now so difficult to grasp, especially in this noisy crowd of ugly people who would not leave her in peace. Porters rushed up, offering their services. Young men stamped their heels on the planks of the platform, talking in loud voices and staring at her. The people that tried to get out of her way always dodged to the wrong side. Recollecting that she had meant to go on in the train should there be no answer, she stopped a porter and asked him if there was not a coachman anywhere with a note from Count Vronsky.

"Count Vronsky? Someone from there was here just now, to meet Princess Sorokin and her daughter. What is the coachman like?"

As she was talking to the porter, Mihail the coachman, rosy-faced and cheerful, came up in his smart blue coat with a watch-chain, and handed her a note, evidently proud that he had carried out his errand so well. She tore open the note, and her heart contracted even before she had read it.

"Very sorry your note did not catch me. I shall be back at ten," Vronsky had written in a careless hand.

"Yes, that is what I expected!" she said to herself with a malicious smile.

"All right, you may go home," she said quietly to Mihail. She spoke softly because the rapid beating of her heart interfered with her breathing. "No, I won't let you torture me," she thought, addressing her warning not to him, not to herself, but to the power that made her suffer, and she walked along the platform past the station buildings.

Two servant-girls strolling up and down the platform turned their heads to stare at her and made some audible remarks about her dress. "Real," they said, referring to the lace she was wearing. The young men would not leave her in peace. They passed by again, peering into her face and talking and laughing in loud, unnatural voices. The station-master as he walked by asked her if she was going on in the train. A boy selling kvas never took his eyes off her. "Oh God, where am I to go?" she thought, continuing farther and farther along the platform. At the end she stopped. Some ladies and children, who had come to meet a gentleman in spectacles and who were laughing and talking noisily, fell silent and scanned her as she drew even with them. She hastened her step and walked away to the edge of the platform. A goods train was approaching. The platform began to shake, and she fancied she was in the train again.

In a flash she remembered the man who had been run down by the train the day she first met Vronsky, and knew what she had to do. Quickly and lightly she descended the steps that led from the watertank to the rails, and stopped close to the passing train. She looked at the lower part of the trucks, at the bolts and chains and the tall iron wheels of the first truck slowly moving up, and tried to measure the point midway between the front and back wheels, and the exact moment when it would be opposite her.

"There," she said to herself, looking in the shadow of the truck at the mixture of sand and coal dust which covered the sleepers. "There, in the very middle, and I shall punish him and escape from them all and from myself."

She wanted to fall half-way between the wheels of the front truck which was drawing level with her. But the red bag which she began to pull from her arm delayed her, and it was too late: the truck had passed. She must wait for the next. A sensation similar to the feeling she always had when bathing, before she took the first plunge, seized her and she crossed herself. The familiar gesture brought back a whole series of memories of when she was a girl, and of her childhood, and suddenly the darkness that had enveloped everything for her lifted, and for an instant life glowed before her with all its past joys. But she did not take her eyes off the wheels of the approaching second truck.

And exactly at the moment when the space between the wheels drew level with her she threw aside the red bag and drawing her head down between her shoulders dropped on her hands under the truck, and with a light movement, as though she would rise again at once, sank on to her knees. At that same instant she became horror-struck at what she was doing. "Where am I? What am I doing? Why?" She tried to get up, to throw herself back; but something huge and relentless struck her on the head and dragged her down on her back. "God forgive me everything!" she murmured, feeling the impossibility of struggling. A little peasant muttering something was working at the rails. And the candle by which she had been reading the book filled with trouble and deceit, sorrow and evil, flared up with a brighter light, illuminating for her everything that before had been enshrouded in darkness, flickered, grew dim and went out for ever.

WILLIAM STYRON

Darkness   Visible

O MANY OF us who
knew Abbie Hoffman even slightly, as I did, his death in the spring of
1989 was a sorrowful happening. Just past the age of fifty, he had been
too young and apparently too vital for such an ending; a feeling of
chagrin and dreadfulness attends the news of nearly anyone's suicide, and
Abbie's death seemed to me especially cruel. I had first met him during the
wild days and nights of the 1968 Democratic Convention in Chicago,

---

With the 1990 publication of Darkness Visible, *William Styron, author of
such contemporary classics as* The Confessions of Nat Turner, Lie Down in
Darkness, *and* Sophie's Choice, *became one of the first writers to grapple
publicly with the devastating effects of depression. This haunting memoir has
played an important role in redefining depression as a treatable disease.*

where I had gone to write a piece for *The New York Review of Books*, and I later was one of those who testified in behalf of him and his fellow defendants at the trial, also in Chicago, in 1970. Amid the pious follies and morbid perversions of American life, his antic style was exhilarating, and it was hard not to admire the hell-raising and the brio, the anarchic individualism. I wish I had seen more of him in recent years; his sudden death left me with a particular emptiness, as suicides usually do to everyone. But the event was given a further dimension of poignancy by what one must begin to regard as a predictable reaction from many: the denial, the refusal to accept the fact of the suicide itself, as if the voluntary act—as opposed to an accident, or death from natural causes—were tinged with a delinquency that somehow lessened the man and his character.

Abbie's brother appeared on television, grief-ravaged and distraught; one could not help feeling compassion as he sought to deflect the idea of suicide, insisting that Abbie, after all, had always been careless with pills and would never have left his family bereft. However, the coroner confirmed that Hoffman had taken the equivalent of 150 phenobarbitals. It's quite natural that the people closest to suicide victims so frequently and feverishly hasten to disclaim the truth; the sense of implication, of personal guilt—the idea that one might have prevented the act if one had taken certain precautions, had somehow behaved differently—is perhaps inevitable. Even so, the sufferer—whether he has actually killed himself or attempted to do so, or merely expressed threats—is often through denial on the part of others, unjustly made to appear a wrongdoer.

A similar case is that of Randall Jarrell—one of the fine poets and critics of his generation—who on a night in 1965, near Chapel Hill, North Carolina, was struck by a car and killed. Jarrell's presence on that particular stretch of road, at an odd hour of the evening, was puzzling, and since some of the indications were that he had deliberately let the car strike him, the early conclusion was that his death was suicide. *Newsweek*, among other publications, said as much, but Jarrell's widow protested in a letter to the magazine; there was a hue and cry from many of his friends and supporters, and a coroner's jury eventually ruled the death to be accidental. Jarrell had been suffering from extreme depression and had been hospitalized; only a few months before his misadventure on the highway and while in the hospital, he had slashed his wrists.

Anyone who is acquainted with some of the jagged contours of Jarrell's life—including his violent fluctuations of mood, his fits of black despondency—and who, in addition, has acquired a basic knowledge of the danger signals of depression, would seriously question the verdict of the coroner's jury. But the stigma of self-inflicted death is for some people a hateful blot that demands erasure at all costs. (More than two decades after his death, in the summer 1986 issue of *The American Scholar*, a one time student of Jarrell's, reviewing a collection of the poet's letters, made the review less a literary or biographical appraisal than an occasion for continuing to try to exorcise the vile phantom of suicide.)

Randall Jarrell almost certainly killed himself. He did so not because he was a coward, nor out of any moral feebleness, but because he was afflicted with a depression that was so devastating that he could no longer endure the pain of it.

This general unawareness of what depression is really like was apparent most recently in the matter of Primo Levi, the remarkable Italian writer and survivor of Auschwitz who, at the age of sixty-seven, hurled himself down a stairwell in Turin in 1987. Since my own involvement with the illness, I had been more than ordinarily interested in Levi's death, and so, late in 1988, when I read an account in *The New York Times* about a symposium on the writer and his work held at New York University, I was fascinated but, finally, appalled. For, according to the article, many of the participants, worldly writers and scholars, seemed mystified by Levi's suicide, mystified and disappointed. It was as if this man whom they had all so greatly admired, and who had endured so much at the hands of the Nazis—a man of exemplary resilience and courage—had by his suicide demonstrated a frailty, a crumbling of character they were loath to accept. In the face of a terrible absolute—self-destruction—their reaction was helplessness and (the reader could not avoid it) a touch of shame.

My annoyance over all this was so intense that I was prompted to write a short piece for the op-ed page of the *Times*. The argument I put forth was fairly straightforward: the pain of severe depression is quite unimaginable to those who have not suffered it, and it kills in many instances because its anguish can no longer be borne. The prevention of many suicides will continue to be hindered until there is a general awareness of the nature of this pain. Through the healing process of time—and through medical intervention or hospitalization in many cases—most people survive depression, which may be its only blessing; but to the tragic legion who are compelled to destroy themselves there should be no more reproof attached than to the victims of terminal cancer.

I had set down my thoughts in this *Times* piece rather hurriedly and spontaneously, but the response was equally spontaneous—and enormous. It had taken, I speculated, no particular originality or bold-ness on my part to speak out frankly about suicide and the impulse toward it, but I had apparently underestimated the number of people for whom the subject had been taboo, a matter of secrecy and shame. The overwhelming reaction made me feel that inadvertently I had helped unlock a closet from which many souls were eager to come out and pro-claim that they, too, had experienced the feelings I had described. It is the only time in my life I have felt it worthwhile to have invaded my own privacy, and to make that privacy public. And I thought that, given such momentum...it would be useful to try to chronicle some of my own experience with the illness and in the process perhaps establish a frame of reference out of which one or more valuable conclusions might be drawn. Such conclusions, it has to be emphasized, must still be based on the events that happened to one man. In setting these reflections down I don't intend my ordeal to stand as a representation of what happens, or might happen, to others. Depression is much too complex in its cause, its symptoms and its treatment for unqualified conclusions to be drawn from the experience of a single individual. Although as an illness depression manifests certain unvarying characteristics, it also allows for many idiosyncrasies; I've been amazed at some of the freakish phenomena—not reported by other patients—that it has wrought amid the twistings of my mind's labyrinth.

Depression afflicts millions directly, and millions more who are relatives or friends of victims. It has been estimated that as many as one in ten Americans will suffer from the illness. As assertively democratic as a Norman Rockwell poster, it strikes indiscriminately at all ages, races, creeds and classes, though women are at considerably higher risk than men. The occupational list (dressmakers, barge captains, sushi chefs, cabinet members) of its patients is too long and tedious to give here; it is enough to say that very few people escape being a potential victim of the disease, at least in its milder form. Despite depression's eclectic reach, it has been demonstrated with fair convincingness that artistic types (especially poets) are particularly vulnerable to the disorder—which, in its graver, clinical manifestation takes upward of twenty percent of its victims by way of suicide. Just a few of these fallen artists, all modern, make up a sad but scintillant roll call: Hart Crane, Vincent van Gogh, Virginia Woolf, Arshile Gorky, Cesare Pavese, Romain Gary, Vachel Lindsay, Sylvia Plath, Henry de Montherlant, Mark Rothko, John Berryman, Jack London, Ernest Hemingway, William Inge, Diane Arbus, Tadeusz Borowski, Paul Celan, Anne Sexton, Sergei Esenin, Vladimir Mayakovsky—the list goes on. (The Russian poet Mayakovsky was harshly critical of his great contemporary Esenin's suicide a few years before, which should stand as a caveat for all who are judgmental about self-destruction.) When one thinks of these doomed and splendidly creative men and women, one is drawn to contemplate their childhoods, where, to the best of anyone's knowledge, the seeds of the illness take strong root; could any of them have had a hint, then, of the psyche's perishability, its exquisite fragility? And why were they destroyed, while others—similarly stricken—struggled through?

WHEN I WAS first aware that I had been laid low by the disease, I felt a need, among other things, to register a strong protest against the word "depression." Depression, most people know, used to be termed "melancholia," a word which appears in English as early as the year 1303 and crops up more than once in Chaucer, who in his usage seemed to be aware of its pathological nuances. "Melancholia" would still appear to be a far more apt and evocative word for the blacker forms of the disorder, but it was usurped by a noun with a bland tonality and lacking any magisterial presence, used indifferently to describe an economic decline or a rut in the ground, a true wimp of a word for such a major illness. It may be that the scientist generally held responsible for its currency in modern times, a Johns Hopkins Medical School faculty member justly venerated—the Swiss-born psychiatrist Adolf Meyer—had a tin ear for the finer rhythms of English and therefore was unaware of the semantic damage he had inflicted by offering "depression" as a descriptive noun for such a dreadful and raging disease. Nonetheless, for over seventy-five years the word has slithered innocuously through the language like a slug, leaving little trace of its intrinsic malevolence and preventing, by its very insipidity, a general awareness of the horrible intensity of the disease when out of control.

As one who has suffered from the malady in extremis yet returned to tell the tale, I would lobby for a truly arresting designation. "Brainstorm," for instance, has unfortunately been preempted to describe, somewhat jocularly, intellectual inspiration. But something along these lines is needed. Told that someone's mood disorder has evolved into a storm—a veritable howling tempest in the brain, which is indeed what a clinical depression resembles like nothing else—even the uninformed layman might display sympathy rather than the standard reaction that "depression" evokes, something akin to "So what?" or "You'll pull out of it" or "We all have bad days." The phrase "nervous breakdown" seems to be on its way out, certainly deservedly so, owing to its insinuation of a vague spinelessness, but we still seem destined to be saddled with "depression" until a better, sturdier name is created.

The depression that engulfed me was not of the manic type— the one accompanied by euphoric highs—which would have most probably presented itself earlier in my life. I was sixty when the illness struck for the first time, in the "unipolar" form, which leads straight down. I shall never learn what "caused" my depression, as no one will ever learn about their own. To be able to do so will likely forever prove to be an impossibility, so complex are the intermingled factors of abnormal chemistry, behavior and genetics. Plainly, multiple components are involved—perhaps three or four, most probably more, in fathomless permutation. That is why the greatest fallacy about suicide lies in the belief that there is a single immediate answer—or perhaps combined answers—as to why the deed was done.

The inevitable question "Why did he [or she] do it?" usually leads to odd speculations, for the most part fallacies themselves. Reasons were quickly advanced for Abbie Hoffman's death: his reaction to an auto accident he had suffered, the failure of his most recent book, his mother's serious illness. With Randall Jarrell it was a declining career cruelly epitomized by a vicious book review and his consequent anguish. Primo Levi, it was rumored, had been burdened by caring for his paralytic mother, which was more onerous to his spirit than even his experience at Auschwitz. Any one of these factors may have lodged like a thorn in the sides of the three men, and been a torment. Such aggravations may be crucial and cannot be ignored. But most people quietly endure the equivalent of injuries, declining careers, nasty book reviews, family illnesses. A vast majority of the survivors of Auschwitz have borne up fairly well. Bloody and bowed by the outrages of life, most human beings still stagger on down the road, unscathed by real depression. To discover why some people plunge into the downward spiral of depression, one must search beyond the manifest crisis—and then still fail to come up with anything beyond wise conjecture.

The storm which swept me into a hospital in December began as a cloud no bigger than a wine goblet the previous June. And the cloud—the manifest crisis—involved alcohol, a substance I had been abusing for forty years. Like a great many American writers, whose sometimes lethal addiction to alcohol has become so legendary as to provide in itself a stream of studies and books, I used alcohol as the magical conduit to fantasy and euphoria, and to the enhancement of the imagination. There is no need to either rue or apologize for my use of this soothing, often sublime agent, which had contributed greatly to my writing; although I never set down a line while under its influence, I did use it—often in conjunction with music—as a means to let my mind conceive visions that the unaltered, sober brain has no access to. Alcohol was an invaluable senior partner of my intellect, besides being a friend whose ministrations I sought daily—sought also, I now see, as a means to calm the anxiety and incipient dread that I had hidden away for so long somewhere in the dungeons of my spirit.

The trouble was, at the beginning of this particular summer, that I was betrayed. It struck me quite suddenly, almost overnight: I could no longer drink. It was as if my body had risen up in protest, along with my mind, and had conspired to reject this daily mood bath which it had so long welcomed and, who knows? perhaps even come to need. Many drinkers have experienced this intolerance as they have grown older. I suspect that the crisis was at least partly metabolic—the liver rebelling, as if to say, "No more, no more"—but at any rate I discovered that alcohol in minuscule amounts, even a mouthful of wine, caused me nausea, a desperate and unpleasant wooziness, a sinking sensation and ultimately a distinct revulsion. The comforting friend had abandoned me not gradually and reluctantly, as a true friend might do, but like a shot—and I was left high and certainly dry, and unhelmed.

Neither by will nor by choice had I became an abstainer; the situation was puzzling to me, but it was also traumatic, and I date the onset of my depressive mood from the beginning of this deprivation. Logically, one would be overjoyed that the body had so summarily dismissed a substance that was undermining its health; it was as if my system had generated a form of Antabuse, which should have allowed me to happily go my way, satisfied that a trick of nature had shut me off from a harmful dependence. But, instead, I began to experience a vaguely troubling malaise, a sense of something having gone cockeyed in the domestic universe I'd dwelt in so long, so comfortably. While depression is by no means unknown when people stop drinking, it is usually on a scale that is not menacing. But it should be kept in mind how idiosyncratic the faces of depression can be.

It was not really alarming at first, since the change was subtle, but I did notice that my surroundings took on a different tone at certain times: the shadows of nightfall seemed more somber, my mornings were less buoyant, walks in the woods became less zestful, and there was a moment during my working hours in the late afternoon when a kind of panic and anxiety overtook me, just for a few minutes, accompanied by a visceral queasiness—such a seizure was at least slightly alarming, after all. As I set down these recollections, I realize that it should have been plain to me that I was already in the grip of the beginning of a mood disorder, but I was ignorant of such a condition at that time.

When I reflected on this curious alteration of my consciousness—and I was baffled enough from time to time to do so—I assumed that it all had to do somehow with my enforced withdrawal from alcohol. And, of course, to a certain extent this was true. But it is my conviction now that alcohol played a perverse trick on me when we said farewell to each other: although, as everyone should know, it is a major depressant, it had never truly depressed me during my drinking career, acting instead as a shield against anxiety. Suddenly vanished, the great ally which for so long had kept my demons at bay was no longer there to prevent those demons from beginning to swarm through the subconscious, and I was emotionally naked, vulnerable as I had never been before. Doubtless depression had hovered near me for years, waiting to swoop down. Now I was in the first stage—premonitory, like a flicker of sheet lightning barely perceived—of depression's black tempest.

I was on Martha's Vineyard, where I've spent a good part of each year since the 1960s, during that exceptionally beautiful summer. But I had begun to respond indifferently to the island's pleasures. I felt a kind of numbness, an enervation, but more particularly an odd fragility— as if my body had actually become frail, hypersensitive and somehow disjointed and clumsy, lacking normal coordination. And soon I was in the throes of a pervasive hypochondria. Nothing felt quite right with my corporeal self; there were twitches and pains, sometimes intermittent, often seemingly constant, that seemed to presage all sorts of dire infirmities. (Given these signs, one can understand how, as far back as the seventeenth century—in the notes of contemporary physicians, and in the perceptions of John Dryden and others—a connection is made between melancholia and hypochondria; the words are often interchangeable, and were so used until the nineteenth century by writers as various as Sir Walter Scott and the Brontës, who also linked melancholy to a preoccupation with bodily ills.) It is easy to see how this condition is part of the psyche's apparatus of defense: unwilling to accept its own gathering deterioration, the mind announces to its indwelling consciousness that it is the body with its perhaps correctable defects—not the precious and irreplaceable mind—that is going haywire.

In my case, the overall effect was immensely disturbing, augmenting the anxiety that was by now never quite absent from my waking hours and fueling still another strange behavior pattern—a fidgety restlessness that kept me on the move, somewhat to the perplexity of my family and friends. Once, in late summer, on an airplane trip to New York, I made the reckless mistake of downing a scotch and soda— my first alcohol in months—which promptly sent me into a tailspin, causing me such a horrified sense of disease and interior doom that the very next day I rushed to a Manhattan internist, who inaugurated a long series of tests. Normally I would have been satisfied, indeed elated, when, after three weeks of high-tech and extremely expensive evaluation, the doctor pronounced me totally fit; and I *was* happy, for a day or two, until there once again began the rhythmic daily erosion of my mood—anxiety, agitation, unfocused dread.

By now I had moved back to my house in Connecticut. It was October, and one of the unforgettable features of this stage of my disorder was the way in which my own farmhouse, my beloved home for thirty years, took on for me at that point when my spirits regularly sank to their nadir an almost palpable quality of ominousness. The fading evening light—akin to that famous "slant of light" of Emily Dickinson's which spoke to her of death, of chill extinction—had none of its familiar autumnal loveliness, but ensnared me in suffocating gloom. I wondered how this friendly place, teeming with memories of (again in her words) "Lads and Girls," of "laughter and ability and Sighing, / And Frocks and Curls," could almost perceptibly seem so hostile and forbidding. Physically, I was not alone. As always Rose was present and listened with unflagging patience to my complaints. But I felt an immense and aching solitude. I could no longer concentrate during those afternoon hours, which for years had been my working time, and the act of writing itself, becoming more and more difficult and exhausting, stalled, then finally ceased.

There were also dreadful, pounding seizures of anxiety. One bright day on a walk through the woods with my dog I heard a flock of Canada geese honking high above trees ablaze with foliage; ordinarily a sight and sound that would have exhilarated me, the flight of birds caused me to stop, riveted with fear, and I stood stranded there, helpless, shivering, aware for the first time that I had been stricken by no mere pangs of withdrawal but by a serious illness whose name and actuality I was able finally to acknowledge. Going home, I couldn't rid my mind of the line of Baudelaire's dredged up from the distant past, that for several days had been skittering around at the edge of my consciousness: "I have felt the wind of the wing of madness."

Our perhaps understandable modern need to dull the sawtooth edges of so many of the afflictions we are heir to has led us to banish the harsh old-fashioned words: madhouse, asylum, insanity, melancholia, lunatic, madness. But never let it be doubted that depression, in its extreme form, is madness. The madness results from an aberrant biochemical process. It has been established with reasonable certainty (after strong resistance from many psychiatrists, and not all that long ago) that such madness is chemically induced amid the neurotransmitters of the brain, probably as the result of systemic stress, which for unknown reasons causes a depletion of the chemicals norepinephrine and serotonin, and the increase of a hormone, cortisol. With all this upheaval in the brain tissues, the alternate drenching and deprivation, it is no wonder that the mind begins to feel aggrieved, stricken, and the muddied thought processes register the distress of an organ in convulsion. Sometimes, though not very often, such a disturbed mind will turn to violent thoughts regarding others. But with their minds turned agonizingly inward, people with depression are usually dangerous only to themselves. The madness of depression is, generally speaking, the antithesis of violence. It is a storm indeed, but a storm of murk. Soon evident are the slowed-down responses, near paralysis, psychic energy throttled back close to zero. Ultimately, the body is affected and feels sapped, drained.

That fall, as the disorder gradually took full possession of my system, I began to conceive that my mind itself was like one of those outmoded small-town telephone exchanges, being gradually inundated by floodwaters: one by one, the normal circuits began to drown, causing some of the functions of the body and nearly all of those of instinct and intellect to slowly disconnect.

—

FOR YEARS I had kept a notebook—not strictly a diary, its entries were erratic and haphazardly written—whose contents I would not have particularly liked to be scrutinized by eyes other than my own. I had hidden it well out of sight in my house. I imply no scandalousness; the observations were far less raunchy, or wicked, or self-revealing, than my desire to keep the notebook private might indicate. Nonetheless, the small volume was one that I fully intended to make use of professionally and then destroy before the distant day when the specter of a nursing home came too near. So as my illness worsened I rather queasily realized that if I once decided to get rid of the notebook that moment would necessarily coincide with my decision to put an end to myself. And one evening during early December this moment came.

That afternoon I had been driven (I could no longer drive) to Dr. Gold's office, where he announced that he had decided to place me on the antidepressant Nardil, an older medication which had the advantage of not causing the urinary retention of the other two pills he had prescribed. However, there were drawbacks. Nardil would probably not take effect in less than four to six weeks—I could scarcely believe this—and I would have to carefully obey certain dietary restrictions, fortunately rather epicurean (no sausage, no cheese, no pâté de foie gras), in order to avoid a clash of incompatible enzymes that might cause a stroke. Further, Dr. Gold said with a straight face, the pill at optimum dosage could have the side effect of impotence. Until that moment, although I'd had some trouble with his personality, I had not thought him totally lacking in perspicacity; now I was not at all sure. Putting myself in Dr. Gold's shoes, I wondered if he seriously thought that this juiceless and ravaged semi-invalid with the shuffle and the ancient wheeze woke up each morning from his Halcion sleep eager for carnal fun.

There was a quality so comfortless about that day's session that I went home in a particularly wretched state and prepared for the evening. A few guests were coming over for dinner—something which I neither dreaded nor welcomed and which in itself (that is, in my torpid indifference) reveals a fascinating aspect of depression's pathology. This concerns not the familiar threshold of pain but a parallel phenomenon, and that is the probable inability of the psyche to absorb pain beyond predictable limits of time. There is a region in the experience of pain where the certainty of alleviation often permits superhuman endurance. We learn to live with pain in varying degrees daily, or over a longer period of time, and we are more often than not mercifully free of it. When we endure severe discomfort of a physical nature our conditioning has taught us since childhood to make accommodations to the pain's demands—to accept it, whether pluckily or whimpering and complaining, according to our personal degree of stoicism, but in any case to accept it. Except in intractable terminal pain, there is almost always some form of relief; we look forward to that alleviation, whether it be through sleep or Tylenol or self-hypnosis or a change of posture or, most often, through the body's capacity for healing itself, and we embrace this eventual respite as the natural reward we receive for having been, temporarily, such good sports and doughty sufferers, such optimistic cheerleaders for life at heart.

In depression this faith in deliverance, in ultimate restoration, is absent. The pain is unrelenting, and what makes the condition intolerable is the foreknowledge that no remedy will come—not in a day, an hour, a month, or a minute. If there is mild relief, one knows that it is only temporary; more pain will follow. It is hopelessness even more than pain that crushes the soul. So the decision-making of daily life involves not, as in normal affairs, shifting from one annoying situation to another less annoying—or from discomfort to relative comfort, or from boredom to activity—but moving from pain to pain. One does not abandon, even briefly, one's bed of nails, but is attached to it wherever one goes. And this results in a striking experience—one which I have called, borrowing military terminology, the situation of the walking wounded. For in virtually any other serious sickness, a patient who felt similar devastation would be lying flat in bed, possibly sedated and hooked up to the tubes and wires of life-support systems, but at the very least in a posture of repose and in an isolated setting. His invalidism would be necessary, unquestioned and honorably attained. However, the sufferer from depression has no such option and therefore finds himself, like a walking casualty of war, thrust into the most intolerable social and family situations. There he must, despite the anguish devouring his brain, present a face approximating the one that is associated with ordinary events and companionship. He must try to utter small talk, and be responsive to questions, and knowingly nod and frown and, God help him, even smile. But it is a fierce trial attempting to speak a few simple words.

That December evening, for example, I could have remained in bed as usual during those worst hours, or agreed to the dinner party my wife had arranged downstairs. But the very idea of a decision was academic. Either course was torture, and I chose the dinner not out of any particular merit but through indifference to what I knew would be indistinguishable ordeals of fogbound horror. At dinner I was barely able to speak, but the quartet of guests, who were all good friends, were aware of my condition and politely ignored my catatonic muteness. Then, after dinner, sitting in the living room, I experienced a curious inner convulsion that I can describe only as despair beyond despair. It came out of the cold night; I did not think such anguish possible.

While my friends quietly chatted in front of the fire I excused myself and went upstairs, where I retrieved my notebook from its special place. Then I went to the kitchen with gleaming clarity—the clarity of one who knows he is engaged in a solemn rite—I noted all the trademarked legends on the well-advertised articles which I began assembling for the volume's disposal: the new roll of Viva paper towels I opened to wrap up the book, the Scotch-brand tape I encircled it with, the empty Post Raisin Bran box I put the parcel into before taking it outside and stuffing it deep down within the garbage can, which would be emptied the next morning. Fire would have destroyed it faster, but in garbage there was an annihilation of self appropriate, as always, to melancholia's fecund self-humiliation. I felt my heart pounding wildly, like that of a man facing a firing squad, and knew I had made an irreversible decision.

A phenomenon that a number of people have noted while in deep depression is the sense of being accompanied by a second self—a wraithlike observer who, not sharing the dementia of his double, is able to watch with dispassionate curiosity as his companion struggles against the oncoming disaster, or decides to embrace it. There is a theatrical quality about all this, and during the next several days, as I went about stolidly preparing for extinction, I couldn't shake off a sense of melodrama—a melodrama in which I, the victim-to-be of self-murder, was both the solitary actor and lone member of the audience. I had not as yet chosen the mode of my departure, but I knew that that step would come next, and soon, as inescapable as nightfall.

I watched myself in mingled terror and fascination as I began to make the necessary preparation: going to see my lawyer in the nearby town—there rewriting my will—and spending a couple of afternoons in a muddled attempt to bestow upon posterity a letter of farewell. It turned out that putting together a suicide note, which I felt obsessed with a necessity to compose, was the most difficult task of writing that I had ever tackled. There were too many people to acknowledge, to thank, to bequeath final bouquets. and finally I couldn't manage the sheer dirgelike solemnity of it; there was something I found almost comically offensive in the pomposity of such comments as "For some time now I have sensed in my work a growing psychosis that is doubtless a reflection of the psychotic strain tainting my life" (this is one of the few lines I recall verbatim), as well as something degrading in the prospect of a testament, which I wished to infuse with at least some dignity and eloquence, reduced to an exhausted stutter of inadequate apologies and self-serving explanations. I should have used as an example the mordant statement of the Italian writer Cesare Pavese, who in parting wrote simply: *No more words. An act. I'll never write again.*

But even a few words came to seem to me too long-winded, and I tore up all my efforts, resolving to go out in silence. Late one bitterly cold night, when I knew that I could not possibly get myself through the following day, I sat in the living room of the house bundled up against the chill; something had happened to the furnace. My wife had gone to bed, and I had forced myself to watch the tape of a movie in which a young actress, who had been in a play of mine, was cast in a small part. At one point in the film, which was set in late-nineteenth-century Boston, the characters moved down the hallway of a music conservatory, beyond the walls of which, from unseen musicians, came a contralto voice, a sudden roaring passage from the Brahms *Alto Rhapsody.*

This sound, which like all music—indeed, like all pleasure—I had been numbly unresponsive to for months, pierced my heart like a dagger, and in a flood of swift recollection I thought of all the joys the house had known: the children who had rushed through its rooms, the festivals, the love and work, the honestly earned slumber, the voices and the nimble commotion, the perennial tribe of cats and dogs and birds, "laughter and ability and Sighing, / And Frocks and Curls." All this I realized was more than I could ever abandon, even as what I had set out so deliberately to do was more than I could inflict on those memories, and upon those, so close to me, with whom the memories were bound. And just as powerfully I realized I could not commit this desecration on myself. I drew upon some last gleam of sanity to perceive the terrifying dimensions of the mortal predicament I had fallen into. I woke up my wife and soon telephone calls were made. The next day I was admitted to the hospital.

—

BY FAR THE great majority of the people who go through even the severest depression survive it, and live ever afterward at least as happily as their unafflicted counterparts. Save for the awfulness of certain memories it leaves, acute depression inflicts few permanent wounds. There is a Sisyphean torment in the fact that a great number—as many as half—of those who are devastated once will be struck again; depression has the habit of recurrence. But most victims live through even these relapses, often coping better because they have become psychologically tuned by past experience to deal with the ogre. It is of great importance that those who are suffering a siege, perhaps for the first time, be told—be convinced, rather—that the illness will run its course and that they will pull through. A tough job, this; calling "Chin up!" from the safety of the shore to a drowning person is tantamount to an insult, but it has been shown over and over again that if the encouragement is dogged enough—and the support equally committed and passionate—the endangered one can nearly always be saved. Most people in the grip of depression at its ghastliest are, for whatever reason, in a state of unrealistic hopelessness, torn by exaggerated ills and fatal threats that bear no resemblance to actuality. It may require on the part of friends, lovers, family, admirers, an almost religious devotion to persuade the sufferers of life's worth, which is so often in conflict with a sense of their own worthlessness, but such devotion has prevented countless suicides.

During the same summer of my decline, a close friend of mine—a celebrated newspaper columnist—was hospitalized for severe manic depression. By the time I had commenced my autumnal plunge my friend had recovered (largely due to lithium but also to psychotherapy in the aftermath), and we were in touch by telephone nearly every day. His support was untiring and priceless. It was he who kept admonishing me that suicide as "unacceptable" (he had been intensely suicidal), and it was also he who made the prospect of going to the hospital less fearsomely intimidating. I still look back on his concern with immense gratitude. The help he gave me, he later said, had been a continuing therapy for him, thus demonstrating that, if nothing else, the disease engenders lasting fellowship.

After I began to recover in the hospital it occurred to me to wonder—for the first time with any really serious concern—why I had been visited by such a calamity. The psychiatric literature on depression is enormous, with theory after theory concerning the disease's etiology proliferating as richly as theories about the death of the dinosaurs or the origin of black holes. The very number of hypotheses is testimony to the malady's all but impenetrable mystery. As for that initial triggering mechanism—what I have called the manifest crisis— can I really be satisfied with the idea that abrupt withdrawal from alcohol started the plunge downward? What about other possibilities—the dour fact, for instance, that at about the same time I was smitten I turned sixty, that hulking milestone of mortality? Or could it be that a vague dissatisfaction with the way in which my work was going—the onset of inertia which has possessed me time and time again during my writing life, and made me crabbed and discontented—had also haunted me more fiercely during that period than ever, somehow magnifying the difficulty with alcohol? Unresolvable questions, perhaps.

These matters in any case interest me less than the search for earlier origins of the disease. What are the forgotten or buried events that suggest an ultimate explanation for the evolution of depression and its later flowering into madness? Until the onslaught of my own illness and its denouement, I never gave much thought to my work in terms of its connection with the subconscious—an area of investigation belonging to literary detectives. But after I had returned to health and was able to reflect on the past in the light of my ordeal, I began to see clearly how depression had clung close to the outer edges of my life for many years. Suicide has been a persistent theme in my books—three of my major characters killed themselves. In rereading, for the first time in years, sequences from my novels—passages where my heroines have lurched down pathways toward doom—I was stunned to perceive how accurately I had created the landscape of depression in the minds of these young women, describing with what could only be instinct, out of a subconscious already roiled by disturbances of mood, the psychic imbalance that led them to destruction. Thus depression, when it finally came to me, was in fact no stranger, not even a visitor totally unannounced; it had been tapping at my door for decades.

The morbid condition proceeded, I have come to believe, from my beginning years—from my father, who battled the gorgon for much of his lifetime, and had been hospitalized in my boyhood after a despondent spiraling downward that in retrospect I saw greatly resembled mine. The genetic roots of depression seem now to be beyond controversy. But I'm persuaded that an even more significant factor was the death of my mother when I was thirteen; this disorder and early sorrow—the death or disappearance of a parent, especially a mother, before or during puberty—appears repeatedly in the literature on depression as a trauma sometimes likely to create nearly irreparable emotional havoc. The danger is especially apparent if the young person is affected by what has been termed "incomplete mourning"—has, in effect, been unable to achieve the catharsis of grief, and so carries within himself through later years an insufferable burden of which rage and guilt, and not only dammed-up sorrow, are a part, and become the potential seeds of self-destruction.

In an illuminating new book on suicide, *Self-Destruction in the Promised Land*, Howard I. Kushner, who is not a psychiatrist but a social historian, argues persuasively in favor of this theory of incomplete mourning and uses Abraham Lincoln as an example. While Lincoln's hectic moods of melancholy are legend, it is much less well known that in his youth he was often in a suicidal turmoil and came close more than once to making an attempt on his own life. The behavior seems directly linked to the death of Lincoln's mother, Nancy Hanks, when he was nine, and to unexpressed grief exacerbated by his sister's death ten years later. Drawing insights from the chronicle of Lincoln's painful success in avoiding suicide, Kushner makes a convincing case not only for the idea of early loss precipitating self-destructive conduct, but also, auspiciously, for that same behavior becoming a strategy through which the person involved comes to grips with his guilt and rage, and triumphs over self-willed death. Such reconciliation may be entwined with the quest for immortality—in Lincoln's case, no less than that of a writer of fiction, to vanquish death through work honored by posterity.

So if this theory of incomplete mourning has validity, and I think it does, and if it is also true that in the nethermost depths of one's suicidal behavior one is still subconsciously dealing with immense loss while trying to surmount all the effects of its devastation, then my own avoidance of death may have been belated homage to my mother. I do know that in those last hours before I rescued myself, when I listened to the passage from the *Alto Rhapsody*—which I'd heard her sing—she had been very much on my mind.

NEAR THE END of an early film of Ingmar Bergman's, *Through a Glass Darkly*, a young woman, experiencing the embrace of what appears to be profound psychotic depression, has a terrifying hallucination. Anticipating the arrival of some transcendental and saving glimpse of God, she sees instead the quivering shape of a monstrous spider that is attempting to violate her sexually. It is an instant of horror and scalding truth. Yet even in this vision of Bergman (who has suffered cruelly from depression) there is a sense that all of his accomplished artistry has somehow fallen short of a true rendition of the drowned mind's appalling phantasmagoria. Since antiquity—in the tortured lament of Job, in the choruses of Sophocles and Aeschylus—chroniclers of the human spirit have been wrestling with a vocabulary that might give proper expression to the desolation of melancholia. Through the course of literature and art the theme of depression has run like a durable thread of woe—from Hamlet's soliloquy to the verses of Emily Dickinson and Gerard Manley Hopkins, from John Donne to

Hawthorne and Dostoevski and Poe, Camus and Conrad and Virginia
Woolf. In many of Albrecht Dürer's engravings there are harrowing
depictions of his own melancholia; the manic wheeling stars of Van
Gogh are the precursors of the artist's plunge into dementia and the
extinction of self. It is a suffering that often tinges the music of
Beethoven, of Schumann and Mahler, and permeates the darker cantatas
of Bach. The vast metaphor which most faithfully represents this fathomless ordeal, however, is that of Dante, and his all-too-familiar lines still
arrest the imagination with their augury of the unknowable, the black
struggle to come:

> Nel mezzo del cammin di nostra vita
> Mi ritrovai per una selva oscura,
> Ché la diritta via era smarrita.

> In the middle of the journey of our life
> I found myself in a dark wood,
> For I had lost the right path.

ONE CAN BE sure that these words have been more than once
employed to conjure the ravages of melancholia, but their somber fore-
boding has often overshadowed the last lines of the best-known part of
that poem, with their evocation of hope. To most of those who have
experienced it, the horror of depression is so overwhelming as to be
quite beyond expression, hence the frustrated sense of inadequacy
found in the work of even the greatest artists. But in science and art the
search will doubtless go on for a clear representation of its meaning,
which sometimes, for those who have known it, is a simulacrum of all
the evil of our world: of our everyday discord and chaos, our irra-
tionality, warfare and crime, torture and violence, our impulse toward
death and our flight from it held in the intolerable equipoise of history. If
our lives had no other configuration but this, we should want, and per-

haps deserve, to perish; if depression had no termination, then suicide would, indeed, be the only remedy. But one need not sound the false or inspirational note to stress the truth that depression is not the soul's annihilation; men and women who have recovered from the disease—and they are countless—bear witness to what is probably its only saving grace: it is conquerable.

For those who have dwelt in depression's dark wood, and known its inexplicable agony, their return from the abyss is not unlike the ascent of the poet, trudging upward and upward out of hell's black depths and at last emerging into what he saw as "the shining world." There, whoever has been restored to health has almost always been restored to the capacity for serenity and joy, and this may be indemnity enough for having endured the despair beyond despair.

E quindi uscimmo a riveder le stelle.
And so we came forth, and once again beheld the stars.